Canons

The Lake District Trilogy
Book 1

ALLAN JONES

OTHER NOVELS BY ALLAN JONES

The Lake District Trilogy
Canons
Compline
Chalice

The Catrin Sayer Mysteries
The Chinese Sailor
The Scottish Colourist
The Falmouth Model
The Carnforth Double
The Powys Deacon
The Stratford Hunter
The Thornham Copyist
The Chiswick Chauffeur
The Pinewood Gardener
The Tavistock Lieutenant

*All novels are released as ebooks
and Kindle Direct Publishing paperbacks*

Canons

CONTENTS

"Yes, there is a theological tradition that says that God wipes our sins out, but you still have consequences. This isn't Eternity. This is Planet Earth. You still have consequences… This is not advanced thinking about forgiveness."

Archbishop Justin Welby, March 2018. From the transcript, an oral response to a question posed during the IICSA public hearing into events within the Anglican Diocese of Chichester.

PROLOGUE

17 July, 4.35 p.m. BST

Even for July it was hot in Keswick and the northerly parts of Britain. London and the south-east of England were worse, the media said, with heatstroke warnings. In the hills of the Lake District in Cumbria the air was cooler. But in direct sunshine both walking and climbing became unpleasant work despite the surrounding natural beauty. Tourists who were not ardent walkers gravitated to the lakes, or the shade of trees, café umbrellas and places with a natural breeze.

The centre of Keswick was still humming with visitors, though, in the late afternoon.

Foreigners, thought Sandra Hardy, looking out of the large front window of Lowell's Bookshop on Station Street at the two men across the road. She carefully placed the two new copies of 'Wainwright's Lakeland Fells' in the space in the display unit. It always sold well. She was being careful about how far to bend in the skirt she now regretted wearing and had just eased herself vertical again.

It was not that the skirt was too short; it was too tight at the waistband. If her husband had not made a 'helpful' comment that morning about how 'we are both facing middle-aged spread', she might have thought twice about choosing to wear this one for work today. Obstinacy won out. His weight, she had responded sharply, was from too many 'working lunches', and too little exercise. Hers, she thought, was simply the results of childbearing, not beer and lunchtime pasties.

As Sandra stood up straight, she wondered why she thought of the two men across the road as foreigners. It was the clothes, she realised. Keswick, a tourist town, was always busy in July, and particularly so during 'Keswick Weeks', the sequence of religious gatherings called the Keswick Convention, organised by a group called Keswick Ministries.

In these weeks in mid-summer, the area was filled with both holidaymakers and religious types attending the convention; hundreds or thousands of them, it seemed at times. Sandra never went to the convention grounds and didn't go to church. Besides, she had to work in Lowell's every summer, as the Lowell family coped with the surge in customers.

They still had theft problems in the shop, but not from the Keswick Convention crowd. What some of those people did, however, was make new books seem second-hand quality in seconds, the way they treated the stock on display. She had to be vigilant.

The two men in conversation across the street were Keswick Convention types, she decided, the American nice, casually dressed sort; people who wear high-end logo sports shirts and pressed full-length pants rather than shorts and T-shirts, despite the warm day.

Just as she reached that conclusion, the man with the

brown hair started gesticulating angrily at the other in a less than churchy fashion, belying her categorization. The other man, dark-haired, seemed to be at first apologetic and then became angry himself. A holy war in Keswick High Street, thought Sandra. But it was over in a second or two.

The brown-haired man reached into his bag, pulled out a small book and slapped it first on to the other's chest, then placed it in his hand. He turned and stalked off, leaving the dark-haired man looking angry, staring at the book transferred to him. He shook his head and turned also, leaving in the direction of the main convention site.

"It's the heat," said a voice behind her, "it doesn't help. My kids are getting fractious with it, too."

A customer, by his voice a holidaymaker from County Durham, was now standing behind her in the shop. He was a walker, she decided instantly as she faced him, complete with hiking shorts, well-worn walking boots, and thick socks. He had a weather-beaten and sun-tanned face, and legs to match. The man had seen the interaction across the road through the window, too, she realised. Her eyes went down to his boots; these were clean, not muddy, at least. Another thing she checked regularly in the shop.

"Can I help you?" asked Sandra.

"I saw you putting the books by Wainwright in the window. You wouldn't, by any chance, have a 'Pennine Way Companion' by him?"

Sandra replied, "It's not in print at present, I think. It was reprinted but we couldn't get any more after a while. I can check on the computer, but I am pretty sure."

He looked crestfallen. "We are walking in the Lakeland Fells this week, not the Pennines, but… my son borrowed my copy; he was using it yesterday as a reference for his own drawings and dropped it in Derwent Water. It's a right soggy mess now. I hate to do without one and mine is fifteen years old, at least. Alfred Wainwright's sketches are so special."

She smiled. "They are indeed. I suggest that you check in some of the secondhand bookshops around here and on-line. You might be lucky. I know that there are still copies in circulation. But we have other books with Wainwright sketches in here, if you would like to see them?"

As she showed the hiker to the shelf providing a possible 'consolation prize' purchase, she thought again of the men they had both seen outside. She had recognized the book that was unceremoniously passed between them; it was a small pocket bible. In the largely Protestant evangelical gathering in Keswick, it was notable for being a Roman Catholic bible edition, to boot. She had been so certain they were part of the Keswick Convention crowd; but at least one of them appeared to be a Catholic in a tizzy.

PART 1

LAKE

Bassenthwaite Lake is the only body of water
in the Lake District to use the word 'lake'
in its name. *Wikipedia*

1 LURE

18 July, 5.36 a.m. BST

Anglers and fly fishermen will never see the world the same, thought Colin.

He was in waders, calf-deep in the water, looking along the stretch of Bassenthwaite Lake as far as the spit of land near St. Anselm's Church. In the new dawn light as he began fly fishing, the little promontory and the silhouette of the pre-Norman church looked to be solid, dark masses with no features really visible yet. It was his magic time, the dawn glimmer on the water, now marred by this bright speckle of light on a stone or branch near the surface of the water.

It was a spoon lure, he was sure. Some angler had lost or discarded it: a chunk of metal with a nasty treble hook to damage fish or spear an unwary kid's foot. Here, of all places.

Bassenthwaite was special for Colin Kavanagh. His family had been holidaying in Keswick every July since he was a boy, always staying in the same bed & breakfast home, the Maywood Guest House. In fact, his landlady now was the daughter of the original owner. She and Colin used to play together as children in years gone by. It felt like a second home rather than a hotel; a place where they weren't strangers.

Part of his ritual pleasure during their holiday week here was to rise well before the crack of dawn, get dressed quietly, and pad down to the kitchen. A short time later, he would leave with a flask of hot tea and his fly-fishing gear. He would return before mid-morning each day, ready for some holiday activity with his own family. The dawn, though, was his quiet time alone. And this week it was a delightfully cool time compared with the rest of the day.

As he finished preparing his rod, the glint of light continued to distract him. It was just sufficiently far away to make it a real drag to plod over in his waders and deal with it. Infuriatingly, also having waders on meant it was not too far out from the bank for him to dismiss it as unreachable. Realising that his mind was now more on the lure than the fly casting to come, he sighed, then edged back out of the water and placed his fishing rod down carefully by his bag.

Striding around the bank until he reached the side of the spit, he re-entered the lake at an angle, keeping the object of his disgruntlement in his sights. As he moved nearer, he saw that it was just slightly proud of the waterline, washed by the surface flow driven by the breeze. That was why the reflection was so intense, he realised. And it wasn't a lure; it was a gold cross of some sort, a lost piece of jewelry on a chain that lay across a stone, the chain tightly turning at the far edge, as if it was held fast.

As he came closer, his feet and lower legs moved deeper into the little pool and he took in subconsciously that the stone was not a rock from the lake; it was large and roughly rectangular, the type found in the many drystone walls that dotted Cumbria. The cross was bigger than he had first thought. It wasn't a woman's necklace; it was more like a crucifix, in fact. As he bent to pick it up the change in angle of the light on the water showed Colin a new sight, diffuse but shocking. An arm was just visible, protruding from beneath the rock, submerged and limp. He then realised that his foot was pressing against something; not hard, like a stone, it was softer, but resilient.

As Colin realised what he had found, he stumbled backwards, feet slipping. He fell, and the rear of his waders started to fill with water. His panic got him out of the lake fast, however. Soaking wet and struggling, he ran back to his pack on the bank to retrieve his mobile phone.

~~

Sergeant Harriet Calder arrived at the lake first by chance; she lived in the village of Bassenthwaite. The Keswick Police Station duty officer on shift was her colleague, Sergeant Des Vickers. In an hour and a half Harriet was due to relieve him, but he knew she would be up and about, so he called her.

"Harriet; it's Des. There's a report come in just now of a body in Bassenthwaite Lake. I've just sent Stella and Mike along to secure the scene, but you'll be getting this one anyway. I thought I would save you coming in here just to turn round again."

He knew she lived in the village, about fifteen minutes' drive away from Keswick itself.

"Where?"

"In the shallows right by St. Anselm's, the man who phoned it in said. He gave his name as Colin Kavanagh, a fisherman, here on holiday. He's on-scene now and sounds really upset. Can you see if he needs attention, perhaps?"

"I'll get down there right now. I was just getting sorted to leave anyway, so I'll be there in less than ten minutes. I'll let you know when I arrive."

Vickers asked, "One thing. I recall it has a pedestrian access to the church from the road. Is that right? Is there vehicle access that can be used? I'm calling Penrith next; they've also been alerted."

The Cumbria Police headquarters was based in Penrith, a town about twenty-five miles east of Bassenthwaite.

"Yes, it's paved and padlocked. I have my cutters; we can't wait to round up a churchwarden with a key."

Harriet Calder arrived four minutes ahead of the responding officers, driving along the narrow country road leading to the paved track to the church. She cut the padlock off the gate, blocked the gate open, and drove down to the historic building.

As Des Vickers had recalled, St. Anselm's was normally a pedestrian-only access, outside service hours. But crossing the adjacent stile to the old lakeside church was not a practical route; there would be more vehicles arriving shortly. A report of a body found in the open and showing signs of a suspicious death would be flagged to the Major Investigation Unit in Penrith, the MIU; it was procedure. Detectives, a pathologist and SOCOs, the forensic Scene of Crimes Officers, would probably be here within an hour.

On their arrival, Constables Stella Keegan and Michael Truman found their day shift sergeant near the church, holding a roll of barricade tape in one hand as she talked to a man in waders, now wrapped in a police blanket.

Harriet said, "Stella, take Mr. Kavanagh into the church; it's open. There is a small kitchen, so look after him there; he's soaking at the back. Make some tea or something?

Mike, let's get this area taped off before MIU arrives."

Constable Truman asked, "And the body?"

"It isn't going anywhere, it's wedged. Mr. Kavanagh was on the bank, sitting nearby holding his phone, waiting for us. I brought him back here."

A few minutes later in the growing daylight, Calder left Truman by the tape barrier, with instructions to secure the area. She returned carefully to the lake edge and stood still, looking again at the body she had seen only briefly as she dealt with Kavanagh. She focused on the stone on the man's chest, and the cross resting on it.

Calder was tall and slim, and in her early forties, a woman naturally veering towards thinness rather than too much weight. An eighteen-year veteran of the Cumbria Police, team leadership and her role in the command structure came from experience. This was not the first body found in waters in the Lake District that she had attended.

She focused, for some reason, on the cross bouncing slightly in the lapping water but somehow wedged firmly, tethered to the rock by the tension in the chain, which must be caught beneath the stone. A religious cross made it worse somehow. The combination of the stone, the cross and the submerged body overwhelmed her, filling her with foreboding.

Not the body alone; Calder had seen enough of those. She had found them in every state, from the dignity of repose of an elderly man alone in his bedsit to a woman in a camping trailer, partly naked, exposed and beaten. Her worst experience in that area was the horror of the damaged and broken body of a child in a traffic accident.

It was the other elements in the scene. All she could do about the thoughts entering her head was to put her hands together and pray.

2 BODY

Detective Constable Samantha Livermore, now Acting Detective Sergeant Livermore, if you please, at least during the rest of July, was about to pick up DC Howard Mooney as her mobile rang. As she heard the details from the MIU duty officer, DC Mooney came down the path from his parent's home and folded his long body into the front passenger seat. The two officers lived within a quarter mile of each other.

He sat in silence as the remainder of the conversation finished. As Sammie started the vehicle, he said, "We are going somewhere else, I gather?"

He was conscious that his more experienced colleague was still adjusting to her temporary role. She had responsibility now for the little sub-team of the MIU that she was normally part of; their own detective sergeant was away with his family camping in Cornwall, probably melting in the heat wave.

Sammie had become tense over this last week, Howard thought, as if the team leader role didn't sit well. Mooney, ever conscious of his height even among a group of police officers, wondered if the reverse sensitivity was true for

Sammie; she was smaller and big-framed, not slim. It enhanced her appearance of shortness, but he knew she wasn't overweight or unfit; a month ago he had seen her sprint after a man who panicked during an arrest, and she beat Howard by a head to intercept him.

July and August were peak 'family holiday' times for police officers with kids, the same as for everyone else bounded by school terms and fines for keeping kids off school. More than a third of the MIU team had holiday leave booked; it was this way every year. It was also, unfortunately, one of their busiest times as a territorial constabulary, given the peak influx of holiday visitors to the Lake District. Yesterday, both officers had been on an investigation into a hit-and-run fatality in Thursby, and he had expected to be assigned there again today.

Sammie replied tersely, "Yes, a new one, it just came in. A fisherman found a body, a male, in the water in Bassen-thwaite Lake. It's not located deep, so we don't need the diving team, apparently. The man is near the shore, a wellies and waders job. The locals are there already, taping it off, and the SOCOs have been called, I gather, as has the locum pathologist. We will be the first from MIU on-scene and I am to take charge, I was told, so we aren't even going into the station first. Trent is arriving at Thursby now and will be along as soon as he can. Everyone else is nearer Carlisle than Keswick, so we are it."

Detective Chief Inspector John Trent headed up the MIU.

Sammie paused, focusing on the traffic at the T-junction, as the light from the low sun was now making her view difficult as she finessed her entry into the the main road.

She continued, "They located just now the vehicle that hit the little boy, they believe. He'll leave the arrest to Neil and come on from there. We are to meet up with Dr. Lee."

Detective Inspector Neil Green reported directly to Trent and led their team within the Major Investigation Unit.

As she glanced across at Howard, taking in his expression, she smiled. "You haven't met Dr. Lee, I take it? No, you wouldn't have. You only started with us at the tail end of last summer, and by then the pathologists were back to full strength. He does some coverage for them, particularly in the summer holidays."

"And?" asked Howard.

"Wait till you see him in his coveralls; he's as round as he is tall. And he has allergies, he says; he snorts, has breathing difficulties. When he is on-scene outdoors he gets irritated, and can get cross with people very easily, so be careful. He prefers the atmosphere at the hospital, I suspect; the formalin clears his sinuses."

They were beaten to the site by the forensic pathologist. That was when the bother began.

The local police officers' job was to seal off the crime scene and not get in the way when the experts arrived; everyone knew that. Providing that the corpse wasn't floating away, they wouldn't be expected to disturb the scene at all.

As Sammie got out of her car, she looked across to the lake edge. They had parked close to the patrol vehicle and two other cars. From the contents of the open tailgate in front of her, this one belonged to the pathologist. She saw Dr. Lee inside the taped-off area walking towards a police officer standing on the bank, a woman.

Neither Sammie nor Howard followed him. They went to the back of their own vehicle and opened the boot.

"I don't have wellies with me," said Howard, stating the

obvious, as Sammie pulled out a pair of her own rubber boots. They would normally have gone first to Penrith and the MIU Headquarters, to pick up a police-assigned vehicle and access their lockers. Sammie said nothing.

Donning forensic boot covers and coveralls would be their first priority, after which they would talk with the local officers who had secured the scene with the characteristic POLICE - DO NOT CROSS barricade tape. There was a standard routine and rushing to the body wasn't it; the deceased wasn't going anywhere until the pathologist had first examined the corpse.

Sammie called to the young constable standing near the tape, blocking access to the water's edge. "Are you the first on the scene? I'm Acting DS Livermore, with MIU."

Her voice carried across to the man, who began walking towards their vehicle as Sammie held up her warrant card.

She had already noted a small, new-looking Ford Fiesta with a rental company sticker parked back on the verge of the narrow road, just before the turn-off to the church. She said to Howard, "That rental back on the road may be the vehicle the deceased arrived in, if he is not local - let's get it secured."

All they knew so far was that there was a body in the lake, a man.

The uniformed officer replied, "No. I was second, I'm PC Truman. Sergeant Calder was here first; she was only a few minutes away when the call came in. She's over there."

He nodded in the direction of the water's edge, just as they heard Dr. Lee raise his voice.

As she expertly donned a set of coveralls, Sammie asked the local officer, "Can you and DC Mooney secure the area around that car back there, also, please? Before our boss gets here. I think it might be relevant."

Howard smiled. He wasn't being asked to get his feet

wet – at least at present.

Her boots covered, Sammie walked over to the bank, ducking beneath the tape. "Good morning, Dr. Lee. It's Sammie Livermore."

The pathologist looked disgruntled. "DC Livermore, good morning. This officer is here for some reason ..."

He left it hanging, just looked at the woman, his eyes fixing on her feet.

As she moved forward, Sammie took in the tall sergeant. She'd seen her before somewhere but didn't know her at all.

Sammie held out her hand. "Acting DS Livermore, MIU. I am now the on-scene commander until relieved by a more senior officer. You were first on the scene?"

"I'm Harriet Calder, from the Keswick station. Yes, I live close by."

Sammie asked, "And the person who reported the find, this Colin Kavanagh; where is he?"

"Inside St. Anselm's – the church there. He's having a cup of tea with PC Keegan from our station. He knows he is going to be interviewed. Stella is good with people and Mr. Kavanagh is still a bit upset and cold from getting wet. I just came back here again after talking to him."

"Does he need medical assistance?" Sammie asked. She hoped not. She always liked to get statements from the reporting person fresh, even if they are jittery. If they are taken away and interviewed later, they tidy it up and in doing so, make changes.

"He says he's OK and I think so; he's upset, but not showing any physical signs of shock or distress."

He was available and being looked after, Sammie thought. Other than this officer being inside the crime scene area without covers, everything seems to be in good shape.

She glanced at the accusatory pathologist, then said to Calder, "You were keeping an eye on the body, no doubt."

"I was praying," Sergeant Calder responded, bluntly, "for the departed."

Sammie could see that Calder's comment satisfied Dr. Lee, made him feel vindicated in raising the matter, so she asked, "Do you know the man, then; is he local?"

Calder shook her head. "No, I don't. And I don't think he is local. I was looking at the cross there. He could be High Anglican or Catholic perhaps, if it belongs to him."

Sammie's brow furrowed as she thought what to say. The last thing they needed was a local copper playing Sherlock Holmes.

"We'll need your shoes, sergeant. You are in a crime scene area. The SOCOs should be here in a few minutes. Until then could you wait by the tape, please, not move anywhere else? Thank you."

Her tone of voice made it clear that she was in charge. As she spoke, she heard the noise of a larger vehicle. The SOCO crime scene van appeared from around the corner. The boys and girls in white would soon be swarming over the place, she knew. Everything seemed in order for when her bosses arrived.

She spoke directly to the pathologist. "So, let's see what we have got."

As Sammie moved closer to the water's edge, she took in the scene little by little, as she had been trained to do. First, she scanned the ground near the edge of the lake. Then she concentrated on the faint outline of a body in the water, the legs more visible than the lower torso. The upper body and head were still too deep to see. The stone was partly in the water, partly exposed.

Only the hand and the man's lower arm, now freed up and moving gently with the water, showed clearly. As Calder had said, the cross was the most visible element of the scene. From a distance she could see the figure of Christ on the cross in gold, real or plated. The working of the detail on the figure of Christ was ornate, which tied in with Calder's comment. Livermore had a Catholic upbringing; she had seen similar crucifixes on priests and nuns.

The pathologist was now calf-deep in his boots, confirming the death and examining the exposed hand. He was a balloon of white on the water, it seemed. Sammie knew better than to ask him anything at this point. They would wait on him and the work of the SOCOs. Bit by bit, the scene would be examined and uncovered. The pathologist would examine the corpse *in situ* and again on the riverbank inside a hastily erected tent, after which it would be taken to the hospital morgue, closely followed by Dr. Lee.

A new investigation was underway. Her team had two new ones in twenty-four hours, she thought; it's July and we are understaffed. It's summer in the Lake District.

Sammie heard Sergeant Calder speak from some distance behind her. "I have some other shoes in the car; sandals."

Sammie said nothing in response, just nodded as she walked past Calder to talk to the head SOCO now suiting up. They knew each other. She said to him quietly, "Can you get the sergeant's shoes bagged? She was by the body but not in the water and has other footwear in her vehicle."

She called back to Calder, "Help is on the way; if you could then wait in the church, too, please?"

She made it sound like a request, but it was clearly an instruction. Sammie felt good that she had taken control.

Then Calder called out to her, "Did you notice the stone?"

Sammie turned back saying tersely, "Yes, I noticed."

She kept her tone even but was thinking, 'It's a bloody big rock; it would be hard to miss', as she walked back to the local officer.

Sergeant Calder said, "It's not from the lake; it's a semi-dressed stone, the big ones often used for topping drystone walls. Someone brought it with them. It took some serious effort, I think."

Sammie kept her face neutral. I should have spotted that, she thought, her confidence dropping a little. She replied, "To weigh him down, it appears."

Calder nodded. "There's a car back on the road, I saw. You'll want people to check that, and the routes here for a wall with a stone missing, no doubt. And there is a landscape environmental architect in Kendal you may want to check with, too. He's a dab hand at knowing the location of these walls and the types of stone."

Sammie looked at the officer. She was starting to sound less like an amateur Sherlock Holmes and more like a member of MIU.

3 TRENT

It was forty minutes later when Sammie heard two more vehicles approaching down the track. They were now waiting for DCI Trent to turn up or, failing him, the lead investigator he assigned to the case.

She had placed another uniformed officer at the corner of the path and the road, denying access to any unnecessary traffic, so these vehicles must be on business. The officer had already turned away two sets of visitors to the church, both early morning tourists.

There was also a Scene Records Officer from MIU in place now, logging the arrivals and departures of all authorised site visitors. The SOCOs had placed stepping plates at the scene, several items near the shoreline had been marked, and the tent for the initial examination of the body had been set up.

Dr. Lee was sitting in his car, having a sandwich and a cup of coffee from a flask he had brought along. Not that he needed nourishment between meals, thought Sammie; it must be his breakfast. If she hadn't been up really early because of the Thursby case she would have been famished herself, but she had at least made time for some cereal and a banana. The hit-and-run case she had been on yesterday was the death of a young boy. Everyone pulled out all the stops for cases involving kids.

Sammie had just come out of the church again after a much-needed cup of tea as she saw the dark blue Mercedes A Class arrive, knowing it belonged to DCI Trent. She headed over to give her status report. The good news was that a minute ago, she'd been told that the SOCOs had gained entry to and checked the contents of the rental car back on the road.

Detective Chief Inspector John Trent was a veteran of the Cumbria Constabulary's Serious Crimes Investigations unit in its various guises, titles, and acronyms. He had no nickname in his team, but if he did it would be 'The Great Delegator'. No-one left his side without more work to do. In fact, he was a proficient people manager and team leader, destined, some rumoured, to be made a super-intendent soon. He wasn't a 'lead the pack, get behind me' sort of guy. But he was in charge; about that, there was no doubt.

What Sammie liked most about him was that he treated everyone with respect and didn't seem to be phased by ballyhoo around the top brass.

As Trent donned coveralls, wellingtons, and overshoes, he listened carefully to her update. At the end he said, "Seems in good shape, Sammie; well done. I'm sorry to take so long to get here."

"They are getting ready to move the body, boss. It's out of the water and in the tent in the shade, with cold air blowers; we were getting worried about the sun rising, making everything warmer. I was about to call to find out who the senior investigator was just as you showed up. Dr. Lee is pressing me to move the body inside."

"Let's go see. Then we can talk."

The deceased was a man with light brown hair, dressed in a black short-sleeved sport shirt and sand-coloured slacks. The slacks still have creases, Sammie had noted. His walking shoes were new, with recent deep scratches, possibly from the stones on the lakebed as he entered. His hair, now drying in clumps and rat tails, was nevertheless trimmed and would be neat, if combed. He didn't strike her as a vagrant or a drunken holidaymaker.

"Dr. Lee says the label on his sports shirt isn't from here; it could be the USA; we haven't searched the rest, yet. We'll check during the autopsy."

The large stone from his chest was now sitting in a covered plastic tray on the grass, to be bagged and examined by the forensic team. Lee had scoffed his sandwich and headed over to intersect with the two officers as Trent moved to the barricade tape.

The pathologist was formal. "DCI Trent, good morning. You have a male in his early-to-mid thirties who, from his skin tones and general physique, would probably be in good health if alive, it seems. There is no significant damage to his frontal areas or his face that I can see. There are no obvious external signs of aneurism, myocardial infarction or stroke visible; again, that is a preliminary observation. There has been a little nibbling around the edge of the left upper eyelid; from some fish or water creature, I expect, but I will check that carefully at the autopsy. Otherwise, at first glance he appears to have died under the weight of that stone holding him down in the water. Accidentally or deliberately is, of course, for you to determine.

"I will check his lungs and stomach to make sure the water there is of the same composition. There are some contusions on his back, elbow and wrists, scratches from the lakebed, I suspect, and some post-mortem lividity. But he hasn't been in the water that long."

He took a breath; Sammie waited for the snort; it didn't come. Dr. Lee was on his best behaviour for the MIU chief, she thought.

"Your team now also has a wallet I found protruding from his back pocket during my initial examination. I will check his clothes more thoroughly at the hospital and pass them to Forensics. "That's about it for now. We are just about to move the body, with your permission."

"Thank you, Dr, Lee. I was detained; my apologies for keeping you. Just before you do, could I see his hands, his nails?"

The pathologist smiled. "Of course; I checked already, but please check yourself."

Sammie followed her boss's careful examination of the hands revealed by the pathologist raising the arms, one after the other. At one point Trent said, "The mark on the proximal phalanx; is that from the chain, do you think?"

"The one attached to the cross; yes, I thought so, too. You have it. He must have pressed very hard with the chain in his hand against the stone. Apart from that knuckle, which may well have been damaged on the stone, there are no obvious defensive wounds visible, as you may have noted."

The men exchanged a long glance and Trent stood upright, arching his back then placing his hands on his waist.

"I'll look forward to your report. DI Green is now set to lead the case and should be here literally any minute, I believe, if you could hold on that long. I'd like him to see the body here also. He was leaving Thursby just behind me. Will the PM be today?"

Lee nodded. "Yes, unless I am called out again. Dr. Caldecott will be back next week from holidays, and we need to keep things tidy."

Trent nodded. "I will be interviewing another man later, tied to the Thursby hit-and run; we have just brought him in for questioning. You did that post-mortem late yesterday afternoon, I gather?"

Lee nodded. "That was the little boy who died from the vehicle impact? Yes, I did. DI Green attended that, too."

Trent said, "I'll let you get on. Thank you."

Once they were alone, walking towards the church, DC Mooney came striding over.

"We have searched the Fiesta and also called Hertz. It is rented to a Duncan Aster from a city called North Bay in Ontario, Canada. He's thirty-four. He gave a local address in Ambleside on his rental details. It's a Roman Catholic retreat hostel of some sort, it says on-line. And there is a mobile in the glove box with a fingerprint access, but we waited on that, for your permission."

Sammy thought somewhere called North Bay sounded cold. After the last few days and the expected heat again today, it sounded quite attractive.

Trent responded, "Have Dr. Lee do it now; open the phone before the deceased is moved; and cover completely the view into the tent while you do it. Just in case. Then get the phone to Linnie or Zoltan – and quickly."

Fingerprint access works whether the body is alive or not. The last thing they wanted, though, was some bird-watcher with binoculars getting nosy, seeing them work with the corpse.

Mooney nodded and continued, "The SOCOs had a

quick look through the wallet. It has money; pounds and Canadian dollars, two credit cards and several ident-ification papers, including a Canadian driving license. There is also an ID card saying he is a Roman Catholic priest, but it has no photo."

Sammie said, "The local sergeant from Keswick, Calder, was right, it seems; she's the one who was praying over there. She said that she thought the deceased might be a priest."

Trent stopped suddenly and looked at her. "I know that name; Harriet Calder, is it? Is she still around?"

Sammie nodded. "She's in the church. She just gave her formal statement, as did the man who found the body, a holiday maker; a regular here. Now Calder is still talking to him, as he was upset. She's the shift duty sergeant in the local station and was just about to head back there, I think."

He nodded. "Let's go talk to her. Then I will assign duties. I need to get back to Penrith to prepare for the hit-and-run interview after that; the detention clock is ticking on that one and I am taking it myself, freeing up Neil to lead this investigation."

It was obvious to Sammie that Trent and Calder recog-nized each other, as if casually; distant acquaintances rather than colleagues or friends.

"Detective Chief Inspector John Trent, Sergeant Calder; you know my wife, I think? And I heard you speak at Wordsworth Street last year. But you had observations on the crime scene, I hear; about the cross?"

Sammie recalled the location in Penrith. There was a large rectangular old church at the intersection of Drovers Lane and Wordsworth Street, not far from the police station.

"Yes sir." Calder didn't acknowledge the earlier part of Trent's opener. "I thought he might be high church; the cross being an ornate crucifix with the body of Christ. I've seen a few, and it looked like one a Catholic priest would have. But it was just a guess."

"Did you think of anything else?" Trent asked, without acknowledging the accuracy of the observation.

"Well, it's the first week of the Keswick Convention, but most attendees will be Protestant. There are visitors of all church denominations attending from across the area and well beyond."

"Good point." Trent pursed his lips, as if he should have thought of that, but hadn't. Sammie knew vaguely of the meeting, but not when it was. She gave an inner groan. It could complicate the investigation considerably.

But Trent was still waiting on Calder, she saw. The local officer said nothing for a moment, but Sammie could read her face as well; she wasn't done. Then her boss asked, "You were praying; do you have something else, more a speculation, perhaps?"

Calder hesitated, then replied, "The stone on his chest; it's not from the lake, as I told DC Livermore; it's a wall stone. I wonder if he carried it in himself, and if he is a priest or a religious person, perhaps... I was thinking of Matthew 18:6."

A bible reference, Sammie noted.

Trent smiled. "Now, that thought crossed my mind, too."

He looked at Sammie and said in explanation, "I don't recall the exact words. But there are bibles around and –."

Calder said softly, "The verse is, 'But whoever causes one of these little ones who believe in Me to stumble, it would be better for him to have a heavy millstone hung around his neck, and to be drowned in the depth of the sea'. It's not the sea and not a millstone, but…"

Sammie thought back to the scene in the tent. Both her boss and the pathologist are working on the premise that this man may have killed himself. It was too soon for that.

Detective Inspector Neil Green walked into the church at that moment, obviously having just arrived and directed here by someone. Green was in his forties and portly. But it wasn't all fat. Sammie had seen him in action; he was a powerful man. Bigger men had fooled themselves and ended up in handcuffs. Recently he had shaved his head, going with the trend; before that his balding pate and the grey in his remaining hair had made him seem older than he was. It was true, thought Sammie; he does look younger now.

Neil was looking a little tired. The arrest of the hit-and-run suspect must have taken it out of him, she realised. Arrests never resulted in a sense of euphoria, as presented in books and films. They were treacherous ground; doing everything by the book with a person who may be protesting their innocence, making excuses, or silently working away at how to escape the charge. Investigations involving dead children amplified that, she knew. The exhaustion sets in early.

Green said nothing, but from his look he expected their boss to give him some direction.

"Neil, you got here just in time. You are to lead this one and, I suggest, head back with Young and Crossley to Ambleside, to the local address of this Father Duncan Aster, the suspected deceased. He's a visiting Canadian; a Catholic priest. At least the wallet with that ID and photo was in his pocket. Confirm his identity, if you can, and break the news. If they know him, we will need a positive identification from someone. Depending on their reaction, see if we need a liaison officer assigned. But go check out the tent, see the victim with Dr. Lee first. You'll be attending the PM this afternoon. Is all in line with this man Kleiber?"

The hit-and-run suspect, Sammie realised.

Green responded, "He's in custody, and they are running forensics on the car and doing his blood work now. He has called a solicitor and is a UK resident. He has a German name, but his nationality is Polish. He's been here for more than three years, though. It's not good, John. He's blaming the boy and calling the kid's friend a liar. You talked to him; that little boy wasn't lying. This one is going to get ugly."

Trent nodded, assessing the potential complications. "I'll take over that one directly now, and flag it to the Super; he will deal with the foreign resident complications."

He paused, thinking. "This Keswick Convention aspect; the man in the water could be here for that, Neil, as Sergeant Calder has pointed out. We need to check that. Sammie, you take Howard and – Sergeant Calder, who is your boss?"

"Inspector Dewar, but he is on holiday. Inspector Robinson from headquarters is the acting commander at present and I think I really need to get back now–."

Trent cut her off. "I'll call June Robinson. You know the ropes at the convention site, I'm sure. I'd like you to assist Acting DS Livermore and DC Mooney there and see if this man is known. Not easy, I know, but I am conscious that the convention people will disperse over the four winds at the end of the week. Sammie, you are in charge, but Calder knows the place. Report back directly to Neil, as the lead. Is there anything else, anyone?"

Sammie replied, "If I'm leaving, we need an on-scene

commander here until the body is moved and the SOCOs are through phase one."

Trent squinted. He's probably thinking about how understaffed we are this week, thought Sammie. He looked at Howard Mooney. "Have you done on-scene command, before, Howard?"

"No sir."

"Well, you are now. I'll send someone over when I get back to HQ. You two head off; Mooney, you join them once you are relieved. There could be quite a few people to interview if Aster was attending the event."

Within minutes Sammie found herself driving to a religious gathering with a local sergeant dressed in uniform other than a pair of tan-coloured sandals. In the back of her mind was Trent's comment to Calder, 'I heard you speak'. About what, she mused?

4 RAWNSLEY CENTRE

"So, you know DCI Trent's wife. How come, may I ask?"

Harriet Calder was sitting silently in the passenger seat lost in her own thoughts as Sammie drove. Sammie had been working out how to approach delicately the issue she had just encountered and gave up. Straight out with it, she decided.

Harriet took a moment, apparently concentrating on the growing traffic, then she answered, "I'm a Methodist local preacher as well as a police officer. That's like a part-time service role with the church. The Trent family attend a Methodist church in Penrith. I go there occasionally to give a sermon or lead a service. It is part of our circuit –."

She glanced at Sammie. "Are you religious?"

"Lapsed Catholic; well and truly lapsed."

"Then our circuits are a bit like a Catholic diocese, our geographic areas. I got to know Mrs. Trent through that."

"You knew he was a police officer, then?"

"I knew the name from prior investigations, but only

saw him once before in person, that I recall. But he may have seen me speak, as he said. I just recognized his face vaguely, that's all. But let's talk about the Convention. It may not be easy finding out anything about Aster there; they don't have lists of all attendees."

Sammie looked surprised. "What, people just turn up? That's not much use! What's this place about, really? Bible lectures, that sort of thing?"

"There are lectures and discussions on bible themes and Christian theology, but it is mainly about things like youth ministry, discussions of faith and spiritual renewal."

Sammie said somewhat tersely, "MIU is more about spiritual depletion than renewal; particularly when half of our lot are away on holiday, getting spiritual something else, most of them."

Harriet hummed a vague acknowledgement, but said, "And if Aster is a Roman Catholic priest, there won't be a wife and kids. It's the kids which have to be registered, for safeguarding compliance. That requirement covers anyone who attends between the ages of three and eighteen, as well as their responsible adult or parent. So with the reception people, we should try to find any registered children from the same area of Ontario, or perhaps just from Canada, I suggest. See if they or their parents know this man. If we had a photo that would help but…"

We may, after DI Green gets to this Catholic retreat hostel, Sammie thought. The photos they had of the drowned man were not for sharing, nor were they suitable to use, with half of one eyelid lip nibbled away.

The traffic was building. Sammie couldn't do anything about that; she was in her personal vehicle, not one fitted with flashers and a siren. At one point, she said unnecessarily, "You are right, there are a lot of people here for this meeting. Keswick is packed. It must be like a football match every day."

Harriet laughed softly. "It's something like that, in terms of traffic and street safety. But you don't get physical clashes between opposing sides."

"Opposing sides?" repeated Sammie.

"It's religion," Harriet said, matter-of-factly.

They made their way along Main Street and turned into the road leading to the Rawnsley Centre, the headquarters of the Keswick Ministries. As they parked, Sammie started to feel uncomfortable. She wasn't just lapsed, she didn't like evangelicals at all; it brought back a memory from her teens and, more recently, while in the job, she had assisted at an arrest of a fundamentalist pastor who had beaten his children. She recalled him to be a right bastard, despite his holier-than-thou ways.

They got out and Harriet said, "We should start with the reception centre people. They process all the three to eighteen year-old attendees; they may know something."

This could be a 'needle in a haystack' job, Sammie thought. Neil Green will get further on with the visit to Ambleside than us messing about here, searching for someone who has heard of this priest.

She was wrong. In fact, they hit gold. Later, Sammie was to tell her teammates that it was only the second time in her years with MIU that she had this sort of luck.

~~

Inside the reception centre, Sammie strode past the people waiting there for help. But it was Sergeant Calder's uniform which did the trick; parting the line like the Red Sea, she thought, with an inner smile.

She spoke quietly to the woman behind the first desk

they saw. "Cumbria Police; we need to establish if a person is attending the convention. Who do we talk to?"

The woman responded, "You should start with Mr. Vaughn. Tom Vaughn is the Reception Centre coordinator. A lot of us on the desk here are volunteers, on shifts. But we have a list of reception centre staff you could talk to, as well."

Sammie replied, "But not a list of attendees, I gather?"

The woman shook her head. "No, we don't have a complete list; just one of the young people and their parents or responsible adults. Hello Harriet."

She was looking at Calder, who smiled. "Good morning, Jean."

They knew each other, Sammie realised. She said to her colleague, "Do you know this Mr. Vaughn, too?"

"Yes, we've met." Her expression was neutral, but her eyes gave away that she was thinking that perhaps the MIU officer should have asked her first, given her earlier revelation of her other role.

Jean led them across to an inner officer area, its door partly open. Still, she knocked. "Tom, some police officers are here, with a query about a possible participant."

Vaughn was a middle-aged man in good shape, it appeared, and with a trim moustache. He offered them seats as Harriet firmly closed the door. He said lightly, "Harriet, wearing brown sandals, in uniform? Is this a new trend?"

"Tan, Tom; they're tan."

Sammie cut across the dialogue. "We are trying to establish whether a man called Duncan Aster is attending this week. He is from Ontario, Canada, and we believe he may be a Roman Catholic clergyman. Can you help us at all?"

Vaughn looked at her. "I am not aware of the name. Sergeant Calder may have explained; anyone can attend the meeting, there is no registration for adults. We register children and young people, so I can check that list. Or we can check the bookshop purchases for credit card payments, that sort of thing."

"Does the list have home addresses; would it identify Canadians?"

"Yes, it does."

"We would like a copy, if you would."

Vaughn looked a little uneasy. "I would need to check with my superiors, if you don't mind."

This was a familiar problem for Sammie. "If you could do that, please? And do it as fast as you can. This is an investigation into a suspicious death, so we have rights of access. If you feel you can't co-operate, I will call my team lead and it will shoot up the ladder very fast."

The man looked still more uncomfortable as he picked up the phone. As he went to dial, he paused. "This is not a child safeguarding issue then?"

Sammie thought of the bible quote Harriet had recited earlier. "We don't know at this point. Why?"

He paused, obviously thinking something through. Harriet Calder spoke up. "Tom, is something troubling you?"

She even sounds like a priest, thought Sammie.

Vaughn sighed. "There is a Canadian clergyman here, but not your man, though; he's an Anglican, a Reverend Andrew Moore. He came to see me yesterday afternoon, to ask about 'child and vulnerable person' reporting obligations in the UK, as he put it. It was unusual, to say the least, and we are always on alert during the convention; Harriet knows that. He didn't say abuse or sexual abuse *per se*, but I asked him outright. He was just interested in the child protection measures here, he claimed. I explained our safeguarding reporting requirements. He wasn't familiar with the term 'safeguarding' but told me that Canada had something similar in place. I thought there may be more to his enquiry, so I was keeping an eye out for him in case he came back with a specific issue. Moore's wife is registered, as the family has two children here. Her first name is Sylvia."

He was reading, it seemed, from a data entry on his computer screen.

Sammie said immediately, "So do you have her contact information? We'll start with her; but I still want that other list fast, please."

Ten minutes later, after a call to a Canadian mobile number, they met up with a casually dressed woman; but one dressed expensively, noted Sammie. The Moore couple had money, she concluded.

"My husband is in the session at the other site, at the main tent this morning; he's been there all week for the morning sessions. I'll call him, if you like? But what's this about?"

Sammie said carefully, not answering the question. "Do you know Father Duncan Aster, a Roman Catholic priest?"

The woman's face clouded over. Sammie's first thought was that Moore knows him, and perhaps what this is about.

"I was introduced by my husband. Duncan is attending the same sessions as Andy."

Sammie pressed on. "Have you visited St. Anselm's Church, on the lake?"

The woman looked more puzzled. "No. In fact, Andy was going to take us there tomorrow, a free afternoon. He really liked it."

"And when did he go there?"

"Yesterday, in the afternoon; he and Father Aster went there to talk."

From her face, Sammie could see that she realised now that something serious was wrong.

"If you could give us your husband's number, please; we will call him ourselves."

Sylvia Moore said, "Why don't I come back with you? The girls are in their sessions now. We can find him together."

"Let's not call, then; let's just go over and you can point him out."

As they walked out, Sammie said to Calder, "I'll catch you up in a minute."

She needed to call in, get another car and some uniforms here right now.

5 MOORE

Reverend Andrew Moore was fascinated by a Pastor Garston Hoag, a speaker from Ohio. His views on the Book of Micah were thought-provoking, but to Moore, they were largely ill-founded and an over-extrapolation. Nevertheless, he was enjoying the sessions each morning as much for the fellowship, the discussion, and the atmosphere, as for anything else. No-one here was bored or disinterested. No-one was checking their watch, as some do during his sermons back home. It had energy to it.

His daughters were similarly energized by their youth sessions, he found, bubbling over with the learnings of each day, and the new friends they had made who had traveled here from different places.

Moore was thirty-eight, dark-haired and clean-cut, a man conscious of his appearance. Small things gave away that he wasn't one to be counted among the impecunious, sacrificing wealth for vocational poverty. His daypack, for example, was a Canadian brand, Roots; but not a cheaper canvas one. It was pebble-grained black leather, probably costing hundreds of dollars, but had been well beaten up over the years. And in addition to a wedding ring, he wore a fancy signet ring, a heavy gold piece with the letter 'A' deeply engraved, bracketed between a pair of substantial diamonds. Like the backpack, it was well scratched and worn.

Talk to him in a social setting, as in the big tent at Keswick or the narthex of a church, and he would engage you in pleasantries or talk about world events, if you wanted. However, raise a biblical or theological point or question, his eyes would light up and give you the correct and only possible interpretation; his tone of voice making it clear that he would brook no other viewpoint, unless you too were an accredited theologian or also ordained. At the end of the conversation, he would still seem a million miles distant and after his departure you may or may not notice that he hadn't bothered to ask you for your name, nor enquire how you are.

Moore's phone buzzed and he frowned, disturbed by it. It was a text from his wife, he saw. It was urgent that they meet just outside the main entrance. His first thought was for his children; it must be to do with them. He stood, picked up his backpack as he shuffled out, apologising quietly to the people who had to let him pass.

As he reached the front of the tent and his eyes adjusted somewhat to the sunlight outside, he saw in the middle distance the distinctive hat that Sylvia had brought with her from home. As he headed in her direction through the people still entering, he suddenly realised that she was not alone; two people were with her. Drawing up at the gate behind was a police car and two officers got out. Moore took in that they focused instantly on the tall police officer in uniform standing with Sylvia.

On seeing her husband appear, Sylvia waved and walked

forward. Harriet Calder was a step behind the wife as they zeroed in on Reverend Moore; the sudden find, this man who had been at the crime scene with the deceased only yesterday. As the gap narrowed, she saw him stop still.

He may bolt, Harriet thought, and instinctively she checked behind her, seeing the Cumbria Police vehicle and the officers exiting it.

In the end, he just stood still as they approached.

Sylvia called out. "Andy, these people need to talk to you about Duncan."

She stopped short as Livermore touched her arm. "We'll do this, thank you. Please wait here."

Sammie moved forward the last few steps; her in a business suit, him in casual clothes, a head taller than her. She said quietly, "Reverend Moore, we need to talk to you about a man called Duncan Aster."

He looked down at her, appearing irritated but didn't speak.

Sammie continued, "We understand you went to St. Anselm's Church with him yesterday; is that right?"

He responded in a clipped manner. "Yes; but I can't talk about that; I'm sorry. I can't talk at all about Father Aster. I need to get back to my session."

Moore half-turned and found that the sergeant in uniform was now blocking his way. They were standing eyeball to eyeball, it seemed. She said softly, "Actually you have to, so please don't move away or I'll be forced to detain you. This detective has some important questions, you see?"

Andrew shook his head. "It's you who doesn't understand. I can't talk about Duncan with you. He's a priest; I'm a priest. I would want to talk to a lawyer before I would do that."

He looked around, first at the shorter plain-clothed

officer, her face implacable, then at his wife, her face a mix of astonishment and fear. They didn't get it; discussions between clergy were out of bounds to lay people, his expression said.

Both Sammie and Harriet were struck by the fact that Moore hadn't even asked what was wrong. Most normal people ask that question straight off when approached by a police officer about another person. Most, not all; the uncaring and the guilty didn't. But he was a priest; they are supposed to care, aren't they? It was enough for Sammie.

"I'd like you to come with me across to those officers over there, quietly and without fuss. We don't want a scene, do we?"

From her expression, Moore saw that the woman didn't care one way or the other on that score. If he didn't cooperate, they would put him in handcuffs, he thought.

He said disdainfully, "If you insist. This is a spiritual gathering, despite your presence."

But he started moving towards the gate as Sammie moved along one side of him and Harriet took the other. Sylvia Moore traipsed along behind.

Five minutes later, with Reverend Moore sitting in the back of the police vehicle and his wife telling him she would stay here for the children, Sammie was calling DI Green to explain the developments. She was instructed to bring Reverend Moore into Penrith Police Headquarters for an interview. Harriet Calder, still in her tan sandals, was instructed to accompany them. The Cumbria Police vehicle then took him over there; she and Calder were going to follow.

"I should stay here, help with the interviews," said Calder.

Sammie responded, almost accusingly, "DI Green said, 'Bring Harriet'. I have the suspicion that you know more people in my team than DCI Trent's wife."

Calder chose not to respond. As they got back to their car, DC Mooney drove up. Sammie went across to talk to him. She said, "We have a photo now. Mrs. Moore had one on her phone of her husband and Aster. First, you talk to her; get her statement about all she knows about Aster. She's worried, of course, but is staying here for their kids. At least she is being open with us, unlike her husband.

"I've just sent the image from her phone to mine, and on to headquarters. Linnie is gussying it up at the office and will release the head and shoulders for general use. Contact her and get copies available for all the interviewing officers. Good so far?"

He nodded.

"Green is arranging some more uniforms to help us here and a Tom Vaughn in the office over there has a list of some of the Canadians here with their telephone numbers; you need to get that list right now. There may well be others here, people who might know Aster, but they could be spread all over hell's half-acre. Work the list; do what you can. I'm meeting Neil at the station to do the interview with this guy Moore, apparently. But you are 'it' here for now; don't screw up."

Howard looked across at Sergeant Calder. "And the sergeant, shouldn't she help? She knows the place."

Sammie rolled her eyes. "Don't talk commonsense to me. 'Bring Harriet', I was told. I'm doing that; you do what you are told, too."

She turned on her heels, giving Calder a scowl. Howard didn't complain. He quite liked this opportunity to show his capabilities without Sammie finding her feet in a command role by treading on his.

~~

In the Penrith MIU operations room, Harriet Calder felt out of place and ill at ease. It was only partly to do with the fact she was dressed in the hybrid mix of her uniform and sandals. She was hoping for the nod from someone that she could head back to her regular duties, although the events of the day intrigued her. Being here awoke old memories, old ghosts.

Neil Green and Sammie had been talking one-on-one on their arrival before they came over to her.

Green said, "I talked with DCI Trent just now, Harriet; he was heading into an interview on another case. How are you doing these days?"

The hit-and-run, thought Harriet. "I'm doing fine, sir, but Keswick is busy. We have a lot going on."

He acknowledged the point with a nod. "Sammie and I are doing the interview with Moore. Trent wants you to observe this one. Your boss, Inspector Robinson, has arranged coverage for you for this shift, I gather. DCI Trent thinks you are more familiar with church law; is he right?"

"Probably more than most, I suspect, but I am not an expert; certainly not on Catholic canon law, no. Anglican is similar to Methodist and safeguarding reporting is common to both, so... yes, I guess I do."

He led her over to an office, where a young female civilian staff member was setting up. "Linnie, Sergeant Calder will be observing."

He addressed Harriet. "You know the ropes. I'll be wearing an earpiece. Anything you think of, tell Linnie."

Harriet found herself watching a muted computer screen, seeing the Canadian talking with a lawyer, in some consternation and apparently asking questions.

6 FIRST INTERVIEW

18 July 11.00 a.m. BST

DI Green was softly spoken and friendly as they settled in the interview room.

"Reverend Moore, thank you for coming. We are sorry to take you away from your meeting, but you wouldn't answer my colleague's routine questions, so we had no choice. This is a serious matter. We are looking into the death of a man. I'm sure Mr. Newbold was able to clarify this for you."

Newbold was the duty solicitor.

"Is this about Father Aster?" asked Moore.

"It is about a suspicious death. We can't say who that is until a positive identification has been made. But why did you say his name? Do you know him?"

The clergyman nodded. "I met him here; I didn't know him back in Ontario. It was a coincidence, really. We were attending the same sessions this week and he heard me talking; he recognised my accent. And my wife, with your officers; they said it was about Duncan."

Green nodded, affirming he understood the basis for

Moore's earlier response now.

"You are from a place called Stoney Creek in Ontario, I gather, from your address?"

"Yes, I am the rector of a parish church there, St. Matthew's."

"And you are visiting Keswick; why?"

"It's my annual holiday. The children are off school. My wife and I came on our honeymoon to the UK years ago on a walking holiday in the Lake District. We visited Keswick then. That's when we found out about the Convention, but it wasn't on at the time. We talked of coming and… this year was it. We are going to take the girls hill-walking here after this week's events, then fly home. That's the plan."

Green smiled. "You look fit; do you do a lot of walking?"

The clergyman returned the smile. "No, not at home; I go to a gym, though, and try to stay healthy."

"No other sports, then?"

"Not now. I play a little golf in the summer; that's it. I'm too busy, really."

Harriet saw on Linnie's computer screen that Moore was looking a little lost with the direction of the questions, but Neil Green was doing a good job of settling the man and probing his physical skills. She knew he was checking whether Moore had the ability to hold Aster under the water.

"So, you met Duncan Aster when, exactly?"

"I first talked to him on Tuesday; three days ago. Afterwards, he walked back to the Rawnsley Centre with me and met my family briefly."

"What did you talk about then, with the family? Can I ask that?"

Yes, you can, thought Harriet. That information is

certainly not privileged.

"Well, we talked mainly about the doctrine of discovery; to explain it to the girls simply. That it is wrong, really."

He realised he had lost his audience. "It's an old church doctrine which grants previously unknown lands discovered by Christians to be their own, so that they could convert the people there. Sylvia and I are evangelical, as is Duncan Aster, but that's different from taking away the rights of others."

"So, it wasn't a conversation about regular things; family, sports, television, what the children were doing?"

Moore looked nonplussed. "No. We are at the Keswick Convention so…" He trailed off.

"And the last time you talked to him was when?"

"It was yesterday afternoon near the convention grounds, along Station Street; I think that's what it's called just there, the main road."

Tone tells everything, Harriet thought. He is lying or hiding something about that meeting. But sitting across from him, neither Sammie nor Neil showed that they saw the same thing; but they wouldn't have missed it.

Green asked softly, "At what time?"

"Around 4.30 p.m. or thereabouts, I think, but I didn't check my watch specifically."

Green looked down at his pad. "How was he then, would you say? Happy or sad, can you describe his mood or behaviour?"

Moore thought about it. "He was preoccupied; burdened might be a better description."

"By what?"

"I can't say."

"Don't know or won't say? Could you clarify that, please?"

Moore looked at the solicitor and then back to Neil

Green. "I can't tell you because it is privileged."

Green looked at him, pausing. "That means you know what troubled him, right? But feel you can't tell us."

Moore nodded.

Sammie butted in. "For the record Reverend Moore nodded. Could you answer please?"

"I know something that was troubling him; yes, but I don't know his precise thoughts at that time, obviously."

Green pressed him. "You are claiming, are you, that the information he provided to you is confidential because you are a priest; is that correct?"

"Yes."

"We'll come back to that. Now, I want a detailed under-standing of your movements from Station Street, the time you say you last spoke to Father Aster, and our officers meeting you this morning, please; if you would?"

He held his pen poised.

As Harriet watched the halting summary of Moore's activities unfold, covering the period in question, she heard a slight movement behind her. Linnie swung her head around and said, "Hello, boss."

DCI Trent nodded and looked at her, then at Calder. Harriet got the impression that he had crept in quietly and had been there for a moment or so, watching.

"What do you reckon?"

It wasn't clear which one of them he was asking.

"He's lying about something to do with his last meeting with Aster," Linnie said.

Harriet nodded. "I thought so, too; and he is hiding behind 'privilege'; that needs to be challenged. Either his conversation with Aster meets the criteria of formal conf-ession or not. In any event, he is still subject to the law to answer."

Trent responded, "Linnie, tell Neil we'll take a break after the 'opportunity window' listing he's preparing, but keep Moore there. We'll take stock. Zoltan has Aster's phone open now and there is an interesting email, I gather."

"And Kleiber, sir?" Linnie asked.

"We are in for the long haul on that one; he's being tricky. I'll go back in with him after we have all had a break in that interview. I'm not worried about the detention clock now; I'll charge him before it expires, and we will be opposing bail."

~~

They gathered around a central table, about six of them. Trent said, "Zoltan first; this email."

The tech specialist spoke up. "His last email was sent from his mobile to a Canadian email address. Quote, '*I can't cope, Hugh. First Susan, now this; I talked with an Anglican priest I met here and thought it would help but it didn't. And he's let me down. I am praying for guidance.*' Then there is a Latin quote, I think, *Ignosce Me*. About forgiving, I think."

"It's 'Forgive me', or 'Lord, forgive me', I think," said Harriet, unprompted.

The technician continued, "That was sent at 2.56 a.m. our time, 9.56 p.m. yesterday Canadian time. I am assuming Ontario time because at 10.17 p.m. Ontario time a reply came from the private email, an H. Tremblay at a Bell Canada domain, a local email address there.

"*Call me, please, Duncan. I want to help. Where are you now? I will find someone there to help you. Hugh.*"

"There were then two calls to Aster's phone over the next twenty minutes from a number in a city there. It's North Bay in Ontario, according to the area code. The first was from a male, an older man, it seems, from his voice-mail. *'Duncan, call me, please, we must talk!'* It sounded urgent. On the second call, no message was left. Then there was a final email at 11.25 p.m. their time from the same address; *'Duncan, call me when you wake up, even if it's the nighttime here. Hugh'*.

Zoltan looked up from his laptop screen. "I'm looking into the details to identify the caller, and we need to consider approaching the Ontario Police. Is that OK with you, boss?"

Trent nodded.

The technician continued. "From the timing, it must have rung in the car. Aster may have been in the water by then, from what I gathered so far."

Trent said, "Thank you. Neil, the update from Aster's local address, please?"

"It's a small Roman Catholic retreat in Ambleside, a large house, but nothing too fancy. They confirmed he was staying there but didn't know him in any detail. They often get priests on retreat, they said; 'recharging their batteries, away from it all'. The person we spoke to, a Malcom Reilly, said Aster had been there five days. The decision by him to go to the Keswick Convention seemed out of the blue, unplanned. He asked about directions and said he would miss the lunch for three days; that there was a lecture series at the convention he wanted to hear. Apparently one of the priests there was put out a bit, it not being a Catholic event, but no-one said anything to the man to stop him. Aster kept to himself otherwise. Reilly is the Centre admin-istrator; he volunteered to identify the body. He should be doing that with DC Howell about now."

Trent said, "And now the interview of Reverend Moore. Sammie, you give it."

"Initially he seemed to be communicating with us once

he was in the interview room, but it then became clear he's hiding something. And we don't believe he is being completely honest about the last contact he claims they had. But he's shutting down now, using this religious privilege thing. We didn't want to push there yet."

She looked at Neil Green, in deference to him being the senior investigator. Green added, "I don't know Canadian law on that, which could be guiding him, but we need to get past it someway or confront his lack of co-operation. He admits he knows more about Aster's state of mind, at the very least."

He looked at Trent, obviously wanting guidance. Trent thought for a few seconds as DS O'Brien, his co-interviewer in the hit-and-run homicide, walked across, hovering at the perimeter. They were ready for the next session with the driver, Kleiber, his body language said.

Trent nodded and stood up. "Everything indicates that this man understands, better than anyone else we are aware of at present, what was on Aster's mind before he died. It is already looking to me like suicide, but I am not firm on that. I think we push Moore a little.

"Sammie, you and Sergeant Calder go back in. You inform him about the manner of death and see his reaction. Calder, after that, not before, you press him on the priest-penitent privilege. See what gives. He will either open up or shut right down."

Sammie glanced at DI Green, surprised that their boss was replacing him, but Neil seemed quite comfortable with it. Calder seemed surprised also.

Trent added, smiling at her, "Your reward for helping us is that you will get your shoes back before you leave; I asked the SOCOs to expedite the checks."

"Fair enough, sir. Thank you."

Moore looked a little put out as Livermore and Calder entered; probably by being kept waiting. People unfamiliar with police procedure often did. Sammie was unfazed. She went through the interview set up and the identification of those present for the record.

"Reverend Moore, we believe that the body discovered earlier today is Duncan Aster. A formal identification is being organised now."

Moore seemed lost for a moment, stunned. He bowed his head, then both officers saw that he was praying silently. They waited until he looked up. They saw the pain in his eyes. It appeared to be genuine, but they were police officers; appearances weren't enough.

"How did Duncan die? Is it alright to ask?" said Reverend Moore softly.

Sammie said, gently, "We don't know for sure. We are awaiting the autopsy findings to determine a cause of death. He was found at Bassenthwaite Lake. You said earlier that he was burdened. Do you think he was in fear of others, or sufficiently burdened to harm himself?"

Moore thought about it. "Troubled, but I didn't know him, so I can't say. It is a tragedy if that was the case."

His voice had taken on a more distant professional tone.

Sammie went on, "You said earlier that his last discussion with you is privileged. We want to explore that further; clarify a few things, particularly whether the scale of those 'troubles' you mentioned were sufficient for him either to take his own life or be a reason for another person to do so. Let me repeat my question. Did he mention anyone he was afraid of?"

Moore shook his head. "No, he mentioned no one who would harm him, I believe."

Sammie looked at Harriet, passing the lead.

Calder leaned forward slightly, engaging the man with a

slight smile. "I'm glad that you prayed just now. I did, too, when I saw him; I was the first officer on the scene once the call came in. It was all I could do for him, really."

The change in direction caught Moore by surprise; that was clear. In the operations room, Neil Green and Linnie watched how Calder immediately started to try to bond with the man.

Harriet continued, "Was Father Aster's meeting with you at any time a form of confession, formal or informal?"

Moore responded. "Not in the formal sense that confession is generally understood by lay people, inside a church, in a confessional. It doesn't have to be that. In content... as I said, I can't speak to that."

Calder pressed on. "Are you an Anglo-Catholic? Do you routinely engage in auricular confession?"

Moore seemed surprised. "No, I'm a more traditional sort of Anglican, but not one who holds to conservative Roman Catholic practices or positions for our faith. I am not, for example, against the ordination of women clergy. Auricular confession; no, not routinely or formally; I don't press that with people. Not at St. Matthew's. But I meet one-on-one with members of my congregation for that purpose, as does any priest."

Calder smiled. "As in the aphorism, 'All may, none must, some should', I take it?"

"Yes; exactly. You seem well-informed?"

"I'm a part-time Methodist lay preacher in Cumbia, so I do understand. As your solicitor will advise you, there is no right of confessional privilege in English law. Each case is judged on its own merits by the courts. Withholding such information is either a serious impediment to an investigation or, at the stage of a court proceeding, disobedience to the instruction of the judge, a contempt of court. The reasons for withholding information from the police may be understood, but it is going to take the establishment of merit for the claim to avoid repercussions if you continue your current stance on this matter.

"It would really be a lot simpler for you to tell us, in whatever manner you feel comfortable, something about Father Aster's state of mind yesterday. His death was not 'natural'. All we are trying to do is establish the events leading up to it."

Calder sounded so reasonable and collaborative, Sammie thought. Moore was nodding. "That seems similar to Canadian law, as I know it. Not that I have ever experienced a situation like this before, you understand. A Methodist. I see."

Whatever he saw in his last comment, it wasn't clear to Sammie what that meant. But as much as his interest had been perked by Calder sharing the information, he didn't seem to warm to it at all – or to her.

Harriet just waited, hoping the invitation would yield something. But Moore just looked at her; thinking. Then she realised he wasn't going to say anything.

After about thirty seconds, she continued equally gently, "The one area, though, that is very clear in our laws is the issue of safeguarding. A member of the clergy must advise a penitent that they have a duty to inform the authorities immediately of any risk to children or vulnerable adults. We understand that you sought clarification on that point from the safeguarding officer at the convention site. Was that related to your conversation with Duncan Aster? A clear yes or no, please, to that question?"

The tone on the last sentence was forceful, pressing the man.

On the computer monitor, DI Green watched the change come over the priest. It seemed at first that he flushed with embarrassment, but Green quickly revised his assessment; the priest was showing intense anger. But Moore said nothing. He just glared at Calder, whose expression remained unchanged.

"Well, what do you know!" Neil Green remarked to Linnie. "She's pushed his button alright."

Then Harriet Calder said softly, "Did he mention a particular name to you, perhaps?"

Trying to contain his anger as best as he could, Moore said, "I have nothing more to say to you. Not without first talking to a lawyer of my choosing instead of your duty solicitor here. I have told you all I can; that's it. I want to go back to my meeting and my family. I want to contact the local diocesan office of the Church of England, seek their expert legal guidance from a solicitor with ecclesiast-ical training and, I might add, register a complaint about my treatment by the police today."

Green was nodding slowly, noting the anger turning into retributive threats. He glanced at Linnie and gestured to her to flick the line open to Sammie's earpiece.

"That's enough for now. Tell him he is released; he can go, but we will want to talk to him again as we still have further questions. And he will need a solicitor of his choosing by tomorrow. In fact, ask Calder if she will give him a lift back to Keswick, we'll get her a car to do so. See what comes out of their conversation on the way back, perhaps."

Sammie gave a slight nod, indicating she had heard and started the wrap-up. Green signalled to Linnie to close the link and said, "You or Zoltan find out when the Moore family are due to fly back to Canada. Check our window of opportunity for follow up without having to hold him."

Linnie asked, "Do we place a flag with Immigration to stop him, if needed?"

DI Green shook his head. "Not yet; there's no basis. I'll

have people check his alibi before we do that. But that flash of anger… and he is a fit man. It didn't look like someone had held Aster under the water, but we need the post-mortem results and the toxicology screen as soon as possible on this one. There's something not right."

As he finished speaking, he watched the four people in the interview room stand and Sammie reach over to turn off the interview recording. He heard Reverend Moore say, "I'd rather take a taxi, thank you," as it cut off.

~~

It was that evening as Sammie was heading home, she suddenly stopped and turned around to pop her head into Neil Green's office. He was lost in reading something.

"Boss, I have a question, if I could? I was surprised that DCI Trent put Calder into the interview, but it certainly stirred it up. She knows Mrs. Trent, I heard. But to turn an interview over to a local, an untrained …"

He smiled. "Not so. In fact, she was a DC here back before John came in from Birmingham and took over MIU, after Murray Cassidy retired. She was in FMI, as it was then, for two years. I had just been made sergeant here. Calder was sharp; good at interviews and had a good nose for the investigations. I thought she would stay."

He stopped, thinking back.

"What happened?" Sammie asked

"Her husband got some sort of terminal illness, his brain, I think. He wasn't in the job; he was an architect or something like that. She took a leave of absence, looked after him. Somewhere along the line she got religion. She's a church minister, or preacher of some sort."

"She said."

Green continued, "She transferred into Keswick, to

work near where she lives, and returned to general duties. Now she is a shift sergeant. A surprise really, but it takes all sorts. Perhaps the boss was sounding her out; see if she was interested in coming back. As I recall, she decided to transfer out officially the week before he took over; I think he must have processed her final transfer papers during the week he started here."

Sammie nodded, thinking about it. "It must be strange; one minute 'holier than thou' stuff from the pulpit, and the next pulling in some of the characters we deal with."

Neil smiled. "I don't think she has much trouble with that, to be honest. At least, that's what I heard. Two years ago, the bookie Larry Trowse in Keswick was fined for duffing up his nephew, Roland. It could have been worse, but I think if the magistrate could have had his way, he would have duffed up Roland, too."

Sammie knew the name of the bookie. "She arrested him?"

"No, she arrested Roland earlier. He had locked his girlfriend in the garden shed as a punishment for some perceived wrong and gone out to the pub. A neighbour phoned and Calder and a young PC were sent to the Feathers to get him. Roland got stroppy and abusive with her and next thing he knew his arm was up his back. When he tried to fight back, she took his legs out from under him and floored him. Calder told the young officer to put him in handcuffs. It was his first arrest; he was very impressed with her."

"So why did Larry Trowse get arrested? I don't get it."

"Roland got a suspended sentence and a fine, but he started telling his mates how he was going to 'settle' with the copper who had decked him; had embarrassed him unnecessarily, he claimed. Apparently, Larry's wife likes Calder's preaching. His uncle heard and decided 'enough was enough', so he went to speak to Roland, talk some sense into him. The stupid sod forgot that his uncle used to box before he became a fat bookie, so when he got truculent that time Larry floored him a second time; and not so nicely as Harriet did, either.

"The bottom line is that I think Harriet doesn't mix her job with her hobby, if you can call it that? Probably not. It's a vocation, right?"

Sammie nodded, still musing on it. "Goodnight, boss; see you tomorrow."

It had been a normal day for her, other than the surprise around the sergeant from Keswick.

7 HAMILTON

18 July 2.20 p.m. EDT

"Good afternoon, James; are you slumming it in your old haunts?"

The familiar voice of Rabbi David Simmons came from behind him. In his wanderings this early afternoon, The Right Reverend James Azikiwe, the third Bishop of the Anglican Diocese of Hamilton-Brant, had turned into a familiar road in the Westdale area of Hamilton, a city at the west end of Lake Ontario. Lost in thought, he had missed that there were people here he knew from years ago.

Azikiwe was in his mid-fifties, an average height, barrel-chested man now with a neat head of greying curly hair. He had just been to his barber for a trim and a chat, a brief respite in his heavy calendar of activities. Work for a bishop was ever-present, never far away.

James stopped and turned. David looked older, thinner; more shrunken, in a sense. Like David, James was also in dark suit pants and a short-sleeved shirt. David's old sports shirt looking a little more comfortable than the pale blue, starched shirt on the Anglican cleric.

David must be in his late seventies now, James thought. Without hesitation, he held open his arms and beamed at the man, bending to fit the embrace as David moved forward.

The old rabbi asked, "What y' doing, *Makher*, walking around here? You should be downtown."

James smiled. "I still get my haircut at Whyte's, as I used to. Then I just started walking, thinking about things. It's a long time since we were together, David, and no-one tries to teach me Yiddish anymore. *Makher*?"

Harry Whyte had established a small barbershop in the neighbourhood forty years ago. Now his nephew was the hairdresser. It never grew any bigger, but it had a loyal local clientele.

David replied, "A big shot, a VIP. Do you have time for a coffee at Timmy's; to catch up?"

If he went to the nearby Tim Hortons, James would be late for his next appointment at the cathedral office, a regular internal meeting on church planning that he sat in on from time to time. He had confirmed only this morning to the Dean and Cathedral Rector, Tom Grieves, who led the meeting, that he planned to attend. He was about to make an elegant excuse – he always had them to hand these days and needed them, it seemed. But behind the old man's smile he saw a need, and it took him back to earlier times; he had been a parish priest around here.

"Sure. For an old *Mensch* like you, Rabbi, I have time. I just need to send a text. Then I am all yours for a little while. Just don't try to convert me; I don't have that much time."

Audrey Lille, his assistant, would sort it out back at the office.

In the coffee shop a few metres away, James let David

buy; he claimed it was 'his turn'. After more than ten years, who would know? When Azikiwe was the parish priest here, the two men met regularly for a chat, ostensibly over pastoral and interfaith issues in the community, but occasionally just for companionship.

"So, James, is it all politics and prestige these days? It must be a year since you were elevated to bishop. Has the newness worn off and left the weight of responsibilities sitting on those big shoulders of yours?"

David had always been this direct with him. In his present role it was refreshing; people tended to tread carefully around a bishop.

He replied, "Something like that. At least, the problems never go away; they just change their shape."

The older man nodded. "I thought so. I must remember to pray for you. Such a Gordian knot."

James responded, "Now that's not in my bible, I believe. Alexander the Great must be in the Torah?"

David smiled at the joke. "Dissent in churches is in both our histories. You have just discerned your new ministry in particularly difficult times. You Anglicans cloak it in fine words and silence; my people tend to be a little more direct when they disagree; you hear about it."

~~

The diocese of Hamilton-Brant had been established in the eighties, as part of the restructuring of the Anglican Church in the ever-growing population of the Golden Horseshoe area west of Toronto. It encompassed areas of industrial blue-collar communities that dated from the eighteenth and nineteenth centuries, as well as wealthy rural villages and newer suburban bedroom developments. The styles and financial robustness of the churches in the diocese were as varied as their populations. These days, approximately half of the employment supporting its families was tied to the City of Toronto or its commuting lifestyle.

Adding to the mix were other divisions.

The first main rift in the diocese had been over the issue of female bishops. Women priests had been accepted by some, not all, but the thought of apostolic succession of bishops passing to a female was too much for a core minority. In the style of Anglicans, the voting at the next diocesan synod covered all the bases – and ended up in a stormy agenda item narrowly voting in Bishop Gloria Holtzbergen.

That Bishop Gloria then embraced not only a range of women's issues, but those of the LGBTQ community by blessing same-sex marriage and advocating marriage of gay couples within the church proved too big a change for the minority. Several church congregations upped sticks to join the breakaway conservative Anglican Network, at least in terms of their congregations and bank balances, if not their church buildings. After some misunderstandings and legal cases, title to those churches remained with the diocese.

The balance of conservatism and liberal change in the diocese sat uneasily and ever-present for nearly a decade, until the run-up to the recent election of a new bishop, as Holtzbergen approached retirement. Her likely successor as a change agent was a popular female priest. The conservatives were represented by a well-liked white male priest with sparkling academic credentials. There were three 'also rans' in the first ballot who would, of course, get complimented and nowhere; or so the *cognoscenti* in the clergy thought.

But synods are strange things; the meeting of all; the houses of bishops, clergy, and laity. In the divisive solemnity and occasional hysteria of the supporters of the main protagonists, in the re-votes and corridor discussions, a quiet black priest of African origin came to the fore. By the final vote, by a narrow legal margin, James Azikiwe was chosen as bishop.

His platform was simple; the diocese must heal and become one, become above all else a true witness to Christ's love for all; it must focus internally to renew, rather than stretch externally to overachieve. People weren't sure what that meant, but for many of the laity and clergy it made sense, it seemed.

On his appointment, James had been shocked at his first attendance at a national church committee event how evident it was, at the level of bishops, that Hamilton-Brant was considered, 'in error'. People shook hands, welcomed him formally and graciously, sometimes with more polite smiles than warm words.

At the lunch break on the first day a white, female bishop from the Maritimes sat next to him at one of the big round tables with open, free seating. She greeted him warmly. By the time they were well into their main course there were three spaces left on her side and two on his. The glances from others while finding a seat for lunch were very apparent; they wanted to sit with familiar friends, or perhaps like-minded colleagues.

She whispered, "I don't know whether you are blighting me, or it's the other way around; whether it's because I am female and gay, or you are black and from a similar left-footed diocese."

He laughed softly. "Welcome to Rosa Parks bus, or is there a different vehicle for women bishops?"

"Oh, no, I should welcome you. I got on two stops before you did, James. And where I come from, we are in

Viola Desmond's theatre, not on Rosa's bus, on that score."

He gave a big laugh. "See, I knew I'd find new friends here!"

But they turned out to be fewer than he had expected. In his first year as bishop, he had more 'hard going'. He worked at healing divisions in his diocese, but with little obvious progress.

~~

David Simmons asked, "And Dodee's arthritis; how is she doing?"

Azikiwe's wife Dorothy had been a runner, a good one, but some years ago she had gone down very quickly with osteoarthritis.

The bishop said softly, "Not good, not good at all. Her sister Ursula lives with us now. She moved in about four years ago. I think without her help, it would be hard. I doubt I could handle this job, despite Dodee's support for me doing it. And you, David? How are you and the family?"

His tone of voice and eye contact made clear his concern.

The older man paused then said, "Michael died last year, in Tel Aviv. He had been there for two years. We had worried, of course, with the situation there, but it wasn't that; it was simply a road accident."

It hit James hard. Michael Simmons had been a teenager at the time James was a priest in the parish. He was David's oldest grandchild. One time, David had asked James to talk to him. The boy was a rabbinical student; fervent. 'Can you round him out a bit?" he had been asked bluntly.

The Anglican priest and the young Jewish scholar had

many discussions about all sorts of things; religion, ethics, and politics among them, during the months before the young man went away to college.

James said softly, "I am so sorry; I never knew. I would have–."

"I know, I know. That's what I feel bad about; out of sight, out of mind. I am embarrassed that I didn't think of telling you at the time. I apologise."

The bishop took the old man's hand, now understanding the need. "Don't be. I will pray for him, and also for your family."

David asked, "Do you still sing? What was the medieval piece that you, Michael, and others did at Milly's funeral? Do you recall it, some old motet? How everyone was surprised by your voice, a countertenor, of all things. It was such a comforting sound, I remember."

James smiled at the memory. It was Millicent Rose's memorial service, not her funeral, he recalled. The woman had lived locally and had been a social worker in Hamilton during some of the darker times there. In her heyday, she had been a loud voice for the underprivileged.

"It was by Josquin de Prez, a French composer. Michael chose it. We performed the Latin version that Martin Luther sang; our French wasn't up to the original, I recall."

"Yes, from Jeremiah, I believe."

James replied, "You know, I don't recall – and me a bishop. But you are right; it was beautiful, the combination of those words and music. I had almost forgotten."

As they sat silently, each recalling the event, James's phone rang. He answered after glancing at the screen. "Yes, Audrey?"

The old rabbi watched the middle-aged priest listen, his face reflecting the news he was receiving. When he closed the call, David just waited.

"I have to go, and we have to meet again. I am remiss in not staying in touch. But… that was my assistant. We have a priest on holiday at a spiritual convention in England, with his wife. There is some urgent problem that I need to help with."

He stood, placed his hand on the old man's shoulder. "Stay; finish your coffee. Give my love to Rebecca. And I promise we will meet again soon to catch up on the years."

David just nodded. By the time he thought of something to say, the Bishop of Hamilton-Brant was heading towards the door.

8 SECOND INTERVIEW

19 July 8.45 a.m. BST

The following morning in the briefing, Sammie noted who was there and who was not. Something new had come up, she concluded. More work.

Trent confirmed it as he began.

"DI Green and DS O'Brien are now in Workington; a domestic. It's touch and go whether the wife will live, I gather. They went over there at four-thirty this morning and will be on that case now throughout. Cranwell, you'll take over the wrap-up of the Kleiber hit and run with me. We need all the ducks in a row, so the interview list needs to be finished properly. I think his solicitor is looking for any process errors on our part so he can throw them back at us in court, so be careful.

"Landry and Mooney will continue the search for further witnesses to the hit and run. They've finished the CCTV reviews of the route the suspect took; there should be some people who may recall something."

Sammie was surprised. She was an acting detective sergeant; she had been expecting to keep Howard Mooney with her.

Trent looked at his jotted notes. "We have to stretch a bit until next Wednesday, I make it, when Burrows, Cargill and DI Nolan are all back off holiday. Since when have people taken their holidays from mid-week to mid-week?"

"Since airlines and travel agents started discounting offers," responded Landry.

"Well, it's a squeeze until then. We've got two obvious big ones, with people in custody; Workington this morning and the Thursby hit and run. And we have the puzzle about the death in Keswick, the Canadian. Sammie, I am giving that one to you for the day. Once the post-mortem is completed, we will have a better idea whether it's third party or self-inflicted. If the former, we will be in for a big one, a homicide investigation of a priest, a foreigner. We'll have to regroup resources if that proves to be the case. But I want that Anglican priest brought back in this afternoon, see if he has mellowed a little, and found a solicitor that he is happy with. So, call him. First, you do the observation of the PM with Dr. Lee. It didn't happen yesterday, as you know."

He added, "And the lab results on the prelim toxicology screen on Aster are in – there's nothing there, that I saw."

Sammie nodded, a little disconcerted that she was on her own on this now.

As he wrapped up, Trent thought of something he had missed. "Sammie, go through the deceased's possessions lists; look for a clue to the name Susan, perhaps."

She responded, "I was thinking about that already, boss. We should also check whether there is a Susan that the man came across in the Convention – if there was a safeguarding concern locally. I am not sure how easy that will be, but I'll get on it."

Trent nodded his approval and signalled that the

meeting was closed.

A couple of minutes later, as Sammie reviewed the new information in the Aster file, Trent walked across to her and said, "I've just called in another favour with Inspector Robinson. Despite it being busy in Keswick, you can have Calder with you today for the convention site visit and the follow up interview with Reverend Moore. She knows the scene and church law, as you found out. But do his interview in Keswick. Once we are through the hump on other things, I'll send Howard Mooney back to you; he seems to work well with you leading. The way things are going, you'll be a full-time DS soon, I think."

He turned around then stopped again. He was overworked, she thought, dealing with too much at once.

"The email with Tremblay in the name; it's in the file. It's a Bishop Hugh Tremblay, the deceased man's boss in Ontario. As is the telephone number he called from. We'll be hearing from his church and his family now, I expect."

As he left the office, Sammie felt a glow of appreciation for her efforts, that they had been recognized.

~~

"Reverend Moore, this is Acting DS Livermore. We would like to interview you again, please, this afternoon at 3.00 p.m., but at Keswick Police Station. It's part of the Town Council office there, so it is a lot closer for you than Penrith."

He sighed. "And I'll miss part of another day here. If I must, I suppose, I must. I talked with a Mr. Selby this morning. The diocese put him in touch with me. I will call him and hopefully he can be here, too. As I said, I won't meet you without him."

"You called your diocese in Canada?"

"Yes, well, my wife called our diocesan office back home. Bishop Azikiwe, my bishop, spoke to someone in the Bishop of Carlisle's office, and they are providing support for me.

"A lot of people at the convention know now about Father Aster's death, I gather. Some of us are organizing a prayer meeting for him tonight. I would like to be available in good time for that."

He's sounding more normal, she thought. Or confident.

"Good. I'll see you and your solicitor at the police station at 3.00 p.m."

She took a deep breath, having checked her watch. And now for Dr. Lee.

By late morning Sammie was on her way to Keswick. Aster had not been her first post-mortem and she wasn't squeamish about them. Dr. Lee had proven to be competent and professional. She, too, was now fairly sure that Father Aster had drowned in the lake under the weight of the stone. Probably by his own hand, she thought, but that wasn't a certainty.

It appeared that small scrapes and abrasions on his hands were consistent with traces of tissues found caught in the stone, as if he was holding it in place as he entered the water. Unless he did that under some form of duress, rather than a physical attack, the most logical explanation for his drowning was a self-inflicted act. There was no evidence from the site, or from his body, of a third party being involved.

She could see an open verdict looming for the coroner's office. But, as a MIU case, it would be over with soon now, she knew.

Sammie met Harriet Calder at the Keswick Police station. They walked from there to the convention grounds; it was only a couple of minutes away.

"We have you back yet again for the day, DCI Trent told me."

Harriet smiled. "For one day. It's really busy here for us, at present. All hands to the pump."

She hadn't missed the inference in Sammie's question, so it was no surprise when the younger officer asked her, "DI Green said you used to be with Major Crimes; you were good at it. Didn't you want to stay? For me, it's a really interesting job. I'm learning a lot."

Harriet smiled again. "Yes, I enjoyed it, but... life happens, things change. I'm happier in this role now. I have a question, though. Did you find Father Aster's bible?"

A deflection, back to the case, away from her, Sammie realised. She thought back to the list of belongings.

"There wasn't a bible in his lodging or his car, I recall, but you are right. He should have one, surely?"

Harriet nodded, "I can't imagine a Catholic priest not having one or more books with him, probably a favorite pocket bible and a breviary. If he died by his own hand, I wondered if he had read and prayed beforehand. I would have expected it to be in the car, perhaps. Or did he have it with him in the water nearby?"

Sammie recalled suddenly, "His smartphone has a breviary app. I saw that, but not an online bible. I'll check again before the interview. Now, back in this melee; trying to find a 'Susan' here that could tie in with the email message; any ideas?"

"Well, the word is out about Aster's death, the location, but not the details. I spoke to Tom Vaughn, and also to Marjorie Hallsworth, the staff director, after your call earlier. They will help in any way they can, but are also really busy, as you can imagine. They are having a prayer gathering this evening for Aster. Has his family in Canada been contacted yet?"

"DI Green contacted the Ontario Police in North Bay yesterday, after the formal identification. They made the local contact. There was an email before I left saying they have also informed Aster's bishop in Ontario, the man Tremblay that Aster emailed, and who tried to reach him. Someone will be calling us soon, I'm sure; they are probably getting sorted out to fly over."

She looked at her watch. "It's not even morning over there."

Tom Vaughn dropped what he was doing and came straight out of his little meeting to invite them into his office. Their first question to him was on the issue of the mysterious Susan.

He replied, "Do we have a female staff member called Susan, or a list of women called Susan who may be here? We have two on staff that I know personally, but there may be more I don't, I suspect, in the volunteers. But I'll check the list now."

The man stared at his computer screen as the spreadsheet rolled down. "Mrs. Susan Rhodes, a long-time volunteer here. Sixty-two; serves in youth ministry."

He looked at Sammie questioningly. She just said, "And?"

"A Susan Gillard, a speaker, but she won't be here until next week for that week's program, I know."

He rolled through the list further. Another highlighted name popped up. "This may be more promising, for you, I think. A Susan Clapham from the London area, a volunteer in the Main Tent giving direction and general help. That's where Father Aster spent his time, you'll recall. She's seventeen and her mother is a volunteer also, in a different area."

He looked up, his face quizzing them. Sammie said, "We'll talk to her. Is she around?"

He nodded, picking up a radio unit. "I'll call her area supervisor and get her sent over here now."

Sammie said, "And her mother, too, please. She needs to agree, or sit in, if Susan is seventeen."

He returned to the computer. "Next, the list of three- to eighteen-year-olds and their responsible adults. After that, it will be a bit more difficult."

They worked their way through the rest of the high-lighted names, noting the names and contact numbers.

As Vaughn closed the file and sat back from the screen, he asked, "Is there anything else I can help with?"

Sammie said, "Yes. Who is organizing the prayer meeting for Father Aster, now the news is out?"

'That's Frank Morton, one of our staff, with two people from Canada – a visitor, Julie Stevens, from Father Aster's hometown or parish, not sure which, and Reverend Moore, whom you've met. They both seemed to want to do something."

Sammie said, "We would like to talk with Ms. Stevens and also attend the prayer meeting, if we may."

She looked at Harriet. From her expression, she agreed.

~~

Susan Clapham turned out to be a slim, olive-skinned girl with a warm smile and a London accent. Her mother came with her, supportive but thankfully not trying to speak for her.

"These are police officers, looking into the death of

Father Aster," explained Vaughn, as they stood together on the steps of the reception centre.

With that, from a single gesture from Sammie, the four women walked away into the anonymity of the people outside as Vaughn returned to his office.

Susan Clapham said, "It's such terrible news, that a person at the convention died so tragically."

Sammie opened her notepad and pulled out a pen.

"Indeed. Can I get your full name, Susan? And where you live, and what your role is here?"

Bring it back to an interview, not a conversation, Harriet noted.

The girl gave them the details and talked on - about the excitement of being a volunteer. Her mother was clearly proud of her. Sammie gently led her to the key questions.

"Did you meet or talk with Father Aster?"

Susan replied instantly. "Just once, when he arrived, the first day. I didn't know his name at first. He wore his cross, though, but not a clerical collar. He looked lost. So, I asked him if he needed help."

She stopped.

Sammie prompted her. "But you knew his name, did you? Before the news broke?"

"Yes, I told him mine. He gave me his; Father Duncan, he said. He just smiled and said talking with me made him think of another person with the same first name."

She stopped again.

Sammie asked, "And did you see him again?"

"A couple of times. He smiled at me, from a distance. I'm always talking with people here."

Sammie didn't want her to get back on the track of her joy of being a volunteer, so she said quickly, "He smiled at you... was he watching you, do you think?"

The girl looked surprised. "You mean, stalking; that sort

of watching?"

Her mother looked alarmed, but Sammie pressed on, "Not specifically, no; but I meant just interested in you, perhaps?"

It clearly wasn't something Susan had considered.

"Not that I felt, no. I didn't feel it like that. He didn't give me any qualms; he was just being friendly."

Sammie smiled. "He probably was."

Harriet asked, "Did he carry a program book, a guide or anything else, do you recall?"

"Yes. He had just bought the guide, in fact. He had a small backpack, as well. Most people have something similar. And the cross."

"But not a bible or a breviary in his hand?"

She shook her head. "Not that I saw, no. Not then, but the third time I saw him he was reading something small. It looked like a bible, in burgundy, a small book. Then he saw me. We both smiled, just as someone else needed my help. I had thought of going over and saying hello but… it didn't happen. I wish I had now."

Harriet asked, "Small as, say, a standard NRSV?"

New Revised Standard Version; a bible edition, recalled Sammie.

"No, smaller again. And I think it had a built-in zipper closure, come to think of it, so it probably was a religious text. But I couldn't say what."

Sammie passed over her business card. "If anything comes to mind, please call me…"

The girl nodded. She asked, "Is it true, though? People are talking about what happened to Father Aster; that he drowned in the lake. They are speculating; some are saying he had an accident but there are whispers that he may have drowned himself."

It was Harriet who dealt with it. "We can't discuss it. Just pray for him, that's all you need to do."

"Thank you for your assistance," Sammie said, closing her notebook.

Susan's mother looked at Harriet and said, "I saw you on the panel here four years ago, at the bereavement group counsellors' seminar. I still remember it. I'm glad to meet you at last. God Bless."

Harriet responded, "God bless you both, too."

They shook hands and Harriet touched the girl's shoulder. "Pray for him, as I said, but don't trouble yourself about how he died or why; that's our job. Remember the smiles, the warmth you exchanged, and that you were here together in the work that matters."

Susan nodded, getting tears in her eyes. Sammie looked away momentarily, not sure how to deal with this sudden transformation of the local officer into a pastoral counsellor.

Julie Stevens turned out to be seventy-one, silver-haired, and talkative. They hardly had to ask questions. No, she didn't know Duncan Aster. In fact, she didn't know too many Roman Catholics at all in North Bay. They came from the same city, but she had never attended anything at Father Aster's church, nor had she attended any event where she recalled him to be present. She just heard the news, and someone said he was from Ontario, as was Reverend Moore, who she also didn't know. But when she found out the dead man was from her own city, she thought something should be done with those gathered here to pray for him. She had spoken to one of the Keswick Ministry staff who had, in turn, introduced her to Reverend Moore from Hamilton, as he was Canadian, too. That's how they met.

"North Bay is as far away from Hamilton and Toronto

as the Lake District is from somewhere like Birmingham or London, I think. There is no reason for us to know each other."

In the end they had to extricate themselves from the woman. Sammie was secretly amused that even Harriet Calder didn't want to get into a protracted discussion of the meaning of 'souls in our midst suddenly lost from us to heaven'.

They were having a light lunch in a crêperie called The Wild Strawberry, talking about people they both knew in the Cumbria police, when Sammie's phone rang. She listened, then said, "Any idea when?" In a moment, she thanked the person and closed the call, as Harriet answered her own phone. It was Sammie's turn to wait.

As Harriet closed her call, Sammie said, "That was an update. Duncan Aster's mother is too shocked to travel, I gather; she's an older person. His father is dead and his only other close relative, a brother called Nigel Aster, is a Canadian diplomat now stationed in South America. Apparently, the man is flying in from somewhere there, but won't be here until tomorrow at the earliest, perhaps the day after. The local Roman Catholic diocese in Carlisle has contacted us; they have a solicitor and a priest mobilized to assist as needed in any arrangements."

Harriet said, "On the home front, that was my friend Kerri Sanders, at St. Anselm's; one of the wardens. They have found a bible. They think it's a Catholic one and they haven't seen it before so… she called me."

Sammie said, "Where?!"

"In the church. It wasn't spotted earlier but the pews have bookshelves. It could have been left in one. And it fits Susan's description, by the sound of it. We should head over now, I think, and find out more."

It would be Harriet Calder who would look the profess-ional one of them as they crossed Main Street, thought Sammie, who was holding her purse awkwardly in one hand and a nearly finished crêpe in the other, wrapped in a paper napkin and now leaking shredded lettuce.

It's a beautiful church and setting, Sammie was reminded, as the woman at St. Anselm's greeted Sergeant Calder with, 'Harriet, love, how are you doing? After all the sadness yesterday. Are you alright?"

The barricade tapes of yesterday had mostly disappear-ed. Bassenthwaite and this church were tourist spots. Based on the preliminary forensic work and his discussion with Dr. Lee, John Trent had been quick to authorize the return to normal for the lake area, except for a zone of fifty feet around the location where the body was found. That was still taped off.

Several people were standing at the tape, praying.

Kerri Sanders looked across. "From the convention. They have been coming all day, in here and out there, paying their respects."

Harriet replied, "This is Acting Detective Sergeant Livermore, leading the investigation. Kerri; I am doing just fine. The whole thing and the poor man are now in God's hands. I'm not fretting on it."

"That's the way. Hello, sergeant. You need to come inside. By the way, you have a piece of lettuce stuck on your front tooth; I thought you need to know."

She turned and led them in.

"We have bibles in many languages here; all shapes and sizes, some of them donated by people visiting, others sent in by them when they go home. Walkers and tourists love the place. We are quite proud of them. Some are lovely, even though I can't read a word. Now we have this new one. I was cleaning up earlier, and there it was on the bible shelf."

She picked up the small bible with its zip closure as Sammie drew out forensic gloves and an evidence bag from her purse. She wished she had told the woman not to touch it.

Sanders continued, "It was when I opened it and saw it was in English, a Catholic bible, and the fact that the man yesterday may be a priest, you had said, Harriet."

She handed it over and Sammie opened the zip, spreading the cover open.

"Careful," said Harriet, "Don't lose the place with the bookmark."

Sammie gave her a scowl. In fact, there were two placemarks, one with the ribbon page marker and, further back, a small card, a gift card of some sort. Sammie opened it there and read the card. 'To Father Duncan, with much love and admiration for your work in the service of Christ. Susan."

Kerri said, 'This may be the gift card with the bible, don't you think? A parishioner, probably. But I think it might also be the poor man's bible from the lake."

Sammie asked, "You didn't move the card or the ribbon, did you?"

"I'm not a detective, but I am not stupid, love." She rolled her eyes at Calder.

Sammie said, "How –?"

She was thinking of the time of death.

Harriet interjected, "St. Anselm's is never locked; it's always available. Anyone can come at any time. He must have come in to pray, then left it behind. I should have thought of that."

Sammie's face clouded over. She hadn't realised that fact

yesterday. She had focused on the lake and the car, assuming the church was locked at the time the body went into the water. No-one left places unprotected these days. They had used the church as a temporary command post; it should have been part of the crime scene until cleared. And she had been the on-scene commander at the time.

Kerri broke the silence. "I should have asked you also, sergeant, how you are doing about all this, not just Harriet. You were here, too. I'm sure it's stressful, your job. Are you okay?"

Her expression showed that she had her doubts on that point.

Trent won't be happy, was Sammie's thought. She glanced around the building interior, vainly hoping that they had CCTV cameras. They didn't.

Harriet told her friend, "We will probably need your fingerprints, Kerri; to eliminate them, once the bible is sent over to forensics. And if the fig biscuits keep disappearing from that tin over there, then we will be able to prove you aren't the culprit. Assuming that you are innocent, of course."

Kerri gave Harriet a sharp look.

Harriet said, "Not a lettuce bit on the tooth; a sticky fig crumb on your blouse."

~~

In fact, DCI Trent wasn't bothered by the mistake when Sammie phoned him while standing outside, as the two friends talked. "We are overworked, Sammie. Don't dwell on it. It looks more like it is self-inflicted, anyway. But we'll check the book for prints; I'm not sure it will help much. What did Calder say?"

"That she should have thought of it, the church not

being locked. She was more interested in the bookmarks in the bible. One is a gift card, from a Susan, probably the one he referred to in the email. But she was looking at the positions of the bookmarks, what they meant to Aster, assuming they weren't randomly placed. We don't know, of course."

"It may be useful; it may also be irrelevant from our perspective, something to be passed on to the coroner."

Sammie saw the two women coming out of the church entrance.

"We are heading back now to the station for the interview with Moore, boss."

"Let me know how it goes." Trent cut the call.

~~

"Is my client here solely as a witness, or is he under suspicion regarding any involvement in the death of Father Aster? And you know what I mean; I don't want the standard line, just want to get a sense of it."

The lawyer, Selby, had asked for a pre-interview briefing; he was entitled to that. Sammie was assessing the solicitor. She didn't know him, but Howes & Denning were a top-line firm of solicitors in the region. Someone knew who to go to.

She said, "He's not a prime suspect, but nor is he totally in the clear. He has an alibi for the period during which we believe this man Duncan Aster died. Death was by drowning; the pathologist concluded this morning. We don't have the final report yet. I saw nothing during the autopsy to suggest the involvement of a third person, but a full forensic review has not yet been completed.

"But your client was among the last people to talk to the deceased, we think. He was evasive during our earlier interview and clearly knows something about the state of mind of Aster he is not prepared to reveal, something which could well be material to our investigation."

The solicitor nodded, satisfied with the briefing.

"I have already explained to him fully the law regarding confessional privilege in the UK. How he responds will be up to him, of course."

As they settled down at the table in the interview room, Reverend Moore said to Calder, "I'm sorry for getting annoyed yesterday. I apologise."

Harriet just nodded, acknowledging the point but looked to Sammie to lead; it was her show.

Sammie said, "Then let's pick up where we left off. Did your discussion with Father Aster lead you to ask the safe-guarding officer at the convention site for guidance about reporting requirements?"

Moore replied, "Yes. It did. But I wasn't absolutely clear whether there was a person at risk here at that stage. And afterwards, of course, it was irrelevant."

Sammie nodded. A good answer. A good start.

"So, something he said to you, that he shared with you, gave rise to that. Yet you didn't know each other prior to the convention, but he shared something with you. Can you tell us what that is?"

He looked embarrassed now, and thoughtful rather than angry. "It related to something in his past, I'll say that. Father Aster and I had been discussing forgiveness. We had enjoyed several discussions on theological issues during our encounters over the last few days. He seemed to hang on to me, hang around me, I felt. I met others at the sessions and talked with them, but he always ended up talking with me. I knew he had something significant on his mind, some burden; that was obvious. I just didn't realise what it was."

Harriet asked, "Forgiveness; that was a topic one morning at the convention session, I now recall? That started it, did it?"

He nodded then remembered to say, "Yes; that."

Sammie asked, "Did he mention a particular person in this context?"

"Yes."

"He gave you a name?"

"A first name only."

"Was her name Susan? We do have other sources of information, Reverend Moore."

He closed his eyes. "I think the answer my solicitor advised I could give is 'no comment'. I consider that to be privileged."

Sammie continued, "You just said, I quote, 'But I wasn't absolutely clear whether there was a person at risk at that stage'. Are you talking about a person at risk here; on site - or a person in his past? A Catholic priest is supposed to be celibate, but it seems as if there is or was another person involved in some way. And the fact that it was a safe-guarding question implies that it was probably a sexual risk concern. So, was the matter to do with a person at risk here?"

Moore replied, "It wasn't the most orderly discussion. Duncan was getting upset; how upset I realised only too late. I was confused for a while and I thought another person here may be involved, but now I think not. I believe it was related to something in his past in Canada."

Sammie said, "But you won't tell us whether you know who that is?"

"No. I consider that to be privileged."

Sammie looked at Harriet and grimaced, partly because she wasn't sure what to ask next, partly to show her dissatisfaction with the man.

Harriet picked up the lead. "If you consider it privileged, you are saying that, to you, it has an underpinning of a confession. Is that so?"

"Yes."

"Did he see it as such? Did he speak in a manner that inferred he was making a confession to you?"

"As I said, I consider it so and won't comment further on it."

Harriet nodded, indicating she understood, then she asked, "In both Ontario law, I looked it up, and here, canonical laws now require a priest to advise a penitent that if anything is said which indicates that a child or vulnerable adult is at risk, the confessor has a duty to report that immediately to the authorities. You are aware of that?"

Reverend Moore glanced at his solicitor who nodded at him then he said. "Yes, I understand it's the same, and before you ask, that is the reason I went to the safeguarding officer."

"Did you inform Father Aster of that?"

The question was asked softly but, as in the previous session, it affected the man greatly. Not anger this time, but loss of composure. His head fell. "That's not easy for me to answer, for the reason I just gave. Let us say that the topic of safeguarding came up in discussion with him later. That meeting was the last time I saw him."

"And where was this?"

"In Station Road. We had returned earlier from our visit to St. Anselm's, to see the church. We went there and prayed. We talked on the way and while we were there. It was later, a chance encounter in that street..." His voice trailed off.

Harriet looked at Sammie, who nodded. Keep going, the look said.

"Did Father Aster have a bible with him?"

Moore looked surprised. "Yes, a small one. Burgundy, leather bound. Quite worn."

"Did he have it at St. Anselm's?"

She was watching him closely as he responded carefully. "Yes, I think so. He kept it in his daypack but took it out at times over the days I knew him. He didn't use a bible when we were at St. Anselm's, though; we just prayed."

Sammie asked, "So that was the last time you saw him, around 4.30 p.m. in Station Road?"

"Yes. I said that."

The solicitor jumped in. "I think my client has been open with you and this is ground already covered. He has been clear on his position on privilege, by his own conscience. The subject of their prayer together is clearly off limits, and I think I must ask now whether there are other material areas or issues of the investigation that you need to pursue with him. If not…"

Sammie took the initiative. "No, I think we are finished, at least for now. If we have anything further, we will be in touch. But we do appreciate your co-operation this time, Reverend Moore."

As they started to move, Sammie saw that Harriet Calder clearly had something on her mind. But it looked as if she had stopped herself and let it go, given Sammie's decision to close the interview. Calder just kept looking at Reverend Moore. Sammie's immediate thought was that Calder would put on her 'preacher' hat and say something consoling to him as she had to Susan Clapham. But Harriet Calder didn't say anything; she just watched him silently as he stood and thanked his solicitor as the two men left the room.

Sammie was sharing her status assessment with Harriet.

"Well, it's all pointing to something in Father Aster's past that he probably shouldn't have shared. If it's a girl or woman, it seems he didn't want the issue brought to the attention of the police through a safeguarding officer here. Or he couldn't face the consequences if it did. He must have been pretty disturbed."

The older woman said nothing for a few moments then she replied, "It seems that Reverend Moore's confusion over whether Susan was a person here or not could have been a contributory factor to Aster's death, if self-inflicted. Perhaps he told him he had spoken to Tom Vaughn. That bit about his discussion of safeguarding with Aster; he seemed to get evasive again, to me. What'll you do now?"

Sammie responded, "I'll still go to the prayer service; observe it and the people there, just in case. I'll report back to DCI Trent; it'll be his decision. I think it will be wound up. Aster drowned himself while the balance of his mind was disturbed, as they say. I bet I'll be assigned to the Workington case tomorrow, on the follow-up interviews of the death there. The wife never regained consciousness, I just heard before we came in."

She looked at Calder. "You don't have to come tonight; it'll just be routine."

Harriet said, "I'll be there. A man died. I didn't know him, but I saw him in death. I'd be there anyway, now I know of it."

Sammie was checking her mobile. "Perhaps I won't be, after all; it'll be down to you. A Catholic priest from Carlisle has phoned MIU. And there is an email from Canada, from this Bishop Tremblay's office. I'll have to meet up with someone from the local Roman Catholic diocese and it looks like it will now be this evening. Trent wants me with him, as I have been leading the case. You know the form. You may be on your own at the prayer meeting as we are so understaffed this week."

Harriet smiled. "So much so that you even had to bring in a local for the day. I should get back to my own duties, busy as it is."

Sammie laughed. "An alumnus; let's call it that."

Harriet said as they parted, "A piece of advice when you meet the clergy; don't tell them you are a lapsed Catholic."

Sammie smiled. "I'm on duty; my best behaviour." Her mind was focused on wrapping this one up. She wondered if she would run into Harriet Calder again. In her line of work, one never knows.

9 PRAYER

19 July, 6.00 p.m. BST

The short prayer service for Duncan Aster was held in the main tent in the Skiddaw Street location. It was positioned at short notice between the late-afternoon and early-evening agenda. Harriet thought it was well attended but given the size of the gathering this week and the venue, it was not crowded at all. Many attendees would be with their children, away after the day's main events and having early evening meals.

Frank Morton from the Keswick Ministries briefly introduced Julie Stevens and Reverend Andrew Moore, the former taking the lead thereafter, either by common agreement or her enthusiasm to hold the spotlight for her non-stop oratory. On the stage here she did not have two police officers breaking her flow with further questions.

Yet despite the relentless soliloquy, Stevens somehow caught the mood and had the right words for healing. Harriet's major concern was that the rumour of a self-inflicted death would surface indirectly in pious or oblique comment, but it didn't. Stevens focused on the suddenness of his departure, that he was now in the care of God and that those who knew him well, his family; his friends, his fellow clergy and parishioners would need support through everyone's prayers.

Harriet had dressed in casual clothes deliberately. She entered the tent in the company of another member of staff at the Keswick Ministry whom she knew quite well. In essence, she would not be seen as a police officer other than by people who knew her. She avoided moving closer to the Moore family, not wanting her role to be flagged by a reference to her title; 'sergeant'. As much as her ear was on Julie Stevens, her eyes were on the crowd, both during the homily and the prayers.

Calder was looking for nothing specific other than the possible presence of someone who stood out. It sounded vague, but it wasn't. People involved in crimes who return to the scene, particularly for funerals of victims, always try to fit in. In doing so, they reveal an artificiality to their behaviour. Sometimes that was easy to misread as discomfort or awkwardness; but it gave a face, a name, or a description; one more element to consider in the information analysis around a major investigation.

On rare occasions, it identified a loner, present but not part of; in a way similar to the police officers present. A fleeting look of satisfaction or pleasure on such a person's face could focus an investigation and lead to the discovery of a motive.

It was precise observation work. Harriet had no qualms whatever about continuing her surveillance during prayers while people stood with their heads bowed and eyes closed. She was now here for her job, not her ministry. As she watched, though, part of her mind was on the speakers, taking in and analysing their messages.

A band with two guitars and a keyboard led the singing of an appropriate hymn before Reverend Moore moved forward to the stage, first speaking briefly to his family, Harriet saw, addressing the younger daughter.

His own testament to Father Aster was more formal, less flowery evangelically than Stevens. He referred to the interfaith bonding and discussions he had held with Duncan Aster, one Roman Catholic with one Anglican, together in the spiritually renewing atmosphere of Keswick. They had already exchanged emails and phone numbers, and each had invited the other to visit, to look perhaps for opportunities to do more together back in Ontario. He wound up his speech with, "I will miss him in the days left here for us in Keswick and miss the oppor- tunity that may have been for our continued dialogue in the service of God once back in Ontario."

He thanked the gathering for the support for him and his family in the last two days and then opened his bible.

"Duncan is now at peace with the Lord. I want to share at this time some words from the First Letter of John, chapter 1, verse 7. '*But if we walk in the light, as he is in the light, we have fellowship with one another, and the blood of Jesus his Son cleanses us from all sin*'. I had the privilege of walking here with Father Duncan Aster in the light we all share. It will always stay with me."

He closed the bible and stepped back.

A strange choice thought Harriet, thinking of other verses from the bible that she would have considered, if she was to speak at a memorial. Why did Moore choose that one, with the specific reference to sin?

There was a final hymn and a closing prayer, followed by a blessing led by Moore. The service was over. People began to move out and away. Staff started preparing for the next event in the revised timetable for the evening segment, as other visitors entered, ready to participate.

As Harriet left the tent thinking about the people she had watched, the one image that stayed with her was the face of Moore's younger daughter, the one he had spoken to. She had cried briefly during Stevens' address. But during her father's own briefer talk she had the expression Harriet had seen at times on other children. The sort of expression on a child's face when a father denies hitting his wife; saying that her claim was exaggerated or false. The expression which says I am scared to say anything, but daddy isn't telling the full truth and it saddens me.

Whatever the daughter had heard directly between the men or secondhand through overhearing her parents talking, his soliloquy tonight was not the whole story, by far. Harriet called Sammie and left a voicemail. She was probably still tied up with the representatives of Father Aster.

~~

It was DCI Trent who called Calder back mid-evening.

"Thanks for the update on the prayer meeting. Sammie let me listen to it and I said I would call. I sent her home; it's been a long day."

Harriet didn't comment; her memory was that all days in MIU could be long in the early stages of every investigation.

"I'll send in my report tomorrow, sir."

"Not writing it now, then, Harriet?" he said lightly.

"No. I am working on a sermon for Sunday at Brigham Methodist."

Afterwards she thought about why she revealed that; to stake my ground, she thought, the life I have made for myself.

His response was still focused on the case. That was no surprise.

"We have a lot of information to analyse now. I was thinking about this comment about the daughter's reaction. A good catch. If Moore was a suspect, we would have her interviewed, and with someone other than her parents as the appropriate adult, if needed. But he is clear on that one."

Harriet said, "He's covered?"

"Solidly. We are sure their rental car wasn't moved overnight. We also have a slot of time for the death between the first sighting of Aster's car parked and you arriving at the church. In the early hours of the morning, the older Moore daughter was having a problem with period pains and like young teenagers, she would only talk with her mother, but she needed help.

"The landlady at the B&B got up, too, a Mrs. Downs. She heated up a beanbag thing in the microwave and wrapped it in a towel, a warm compress to help the girl cope with the cramps. She also made a warm drink for her to take with some pill her parents had for her, not aspirin.

"Andrew Moore had got up and put on some clothes, in case he needed to go to an all-night chemist for something, but the warm pad and her mother's presence helped, and the girl went back to sleep. So did the Moore couple and the landlady, but Mrs. Downs sleeps lightly, she said, particularly after her sleep is disturbed. No-one left the house in the window of time that Aster arrived at the lake until he was discovered by Kavanagh.

"Still, it is one more example that Moore is not being open with us. But we knew that."

Harriet said, "I take it I am back on my regular duties tomorrow?"

"Yes; thank you for your help over the last couple of

days, and I will tell Carol you are at Brigham on Sunday. Goodnight."

"Goodnight, sir."

She closed the call. Carol Trent already knows, she thought, being part of the circuit speaker organizing committee.

As she returned to her sermon preparation, she was distracted by the events of the last two days and the re-awakening, in a sense, of her time in MIU as a detective constable, the case still playing on her mind.

She couldn't quite pin down the reason. As she mused on it, she realised that part of the answer lay not in Reverend Moore's actions, but in the man as a member of clergy. He epitomised, she realised, the type of priest she mistrusted most; analytical, intellectual, wealthy, and self-confident. It was as if humility and personal doubt were never factors in such people. She had met over the years both clergymen and clergywomen who fitted that profile; their warmth was reserved for the like-minded, their advice shared too quickly with others whom they saw falling short of their own standards of faith and worship. To her, all religions attracted such people like flies to cowpats.

As a police officer, she had a lot of experience of self-doubt that could only be dealt with by doing her duty by the law. The woman who lashes out at a husband and is arrested for assault, when she has been subjected to years of misery by the man. The teenager caught during a break-in, while knowing from previous experience of the family that the boy had no compass on life other than the bright light of money obtained by any means he could use to get it.

She realised that she was mixing up her own prejudices with the case experience; it was a reminder that she was best out of it.

Harriet stopped writing and went into the kitchen to put the kettle on for some tea. She picked up a favorite book, 'An African Prayer Book' by Desmond Tutu. The tea would sooth her body, the book her mind and spirit. Only then would she return to her preparations for Sunday.

PART 2

RECOVERY

"The basis of the technique of Alcoholics Anonymous is the truly Christian principle that a man cannot help himself except by helping others."
'The Religious View on A.A'.
Alcoholics Anonymous, fourth edition.

10 HAYDN HOUSE

19 July 9.45 p.m. EDT

In the late evening of the same day in mid-town Toronto, on a street near Summerhill subway station, two women walked down the paved front path of a residential dwelling. Near the double doors at the entrance was a small brass plate identifying the street number and the name of the home, Haydn House. The neighbourhood was wealthy; these were larger, older houses with solid construction and quality exterior brick and stone.

The neighbours knew the role of Haydn House, of course, but were not disturbed by the fact it wasn't a family home. Dotted along the street were a few other houses of similar vein: a dentist, a high-end chiropractor and two medical offices; other residents who wanted their own privacy for health-care businesses, and who respected that of others.

A passerby might think the house to be a music school of some sort from the name, but no instruments sent out fragments of tunes or scales. Few would connect it with Sarah Haydn, a soprano of international repute in the sixties, whose career ended early in a blaze of booze. Only Canadian opera fans would probably recall the name, generally in tones of 'what could have been'.

Haydn House was an addiction recovery centre for women, one firmly rooted in the steps of Alcoholics Anonymous. They offered no experimental new approach, no alternative therapies around alcohol reduction or drug maintenance programs; none of the trappings of the wave of new treatment centres that separated clients from large amounts of money.

There were hefty fees at Haydn, sometimes waived. They also received significant donations, many from past clients showing their gratitude. But Sarah's family had been wealthy; she had been their only daughter, and their substantial bequest was well-invested and managed.

The hallmark of Haydn House was that to receive treatment there you were female, an alcoholic or drug addict and importantly, that it was never your first treatment program for addiction recovery. It only took in women who had failed to regain sobriety after participating in at least one other recovery program for substance abuse.

In many ways it was a centre of last hope.

Susan Carlson could see that the two women who entered knew they had been caught out. That Beverley, the duty nurse, and herself were waiting together in the lobby area was the giveaway.

The days at Haydn were structured and busy, a mix of group and individual therapy for residents, as they termed their patients. On three evenings, there were in-house activities. On the other evenings, residents went out in pairs to an Alcoholics Anonymous or a Narcotics Anonymous recovery meeting in the city, chosen by them from a specified list; there were quite a number of these meetings in Toronto.

Residents had specific instructions, including the travel route to and from the church or social centre hosting the recovery meeting. They were told where to walk, detailed down to the side of the street they could walk on - and they had to walk or take public transport together. No bikes, cars, or taxis were allowed, unless they were required for other health or ambulatory reasons. For that, prior approval had to be given by the director of the facility. Above all, each pair of residents had to stay together and look out for each other.

It was highly prescriptive. A city is a dangerous place for people early in addiction recovery, but the residents had to learn how to survive there. They were trusted - but only to a point. It was well understood that alcoholics and addicts craving a high would turn to anything to achieve it if their obsession took over.

Break the rules and you would be interviewed. If you had lapsed and found a way to drink alcohol or use any unapproved substance, you were out of Haydn immediately, no matter whether it was day one or day twenty-eight; the standard term. And fees were non-refundable. The person could come back in due course, get the remaining value of their fees, but they could not be there while they were intoxicated or unwilling to try to stay clean and sober. Like measles in a confined, unprotected community, a person's intoxication could awaken cravings in others for alcohol or drugs. It was highly infectious and could be equally deadly.

"How was the meeting?" Susan asked brightly.

As each woman made a response, she watched their faces carefully, moving forward into their breathing zone. Then she came right out with it. "You were seen crossing over Yonge Street, Jemma. Just by the Shoppers Drug Mart. Did you buy anything?"

Anywhere selling alcohol or medications was off-limits. Tim Hortons was fine; Shoppers Drug Mart was not.

"Personal stuff," Jemma replied, her hostility increasing. The whiff of the cough syrup caught both the counsellor and the nurse. It was either cough syrup or mouthwash generally if they went into Shoppers. For that reason, no mouthwash was allowed at Haydn, even the non-alcoholic sort.

Beverley said, "Jemma, you are coming with me; Alison, you go with Sue."

Alison was looking wide-eyed, not sure what was now happening. She moved forward as Jemma seemed to crumple; the confidence shown on their walk back had just evaporated.

Jemma asked quietly, "Don't. Don't send me back out; please."

As Beverley moved down the corridor to the medical office with her hand on Jemma's shoulder, Susan and Alison heard the soft voice of the nurse say, "First things first; I need to check you, make sure you are alright. How much of the bottle did you drink?"

The older woman was now in tears and didn't answer.

Susan asked Alison the same question, now they were separated and couldn't collude on the answer. "How much, we need to know; you understand? And what brand?"

Alison said, hesitantly, "About half the bottle. I don't know; a green box with a yellow name and a brown bottle inside. Then she threw it away in a garbage can. I never took cough syrup for kicks."

"One like this? Or this?" Susan's fingers showed the different sizes of the packages she had in mind.

Alison nodded, "The first one."

Susan called back down the corridor. "She took about half a 170 ml. bottle of the generic dextromethorphan liquid syrup, by the sound of it."

More than a daily allowed adult dose of cough syrup in a single swig. The nurse nodded as she followed a now tearful Jemma into the medical room.

Susan asked, "Did you have any?"

"No."

The counsellor's voice turned hard. "Honestly; not even a sip?"

Alison shook her head vigorously. "No, not even a sip, I swear. She offered, and I didn't want it. I told her not to, but I didn't know what to do."

Her voice had become panicky. They had reached Susan's little office.

"You looked after yourself, that's what you did; what you were supposed to do. In here, now."

The door closed.

Carlson had come on shift at 8.00 p.m. and would be there until the women had breakfast the following morning. She was assigned night duty all week. She thought of herself as part-warden, part-therapist, and part life-skills counsellor for the group of women in the treatment program.

She now needed to get Alison back on to an even keel before bed. All women shared bedrooms, two to a room. Tonight, Alison would be sleeping alone. Beverley and the Haydn House director would be deciding Jemma's future now; either to the hospital, if her dose and symptoms merited it or, more likely, now they knew what she had taken, a night's sleep in the medical room under nursing supervision, her bags packed while Alison was at breakfast and a ride in the morning to the detox centre off Bloor St.

Susan sat next to Alison, not across from her, for bonding and verification that she hadn't consumed any cough syrup.

The younger woman asked, "What will happen now to Jemma?"

"She'll go to rehab tomorrow or to the hospital earlier if any adverse symptoms appear while she is under observation. She has had a narcotic dose, but she has had a lot worse; you know that."

The young woman shook her head. "I didn't want to be involved; she was my outside partner but… she got angry. I am not responsible for her!"

"Would you have told us, if Jemma hadn't been spotted?"

"I was torn about it all the way back. She had only three days left before she graduated and… I think I would. She is very bossy, strong; I am … passive. I needed to get back here, I felt. But I would have told someone here after we arrived. It scared me so much."

Sue said, "We'll be taking a blood sample, checking you; you know that."

Alison sounded more confident now. "No, I'm clean. I'm shaken by it all. I am only just under half-way through but… it's harder out there."

Susan smiled. "I know. But a treatment centre is not an escape. You are given specific places and routes you can go, and you always have a partner. The times are set for return. We have to prepare you for the real world."

Alison nodded. "As we walked down to the church holding the AA meeting, I looked across the road at the people in the pub, drinking and laughing."

"We know. We walk every route ourselves, see the things that help and those that stall recovery. You are expected to. How did you feel; envious?"

The young woman shook her head firmly. "Not this time. Scared, I think."

Susan nodded. "A week after I got out of here, I went back to university on the subway. In Union Station there was a billboard showing through the window just where the car stopped. It had a Gordon's Gin ad and it looked mesmerizingly beautiful. I sat transfixed the whole stop, until the train moved again. Then I shook with anger, and I got really scared, too."

"Anger?"

"That it was there, looking so good. That the world I lived in was trying to kill me. And out of my fear and anger came the will to learn to live as an alcoholic who wasn't trapped by booze anymore. Fear is a good sign, Alison. You are improving."

She stood up.

"Now we go to see the nurse and you can empty your pockets and bag here before we do."

Alison looked momentarily angry, then laughed. "To make sure that I don't have the bottle with the other half, carrying it for Jemma?"

Susan nodded. "You also can't go back to your room until it has been searched. Then tomorrow you will get a new roommate. As you said, you are half-way through. We can put someone brand new to Haydn in with you. You will be helping her, be her outside partner."

Alison said, almost wistfully as she emptied her purse and pockets, "Jemma will die out there. She's got nowhere to go; nothing left, she said."

Susan checked everything then said gently, "The director is looking at options right now and we will do what we can but, yes, that is a possibility. We have only fourteen beds. We are booked up for at least two months. We can't just recycle people who slip; it wouldn't work. But concentrate on your own recovery, not hers. Now wait here please; I need to check with Beverley that I can take you in."

She got up and left. As she walked back to the medical room, she thought about what would really happen to Jemma after rehab. The director, Consuela, would call one of her volunteers; 'Ladies of the Last Chance', as they were known; probably Alice. Like Jemma, she had done prison time back in her day.

If Jemma worked hard enough with Alice, then she could survive until she got back to Haydn. Alice was in her sixties and was 'old school' recovery; she wasn't into the role of sponsors only making 'suggestions' to the people she mentored. It would be, 'do as I say and there will be a reasonable possibility you will make it. Don't and you will die'. It was the tough end of loving care, brutal on sponsor and sponsee alike. But Alice had some good successes and was always willing to help.

It was three in the morning when a text came in. Her Alcoholics Anonymous sponsor knew Susan was on night duty this week. It said, 'I can't sleep. If it's convenient, call me'.

She did. "I'm the one that's supposed to be awake now, not you!"

The older woman laughed. "I know. Look, some news, bad news really. I was going to leave it until the morning but… I saw a news article on CBC; have you been on-line?"

"No, we've been busy."

"Duncan Aster has died, in England, it says. Police are looking into it."

She waited, listening. "Are you OK? It's a shock. I'll come over if you want?"

"How?"

"He was found in a lake, in the Lake District. It's summer. Perhaps he was swimming or something, but I don't know, to be honest. When was it you saw him? About two weeks ago?"

Sue said, "Less than that. A week and a half. But it can't be…"

Her sponsor butted in. "Linked. I thought you would jump straight there. No, you can't think that. Whatever it is about, it's nothing you need to feel any guilt over. Now, shall I come over?"

"Yes. No."

"Which?"

"No. Someone just came downstairs. I need to go, talk to her. I'll call you mid-afternoon; let's meet then, after I have slept."

She closed the call and looked up.

Alison was standing there in her dressing gown and slippers. Susan asked with a smile, "Can't sleep? Want some juice or a tea?"

The young woman nodded. "And can we talk?"

Sue smiled. "That was my own sponsor; I was just doing that. When you get out of here, you make sure you find one. Let's go to the den. You put the kettle on, and I will be along."

She quickly pulled up CBC news on her cellphone and thumbed through. The article banner read, 'Tragic death of Canadian priest in the English Lake District'.

I'll read it later, she thought. But it was already the central issue in her mind, raising old and deep wounds, as she headed across to the den.

11 LOWELL'S

21 July 9.45 a.m. BST.

Two days later, Sammie Livermore was in Penrith waiting to see her dentist when her phone rang. Despite the stares of disapproval from others, one person markedly glancing at the sign saying 'Please silence all mobile phones', she stood up, took the call, and headed out of the waiting room to get a little privacy in the empty lobby.

Howard Mooney said, "A call came in from a bookshop in Keswick. The woman wonders if it is worth reporting, but she says she recognizes the photo of Aster. She saw him with a man – and a bible was mentioned. Linnie flagged it, but I am on Workington follow-ups."

Sammie thought for a moment. It was her precious day off. She had a lot to do after the dentist. Howard was tied up on the Workington case, she knew.

"Give me the contact info and I'll deal with it."

Once she had the name and number, she thanked him and cut the call. She checked her call log and dialled Calder. "Harriet; it's Sammie. Can I ask a favour from you, assuming you are on duty now?"

"Fire away. But I'm busy, too."

"A report from Lowell's Books in Keswick, a Sandra Hardy. Can you pop in and take her statement? She says she recognized the photo of Aster and saw him with a man in the street. It seems to tie in with Moore's statement but… I'm just being called into see the dentist – right now, in fact, and it's not a routine check-up I'm here for, I tell you."

Harriet's interest was piqued. "I'll get straight on it. Good luck with the tooth."

The presence of a uniformed police officer in the bookshop caused a stare or two from customers, but the assistant knew exactly what it was about. She led Calder over to a room at the back.

"I didn't connect it with the death at the lake until I saw the police request on the TV. The two men were across the road, and I was moving some things in the front window. The man in the photo – he was the one who died, right?"

"Yes, Father Aster, he's the man we are asking about."

"He was with another man and they both were angry, I could tell. It didn't last long, but Father Aster walked off in a huff, I think. The other one was left standing there glaring for a moment. Then he turned around and walked back towards the convention grounds."

"What time was this?" asked Calder as she made notes. It all seemed to tie into the statement made by Moore, she thought, but Moore hadn't mentioned the anger bit. That was significant.

She went on, "Was there anyone else, perhaps someone you know, who was outside and closer to them?"

The woman shook her head. "Not that I recall, no. There are so many visitors. A hiker inside saw it, but… where he is, I have no idea. If he had bought a book, he could have left credit card information, but he didn't."

She had been glancing out of the door of the office frequently; she was the only staff member there at present.

Sandra called out, "Could I ask you to be more careful with that book, please? Don't bend the spine back like that unless you plan to buy it."

She shook her head and said softly, "We get a lot of damaged stock during July."

She picked up where she left off. "No, no-one else was around who I know. The other man, not Father Aster, just put the book in his pocket and went off."

"Book?"

"Yes, Aster's bible, I should say. It had been passed over in the heated argument or whatever it was. I suppose it was his. He pocketed it and went off."

Harriet said neutrally, "Could you describe the book."

Sandra replied, "Well, I know an Ignatius Compact RSV when I see one. Burgundy, with a zip, probably the leather one. But I can't say I saw the zip; just that the edges were cloth, as zippered books look, right?"

She sounded so certain; the same bible they had found in St. Anselm's. As Harriet made her notes, Sandra was keeping her eyes on the potential vandal in the shop.

"You are sure?" asked Harriet, "About the book?"

"It's my job. I've ordered enough religious works for you, Harriet; I know my trade."

Harriet smiled, still writing. "Just doing mine too, Sandra. You may find one of the Penrith detectives coming to take a more formal statement, perhaps; or perhaps not."

She moved into the doorway making her presence felt and giving the customer her 'no nonsense' look. He closed the book he had been mashing up and moved towards the sales desk with it.

"I'll go now," said Harriet, louder than she needed to,

really, "But you'd better come out here. You have a customer wanting to buy."

She smiled at the man as she passed. At the door she waited, looking back as she sent Livermore a text to call her, so that the villain at the sales desk didn't change his mind and scarper before he had paid Sandra for his misdeed.

~~

"Well, we've had the bible checked for prints, but I haven't looked at the report," was Sammie's first thought, expressed out loud to Harriet.

"How's the tooth?"

"Not good. I need a root canal," Sammie replied. "I quote, 'They want to do all they can to save it', but the tone of voice wasn't encouraging. And I am on the Workington case tomorrow, unless something new drags me in. I'll pull the Aster file together once the forensics are complete and see what the boss wants to do next. My money is on him passing the stuff on to the coroner and moving on, despite this anomaly about the bible. Do you think Moore, not Aster, put it in the church, then?"

"I don't know; it could be, but why? I thought Moore was looking too relieved for my liking when the second interview finished."

Sammie said, "Well, thanks for doing it. How's your day been?"

"Three medical-related callouts including a broken ankle and a collapse from heat stress; a call about a dog-bite in Great Crosthwaite and a break-in of a visitor's rental car; they will leave stuff on view. We think that there are a couple of thieves from a gang in Blackpool operating here this week, working the cars. The usual stuff during

Keswick Convention weeks. Oh, and a man in the book-shop you sent me to was breaking in the spine on a new book, a serious crime. I came over the heavy and made him pay for it."

Sammie laughed. "Well, thanks again," as she closed the call. The varied nature of police work, she mused.

~~

It was three days later. Sammie was completing her period of 'Acting' DS as her own team leader, DS John Burrows was back off holiday tomorrow. She wasn't sure what would happen next. In Trent's office were his team leaders, two sergeants and herself. Trent was being briefed on the latest status of several investigations.

When it came to the Aster case, she gave a status report.

"Dr. Lee's final report was death by drowning. There are no signs of foul play. There appears to be, from Aster's email to his bishop, a woman involved back in Canada that may be a factor. Safeguarding has been informed and will contact their Canadian counterparts in Ontario. We inter-viewed Reverend Moore, the last known contact, as you recall. He was pretty evasive, but that could be because he didn't want to reveal Aster's confession. You saw, that, sir."

Trent nodded.

Sammie continued, "The bible that turned up is Aster's; both from an inscription on a card and the forensics. The fingerprints on it are mainly the deceased but there are prints from two other people, recent ones they believe. How it got into the church, we don't know, but we suspect it was via Andrew Moore.

"Finally, Moore and his family went back to Canada earlier than they planned, based on his original interview. I looked into it. It wasn't a little fare supplement to change his tickets; he bought four full fare tickets in premium economy, one way; a significant cost."

"That's it. I feel that at this stage we present the information to the coroner and leave it to her, unless we want to follow up with Moore somehow. Is that worth it?"

Trent nodded his agreement then wrinkled his nose. "Now you mention it, I recall the tail end of that first interview. I didn't like the man; he was hiding something and was uncooperative. For a clergyman, that didn't seem right. Nor does heading back early; he skipped town, it seems to me."

He paused then sighed, "But I agree; nothing else to do at our end at this stage; leave it to the coroner."

He looked at Green. "Neil, catch up on this one; go through it with Sammie and then you can become the ongoing contact with the Canadians and any others. It will quietly slip away, I expect."

Sammie was sure now that she was back in her regular role.

Trent looked at the team. "It looks like some people have had good holidays – now it is my turn. I'm off for a week. DCI Shearing is getting her feet wet in our area and will join the morning briefing today to be introduced."

He looked at DI Nolan, now back from holiday. "Ken, you will be with her making sure she is on track and doesn't trip over; it's not her field. Don't let her – or me – down."

His gaze switched to O'Brien. "Dennis, you take on acting DI for Ken's team. Sammie, you continue as Acting DS, but with Dennis. That's it for now; let's go and join the rest."

As they stood and started out of his office, Trent said to Sammie, "I told you I wasn't letting you off the hook, didn't I?"

12 MEMORIAL MASS

28 July, 11.00 a.m. EDT

The Memorial Mass for Father Duncan Aster was held at the Pro-Cathedral of the Assumption in North Bay, Ontario, an imposing church of white limestone dating from the late nineteenth century.

Many had gathered for the occasion, including Bishop Hugh Tremblay, Aster's fellow priests and nuns, family members and parishioners. Two Anglican clergymen were also in attendance; Bishop James Azikiwe and Reverend Andrew Moore, both dressed in dark suits and clerical collars, but not wearing any other vestments. They were part of the congregation, seated at the front with other clergy and family.

It had been Bishop Azikiwe's decision that they should attend.

That arose from the meeting Bishop Azikiwe held with Reverend Moore and his wife at his own cathedral two days after their return from England. Azikiwe had been hit by the sadness of it all; that a man who had dedicated his life to God and had been so engaged in theological discussion one minute, had died under such tragic circumstances the next. His own priest seemed to have coped well, he thought, particularly with the added imposition of police interviews immediately afterwards.

Andrew Moore and his wife expressed their gratitude to the bishop and the people in the Carlisle diocese office for their help.

He said, "It was very much appreciated; we needed it and when we asked, the support came. We are grateful for that blessing."

Sylvia Moore added, "We came back early. I don't think we could face the idea of the walking holiday section of our plans, Andy and I, or the children. But the prayer service at Keswick for Father Aster was so… healing. People from all over the world were praying for Duncan; it was very special. I am proud of Andy for co-leading it. We have sent a note of thanks and flowers already to the co-celebrant from North Bay, Julie Stevens."

James Azikiwe decided there and then that both he and Reverend Moore should attend the memorial service. Mrs. Moore smiled and nodded but soon made it clear that she was sorry for Duncan Aster and his family, but quite simply had too much to do, now she was back. Her tone suggested that she thought her husband had, too, rather than make a trip to North Bay. But she wouldn't be the one to question the bishop's decision, her eyes said.

Conscious of protocol and interfaith relationships, James had first organized a telephone call with his counterpart, Bishop Tremblay, leader of the Roman Catholic Diocese of Greater North Bay.

After the preliminaries of the call were over, the Catholic leader said, out of the blue, "Now, James, if I can call you that, and I am Hugh, are you thinking of participating actively in some way in the service?"

Glad to put the formality aside, James said, "Oh, no! Not for the funeral of your priest. No. It's too… personal; not appropriate. I just felt, based on what Reverend Moore told me, that we should have some representation to show our respect and support. Perhaps Reverend Moore alone, or with one of my deans, might be a more appropriate choice, if you wish? I don't want to complicate things for you or anyone else."

The Catholic bishop's response was instantaneous. "No, you yourself, if you would, please, James. It would be very much appreciated. Indeed. In fact, bring Reverend Moore of course, as well; it will be a comfort to him, I hope. Such a sad affair.

"But could I also impose on you for a meeting, one-on-one after the service, I suggest, early in the afternoon? I could arrange a schedule for your man. Perhaps a visit to Father Aster's own church, or he may want to visit the local Anglican community? As might you, I know, but an hour of your time would be appreciated."

He was warm toned. James took to the man, reading that he could be a bit of a chameleon, as circumstances dictated.

By the end of the call, it was sorted out. He thought back to the worried call from Sylvia Moore, concerned about the police taking away her husband; his own call to the Diocese of Carlisle and the more restrained phone discussion with Reverend Moore later, saying he had just talked with the police again and was feeling relieved about how that went.

Attendance at the funeral is a proper closure to this sad episode, James concluded. Or so he thought at the time.

~~

The drive to North Bay from Hamilton took about five hours, all told, during the late afternoon and evening the day before the service. James liked to drive, but he ceded to Reverend Moore's offer to do so. It freed him up to make some calls and read some documents he had to catch up on – and Moore had a top-of-the-line Lexus, more suitable for the road trip than the bishop's own smaller vehicle.

It was Moore's suggestion that James take the back seat for a good part of the way, to be chauffeured in a sense, and allow him to spread his documents out on the seat as he worked. By Gravenhurst, when they stopped for a break, James had finished the things with time-sensitive elements and he felt that talking further with Moore, getting to know his priest better, was the right thing to do. When they returned to the car, he sat in the front passenger seat.

That Andrew Moore was a traditionalist who had supported another candidate for bishop didn't disturb him. He was past all that. St. Matthew's in Stoney Creek was a well-run church, a strong contributor to the diocese in funds and people volunteering for diocesan work. A retired banker there, Donald Pernell, was chair of the Finance Committee for the diocese, an important role. James had other churches more in need of his attention.

He had visited St. Matthew's during his first year of office and enjoyed the welcome and the Sunday morning experience. Moore was well thought of there, he saw; and he was a good orator. The only note of concern on the diocesan file was that the church was too cliquey, not open enough. New people found it hard to fit in and tended to move if they didn't feel part of the crowd.

During the remaining trip north, after talking about parish issues, they covered again the ground of the UK trip and the pall over the family's UK holiday plans. Regarding the sudden curtailment of the holiday, Moore said, "You wouldn't think that the summer heat would bother the girls, compared with here, would you? I think it was the nights without air conditioning; they didn't sleep so well."

Azikiwe responded, "And perhaps with the tensions and weight you two were under… children are very sensitive, even if they don't understand it all."

"Tensions?"

"Well, it must have been tense, going through two police interviews? It would be for me."

"I prayed a lot," was the response.

But still, they came back to Canada early, Azikiwe thought. It must have been stressful enough to finish the holiday early.

As they drove into North Bay, James said, "I've not been here since my early teens, at a church camp a little north of here. I haven't a clear memory of the place."

Moore responded, "We have a cottage in the Kawarthas; it was my parents, so we all share it. Sylvia, the girls, and I go in the summer often, generally mid-week."

Knowing that Moore was from a wealthy family, James wondered whether it was a cottage in the sense he would know one, or a more palatial home on a lake. The area was full of multimillion dollar homes which people called their cottages.

~~

The memorial service was a solemn mass. It was clear to James that the congregation was a large proportion of clergy, with a mix of laity from the cathedral and members of the two churches in North Bay where Father Aster had served. James had also cleared his own presence with the

Anglican bishop of the overlapping diocese, who was happy to see him attend, as he simultaneously apologized that he was away on a 'summer retreat'. In his first year in office, James found himself too busy to 'retreat', although he was feeling at present in need of a good holiday.

In the immediate aftermath of the service, as the clergy mingled with the laity, Bishop Tremblay was led over by two aides to meet the visiting Anglicans. James thought that Tremblay looked patrician; his silver hair and fine robes sat well and easy on him and he was comfortable in them. Moreso than James felt in his own at times, was the guilty thought.

There was a formal introduction, which an aide polished off proficiently; 'Most Reverend Excellency, Bishop Hugh Tremblay, please welcome the Right Reverend James Azikiwe, Bishop of the Anglican diocese of Hamilton-Brant'. Tremblay then spoke to Moore.

"Reverend Moore, our sincere thanks for the time you took to talk to Father Aster in Keswick. It was such sad news for all of us. And no doubt, a deeply disturbing one for you?"

Moore seemed pleased to receive the attention. "Thank you, Your Excellency. It was – still is – a troubling matter. I pray for Father Aster daily. But it was a beautiful service."

"Indeed. As do I," the Catholic bishop countered. "That you met at a spiritual meeting, too. I hope this service has provided some healing for you."

He sighed and addressed Bishop Azikiwe. "Father Aster was buried in Cumbria two days ago; may he rest in peace. He had only one relative living over here now, his mother, who was not able to attend the funeral, but his brother Nigel did. Nigel's back now, here with his mother. He works in South America at present, a fine young man."

He nodded in the direction of the cluster that was

obviously the gathering of family and personal friends.

Azikiwe nodded, not sure what to say. It costs a lot of money to get a body across the Atlantic, he knew, but still...

Tremblay continued, "Duncan's parent's family were from England, and he had other family there so, under the circumstances, it seemed... for the best. To be surrounded by family there. But we had a good attendance here today."

James said, "It was indeed a fine service."

"I will look forward to seeing you later, Bishop Azikiwe."

As they exchanged looks, the aides efficiently moved the Catholic bishop on to others waiting for a word.

People were moving slowly towards another room. Finger food and refreshment, it seemed.

~~

In his office later, with the door closed, Tremblay was more at ease. "Some sparkling water... or something a little stronger, perhaps? I could offer you a glass of sherry."

"Water would be fine, Bishop, thank you."

"It's just us. Hugh, remember?"

As they compared notes about their own backgrounds, it turned out Tremblay was originally from Alberta, as was James, but Hugh was a francophone from even further north in the province than Edmonton. He thanked James again for coming and paused. "I have a little problem that I need to share with you, bishop to bishop. Is it Jim... or is it James, really?"

Azikiwe looked surprised, but said, "It's James; I go by that, Hugh. A problem, in what sense?"

"Well, I have a problem and you may have a different one. And I am going to confide a little in you on a strictly need-to-know basis. Between us two, is that understood?"

James nodded but said nothing. His antenna was up.

Hugh began, "We may have to do this more formally, but I hope not. First you need the background. I received an email from Father Aster shortly before he died. A short one, but very significant. I tried to contact him immediately but… the police found it, obviously, on his phone. I'll show it to you, but I would rather that you didn't keep a copy."

He pulled a sheet of paper from a file on his desk and passed it over. James scanned it quickly then, in disbelief, read it again more slowly.

I can't take it anymore, Hugh. First Susan, now this; I talked with an Anglican priest I met here and thought it would help but it didn't. And he has let me down badly. Ignosce Me.

James passed it back, his face revealing his shock. "I understand what it says, I think, but I don't see, in a sense. That Father Aster was troubled; Reverend Moore told me that, but he gave no context. This reference to a woman called Susan? And to Moore letting him down? And *Ignosce Me*; how terrible! I don't know what to say."

The Catholic cleric paused, looking out of the window for a moment, then back at the visitor. "Probably nothing; it would be best at present, I suggest."

He continued, "There is an Ontario court settlement, a civil court matter, a secrecy agreement between the church and a family in North Bay, former members of Father Aster's church. They have a daughter called Susan. I can't say more. It relates to that email message. Our priests, as you know, live a celibate life or try to. But they are human."

James concentrated on keeping his face impassive, finally getting the full gist.

"This is quite a shock, as I said. From this morning's service, I would have said that Father Aster was dearly loved and a wonderful priest, highly valued by his colleagues and congregations."

Tremblay nodded. "He was. He is. But he was a man with an event in his past that was a burden; to some others, too, but particularly to him."

Hugh was assessing him, James realised. The older man said quietly, "I hate to do it to you, really, after such a wonderful memorial mass. I prayed on it."

He gave Azikiwe a searching look. "Whatever the man did, I want you to know that he wasn't... wasn't one of those priests who have so marred both our churches. Never that. I wouldn't have stood for that."

There was an energy and sense of conviction in the man. James didn't know what to say. This was his first formal encounter of the issue of sexual abuse by clergy since his appointment, and he was holding it with, of all people, a Catholic counterpart. He simply dreaded this sort of issue possibly arising in his own tenure as bishop.

Tremblay continued, "We both have far too much on our plates already. But I would rather you know and that we try to build a relationship based on trust, I feel. I don't know what will unfold."

All James could respond with was, "I appreciate that."

He said nothing else, seeing that Hugh Tremblay was going to continue.

"We understand from our contacts in the UK that the police looking into Duncan's death have more or less concluded that he took his own life. Our advisors there tell us that the coroner's jury will likely arrive finally at an open verdict. But the chief inspector in charge of the investigation, in closing the case, referred the file to the Cumbria Police Safeguarding Unit, given this email. That is a child or vulnerable adult sexual assault investigation unit, in our parlance. They will be obliged, we understand, to forward it to the Ontario Provincial Police.

"But Father Aster is dead, why…"

Then his face showed he had thought through to the answer.

Tremblay appeared to read his mind. "Duncan never forgave himself; he struggled with that, right to the end. But some of his holidays were taken in the UK, in various places, often at retreats."

They would worry about him being a predator; that there would be other victims, other names than 'Susan' in the man's past, James had realised. And not only in the UK. Perhaps Tremblay's assertions were more in hope than reality; the blinkering that their churches were often accused of hiding behind.

Tremblay continued, "They have no details, or basis for further enquiries, I sincerely believe, just a suspicion. The OPP will soon have some information, to whatever degree their UK counterparts share files. Our own secrecy agreement is, of course, a matter of sealed record, but a record that can be identified, if not accessed. I must be prepared. So must you."

James asked immediately, "For me, in what context?"

Tremblay replied, "I talked with my legal counsel, Simon Nugent, an experienced man. It may be highly relevant whether Duncan's last discussion with Reverend Moore meets the criteria for confession, as defined by either church, as both men are ordained members of clergy. Apart from the issue of a stain on Father Aster's reputation, there are other people involved. We have no wish for this to surface and bring embarrassment or pain for them.

"I hope, in burdening you, I have also prepared you for when your man comes to you; as he will, no doubt, if approached by the Ontario police. He will need your help and wisdom. I can't do more than that and must leave it in your hands to guide Reverend Moore both by your canons and your conscience."

He stood, signaling he was done.

"I do truly appreciate you making the offer to come today; I didn't expect it, but it was so meaningful to me. I couldn't let this opportunity pass and have it hit you unawares."

James stood also and gave a small sigh. He hadn't expected this at all.

Tremblay smiled. "I will pray for your work as I hope that you will pray for mine. You are at the beginning of your lonely journey, I feel. I am nearer to the end of my own. Fifteen years have taken their toll, so all I can do is say that I understand and wish you well. Go in God's Grace."

James reached out his hand and Hugh Tremblay took the offered handshake in both of his own hands. He held him tight as he looked him in the eyes. "A piece of advice from an old man, if I can be so bold?"

James's eyebrows rose and he smiled. "Gladly, thank you."

"I'm sure you will keep the information I just gave you to yourself. But I suggest while it is milling around fresh in your head, as it does in a not-so-fresh way in my own, don't discuss Reverend Moore's interactions with Father Aster at all today on your long drive back together. You have a legal advisor, of course?"

"Of course. I had thought of that, actually. We are on the same wavelength. She will be my first stop on this one. And thank you. I am touched at your warmth and consideration, even during such a sad moment."

A car organised by Tremblay had driven James to the

Anglican church that Andrew Moore had visited after the reception. His mind was only partly on his task as he talked with the clergy and some of the people present before they set off home. On the drive back to Hamilton, they stopped at Gravenhurst again for an early evening meal. The finger food after the funeral had been varied and interesting but they were mainly occupied with talking to people.

After the stop, it would be a straight drive south to the outskirts of Toronto, then west, hopefully missing the worst of the rush hour traffic. The conversation after leaving North Bay had reflected on the service, and the people met there, but not the events leading up to the funeral.

James's mind was spinning with the information provided by Bishop Tremblay, and he took to heart his advice on letting it alone until he talked further with Anne Lieberman, the Diocesan Chancellor. But his new insight also showed him that, in the reflections on the memorial service, Andrew Moore was being very selective with his comments. Considering what he must know about the deceased, he was steering his own course carefully, James decided. He hadn't seen that in earlier discussions, and on the drive to North Bay.

They then moved on to matters around the planning for the next synod, the issues facing the diocese.

Suddenly, Moore said, "May I say something, Bishop, that might not sit well?"

James stiffened, thinking of his discussion with Tremblay and the man's final warning, but replied, "If you wish, Andrew. Feel free."

"I originally wanted Joe Carrington to become bishop. The issue of protection of our church's rites and traditions is very important to me, and to my congregation. I know it is seen by others as a 'head in the sand' attitude towards change, but we are worried about the erosion of our identity as an Anglican church."

He glanced across at his bishop, checking his reaction. He got none; the man was impassive. He waited, testing whether he should proceed.

James suddenly said, "I remember Joe using that term, 'erosion of our identity' a few times when he spoke. It's from Bursell."

"Bursell?"

"Rupert Bursell, a Church of England Canon Chancellor, a lawyer; the foreword by someone else to his book, '*Liturgy, Order and the Law*', not sure who. Have you read it?"

"Well, no."

Azikiwe held back his next thought; Andrew, don't lay tripwires that are bright, shiny steel. If you lay a tripwire, make sure it is dull and invisible.

Moore continued with, "I am not in any way against our stance on gay rights and same sex marriage, I might add, but I felt that Monique Hall was so aligned with Bishop Gloria that our diocese would continue to be monolithic in its focus on the issue, to the exclusion of other, equally important matters to the church. It's fine to be in the vanguard supporting such issues but is, I feel, too consuming of the energy of the diocese, too much a focal point. In the divisions between these two candidates, you sailed through the centre in the re-votes, on the theme of unity and tolerance of all diverse viewpoints."

James nodded; it was familiar ground. He was thankful that the point Moore thought wouldn't 'sit well' wasn't the Aster issue, it seemed. He watched his companion carefully as the man worked through the wording of his contentious point.

"Well, we are a year into your term as bishop. People

talked about a settling-in period. Some people think it's getting a bit long; we don't know what your 'agenda' is, for want of a better word. Is that too forward?"

The bishop asked, "What issue or cause do I nail my banner to, do you mean? My sister-in-law is asking me the same question, so no; I appreciate your candour."

Andrew Moore focused on the road and waited. After a moment, James said, "Frankly, I don't have one. My vision is a healed, coherent diocese and the growth which could come from that. I said that during the synod that chose me, bland as it seems to some people. That's what I have been working towards; pulling people together. In unity, we can focus our collective energies outwards, for service to all in the love of Jesus Christ."

He sighed and stared out the window. "Though it's not that visible yet, I suppose. Not a brand, as they say."

"Although I will say I worry more about our present and our future as a church and a diocese than I do about our past. I abhor seeing our children lost in expensive video-games featuring assassinations and bombs, these thinly veiled promotions for American gun culture. I ponder about our role in a modern Canadian society, our relevance. I get annoyed when I read, as I did only two days ago, about people explaining the cultural significance of FGM as some sort of expiating mitigation for people mutilating little girls. Here, in Canada! I want to know what I and our church can do to help address issues like these. Does that answer your question?"

James realised that in his tiredness, worry and the return to the issue of the old divisive agendas of the diocese, he had just sounded argumentative and annoyed.

Moore just responded politely but neutrally, "Yes, bishop. Thank you."

Well, that didn't seem to go down too well, thought

James.

As they drove in silence, the bishop mused on it and returned to the topic. He said softly, "I'm sorry; I have had a long week. I pray for guidance. I will continue to try to achieve my stated aim. If I find a banner which fits, that is visible to people, I will wave it. Until then, I will just do my job as best as I can, with God's help."

The light was changing as the sun lowered in the west. They would be home before dark, but driving was becoming more difficult. Moore chose not to comment further and as they entered the busy section of multi-lane highway north of Toronto he concentrated on the road and the building traffic. There was little more to say.

James concluded that he had just picked up the shiny steel tripwire and tightened it a little around his own neck with the St. Matthew's crowd. He was tired. It had been a day with very disturbing news.

13 FAMILY

Susan asked, "How did it go?"

She knew her mother would call her after the memorial service and had been waiting for news, yet she was apprehensive about hearing it. The call came as she had got off the streetcar, as she was going to the bank and doing a little shopping after her shift.

"It was a good Mass. The bishop was wonderful and Father Wesley, his friend from seminary now in Toronto, gave the homily. It was beautiful, truth be told. Duncan had a good send off. Your father and I had a word with the bishop later; he specially made the effort. I appreciated that gesture."

"Nothing about how Duncan… died?"

"No. It was completely avoided. But many knew, you could tell by their faces. If they had said it was an accident, even a suggestion of it being one with him being found in the lake, we all would have latched on to it. There was just a reference that the police were still investigating."

They stayed on the line, silent for some seconds.

"And the conversation with Bishop Tremblay?"

"Nothing was said then, other than he was appreciative of our attendance. He was warm and welcoming; it made it a lot easier for me, at least. He asked after you and I said how well you are doing."

An easier conversation than it would have been for me, thought Susan. But that was well-trodden ground. Instead, she said, "I'm glad that you went, then."

Her mother said, "And how are you today?"

"Up and down a bit. We had one resident who had been taken to rehab looking like she may make it back here. She popped in with her sponsor. I'm glad she is doing better."

Jemma, the woman Susan had caught taking cough medicine, had seemed brighter and better balanced today than at any time during her stay at Haydn. Alice, her sponsor now, had said to Susan, "She's focusing on staying sober a day at a time, at last; it's a good sign. Consuela is seeing when she can return and complete the course."

Neither of them said it; Jemma would probably do just as well now, working closely with Alice, if the older woman's assessment was correct. But Jemma needed to complete the Haydn House program to convince the authorities that she could have access to her children again.

Susan knew that her mother's question had been more directed to Susan's feelings about Duncan Aster's death, but she didn't want to discuss that with her.

Her mother said, filling the growing silence, "We even had two Anglicans attend the service, from Hamilton; a priest and a bishop, no less. I wasn't sure why, but I heard later that the Anglican priest and Duncan had met in the UK on holiday; they had got on well. It was nice of them to come all the way to North Bay for the service."

Susan wasn't quite sure what to say. "Duncan and an Anglican priest?"

It was all she could think of.

"Yes, they met at some Protestant religious gathering in the UK, near where Duncan died. Duncan had decided to attend the meeting, for some reason."

The noise of an irate driver suddenly honking his horn at the intersection made Susan look up, and clearly carried over the phone to her mother, who asked what was going on.

"A blocked intersection. I'm at Yonge and Wellesley, just by my bank. Look, I'd better go, I've a lot to do and it's not easy talking here. I'll call later or tomorrow. Thanks for the news. I'm glad the service helped you and Dad. Give him my love. And you too, of course."

She waited for her mother's similar response before closing the call, grateful for the traffic disruption. As she entered the Scotiabank branch, her mind was questioning what sort of relationship Duncan Aster had struck up in the Lake District with an Anglican clergyman? What had caused not only the priest but also his bishop to make the drive north to attend the memorial service?

~~

29 July, 11.00 a.m. BST

"Make me a channel of your peace; where there's despair in life, let me bring hope…"

Harriet was struck by the beauty of Kerri's voice, a deep contralto balancing beautifully with the tenor notes of the man also playing the guitar. They were leading the hymn set to the words of St. Francis in the gathering at St. Anselm's Church.

Calder had a passable voice and could hold a tune well enough to sing out at services she led or attended, but Kerri, trained or not, was in another league as a singer.

Fleetingly, she wished she had known her before Ian died; she would have asked her to sing something at her husband's funeral. Her voice was so calming.

Calder was in uniform, as were Constables Stella Keegan and Michael Truman. Inspector Dewar felt, as they were the station officers on scene at the discovery of the body, they should attend the service. He had been contacted by a Reverend Christopher Willard.

If it hadn't been a duty requirement, Harriet wouldn't have been able to attend the service that morning. She knew vaguely of Willard. He had responsibilities for a number of smaller Anglican churches in the area but, other than he looked too young for the job, she hadn't had any contact with him.

What surprised her most was the quality and informality of his homily; the maturity and insight into loss that he showed.

"The police tapes are gone. Other than several bunches of flowers, there is no sign of the events of the day Duncan Aster died. The first I heard was a phone call from a warden. By the time I got here, I couldn't do anything, not even get past the barrier. A number of us gathered and prayed; that was all we could do, and it was necessary; a man had died close to our church, in the waters just there. He died tragically, unexpectedly, and for reasons we don't understand. We didn't know him, but that doesn't matter. He was here.

"He is now buried elsewhere, cared for by his church, his family, and his friends. Back in his parish in Ontario, Canada, in a place called North Bay, they held a memorial service yesterday, to celebrate the man's life, his service to God, and to remember him."

"What do we do now? How do we deal with a death on our doorstep of someone we don't know? Time, of course, will help. We'll move on, at least most of us will. But for some, this spot will always bring back a memory of that sad event. Our faith in God will be restorative; we will ask his help at this time, as we would during any anxiety or sadness. We will place our trust in him completely. That works, we know, if our faith is strong."

In her professional capacity as a preacher, Harriet could see that the priest had caught his audience, from their expressions, the focus, and the silence.

Across the church, in the back, she could see Sammie Livermore doing the same thing Harriet had done during the prayer meeting in Keswick. Sammie's eyes were roving, taking in the attendees.

Outside the church after the service, Livermore came across to speak to Harriett and the two officers with her. Some people had left, others were having coffee, and several were down at the lake. Reverend Willard had suggested that anyone burdened should go down there, pray quietly, and simply touch the water, asking for healing.

As they caught up, Stella Keegan said, "I'm glad we got to do this. It helped me, I think." Her eyes were on the lake edge, where people were bending or kneeling to touch the water.

Sammie said to Harriet, "I didn't see anything that particularly stood out."

It confused Stella, who interpreted it as a criticism of the minister or the service. Seeing her face, Harriet explained, "She saw nothing related to the investigation, no person of interest. That's what Acting Detective Sergeant Livermore means."

Sammie laughed. "You make that title sound such a mouthful."

"It is," responded Harriet.

"John said come over; you never know. So, I did." Her head moved. As Harriet turned to follow Livermore's gaze, she saw Kerri Sanders approaching, ready to leave.

"You sang well," called out Harriet, with echoing agreement from her colleagues.

"Thank you, it was Gerry's playing and singing that did the trick; I can always sing easily with him. It was a lovely service, I thought."

Harriet agreed. "Reverend Willard spoke well," she added.

Kerri nodded, but didn't say anything for a moment, her eyes on the people at the lakeside. "Our Reverend Chris; yes, he did. He spoke from the heart on that one, I think. His parents died in a sailing mishap when he was nine. I think he knows a bit about coming to terms with tragedy around water."

She smiled briefly, glancing at Sammie, sensing the police officer wanted to talk further with her colleagues. "I'm heading home."

When she was out of earshot, Sammie said to Harriet, "John made a call yesterday to the Ontario Provincial Police in Canada. They have agreed to do some digging for us. He also talked earlier with someone in the Crown Prosecutor's office. I guess the file is not yet closed, after all."

Harriet nodded, showing her understanding, but she said nothing, with two of her team in tow. It wasn't about Aster's death; it was whether this issue of a girl or woman called Susan had any ramifications for their investigation.

14 BRANTFORD

30 July, 5.00 p.m. EDT

It was a point of principle now that James Azikiwe
would not wear his clerical collar when he drove his wife
and sister-in-law to visit their daughter Rowena and her
family. Rowena Azikiwe and Gavin Atkinson lived in
Brantford, a small city forty kilometres west of Hamilton.
The reality was that his sister-in-law Ursula drove Dodee
there far more often, to see their only grandchildren, and
they had a close and informal relationship with Rowena
and the family. Adding James to the mix didn't change that,
but adding his formal attire did.

Rowena Azikiwe had grown up in the Anglican faith;
being the daughter of a parish priest, that was natural.
James had fully expected, given her personality, that she
would rebel at some point, perhaps, probably in her teens.
It didn't happen. She became more active in the church
and threw herself into pastoral work while studying hard,
making good grades. When she rebelled, it wasn't against
the church; it was against what she saw as its fossilization
and rituals.

She chose Mount Allison University in New Brunswick for her tertiary education. Her parents would have preferred Queens University, in Kingston, only a three-hour drive away rather than a two-hour flight, but it was at university that she found her calling, social work with children in need. Her first job, in the Nation's Capital, Ottawa, was with DFAIT, the Department of Foreign Affairs and International Trade, as it was then known, with her sights on overseas children's aid. It should have been a stepping stone. It became a stumbling block. She stayed two years before transferring to the Ontario provincial government Department of Child Welfare, now engaged to Gavin, similarly disenchanted with the Ottawa bureaucracy.

They bought their first small home in Brantford when Gavin got work there with the regional government and Rowena landed a post with the city. There, they joined a small, relatively new Anglican church, one that had started on the principles that they would not be bogged down with the ceremony and trappings of the past. It fitted well Gavin and Rowena's philosophy and pastoral care mission. They had both their children baptized there with her father co-celebrating the baptismal services.

Over the years, however, the church seemed to lose direction. In constantly seeking new ways to celebrate the liturgy and establish a fresh pastoral mission they settled on only a few elements that satisfied all, and the congregation started to fragment. Gavin and Rowena felt less happy there and, some months earlier, had started church-hunting again. That her dad had overall responsibility for their church now it was 'a mess, becoming more traditional by the day' didn't sit well with Rowena.

James had allowed Justin, his older grandchild who was

now eight, to beat him at chess, sitting on the floor in the boy's bedroom, albeit with some moves far less than legal. Rowena came in, smiled, and gave her father a hug. "You are looking tired. I want to apologize for last week; I shouldn't have blown off steam with you. But you are my dad, and I did."

He held her to him for a moment. "It's alright, I understand. I love you."

She smiled, "And I love you too. Mom worries about you, you know? The constant pressure."

He nodded. He knew. But he wasn't going there. He winked at Justin who sat there silently, taking it all in.

Rowena said, "What I miss, I really miss, is our old church in Westdale, being with you there, being... part of everything. So, Gavin and I are going back to church in Hamilton, to Park Royal, to be part of Ginny's church, I just told Mom. It's... where we fit, I hope. But mom's a bit put out. If we are going to commute to Hamilton for church she said, why not attend the cathedral?"

James replied, "You need to go where you feel right, where you and Gavin feel spiritually at home. It's your journey, Ro, I've always told you that. You have my blessing. But it's a longer drive each Sunday and you aren't simply a Sunday Christian, either."

"It's easier than my daily drive to Oakville, when I used to commute to work there from Hamilton."

He smiled. "And Ginny will put you to work, too; count on it. She did me, last week."

Rowena and Genevieve Farmer were similar in age and had worked together in church activities during their teens. "Ginny put you to work. You, the bishop! You shouldn't let good-looking young women twist you around their finger; it's not seemly for a man of the cloth."

He smiled, ignoring the jibe. "It was for the Okafor

family, the young man beaten and killed last week, Benjamin. If you go to Park Royal, you will find that his sister goes there now. It was in support of them."

Rowena said, "The man killed outside the cleaners? I didn't know. It makes me want to go to Ginny's even more now. Why you; because you are bishop?"

"No, because I have some Hausa in my vocabulary."

Rowena knew that her father had spoken the Nigerian language as a boy; his mother had insisted on it.

He nodded. "It was my dad's first language. Benjamin was the first one to get work since they obtained landed status; he wanted to study. His sister goes with a friend to Park Royal and so Ginny went round to see how they could help the family. The grandmother speaks only Hausa. Being from Nigerian parents, Ginny had the idea of calling me."

His daughter replied, "I gather he was mistaken for some person in the drug trade, that's what the news said. You still speak Hausa?"

"A little; more fragments, really. There are hundreds of languages in Nigeria; I am rusty now. But I went with her to try to help."

His daughter smiled. "It sounds like our Reverend Genevieve wanted a translator, not a bishop! But you needed this, really, I can see. You are missing it, aren't you, the pastoral work?"

He nodded. "It's not my place to do what I want, but what I am called to do. It's a lot more fulfilling than diocesan politics, I have to agree."

He suddenly recalled his discussion with Rabbi Simmons. "I ran into David Simmons recently. We had coffee together. He told me that Michael Simmons was killed in a car accident in Tel Aviv last year. It's so tragic for them."

The Azikiwe and the Simmons families had got along well.

"I know, I heard," she said. "I thought you and mom knew already?"

He shook his head. He, too, missed his old parish. But tomorrow afternoon, he would meet with the Diocesan Chancellor on headier matters, church law and the issue of Andrew Moore's encounter with Duncan Aster.

He was no longer a rector, working with lay volunteers on the plan for the week's services and the pastoral work of the parish.

~~

Every diocese has a bishop; all Anglicans knew that. Relatively few, even amongst regular churchgoers, were aware that every diocese also needs a chancellor. Generally, a lay person, a lawyer, they are often called Canon Chancellor; the age-old term of 'Canon' relating to people who provide service to the diocese, the bishop and the cathedral, whether ordained or not.

A Canon Chancellor's area of expertise is also not that visible at the level of the congregation; it is in both civil and canon law, the latter being the ecclesiastical law system of the church, with a history predating virtually all civil law. Canon lawyers were faithful members of their church denomination, generally providing *pro bono* service year-on-year to the diocese. Some cynics said it must be an act of divine intervention to get so much expensive legal service support for free.

In his first year after appointment, James Azikiwe had come to know and respect Anne Lieberman, the Canon Chancellor of Hamilton-Brant. She provided immediate support and guidance to him on the diocesan legal aspects of his new role, in a manner that still treated him as her spiritual leader. After the synod which appointed Azikiwe, she had taken him quietly under her wing to prepare him for the various committee and legal duties associated with his office. It was then he had said to her, "Anne; I'm James. You can call me bishop when we are with others, in public or in meetings."

He knew she was a talented and wealthy lawyer, with a home in Hamilton and a partnership in a large civil law practice in downtown Toronto. His predecessor had told him she was known to be one of the foremost experts on ecclesiastical law in Canada. If she ever moves, said Bishop Gloria, there will be an Anglican bishop knocking on her door with flowers and smiles of entrapment before the movers have arrived to deliver the furniture.

Their first meeting in which he sought legal advice included an item arising from the audit of last year's financial report to synod. A parishioner was querulously contesting the level of travel expenditure by Bishop Gloria.

After discussion of the parishioner's concern, in which Lieberman had reminded him that the auditors had no problem with the expenses, and that Bishop Gloria was very committed to international support, she asked, "James, there is something not sitting quite right for you, I can see. What is it?"

Azikiwe hesitated a moment, then said, "The international trips were business travel fares; costly."

She looked at him, her expression saying 'and?', then she said, "They were long-haul trips over relatively short visit durations."

He sighed. "It's a memory of my dad; from when I became a curate. I was thinner then. He was a passenger agent in Edmonton but on sick leave from Air Canada. It was how we came to Canada, actually. He had been laid off by British Airways from their Lagos office and people he knew told him to talk to a person with an Air Canada link at the Lufthansa office. But there was a big 'no-no' with it as well, they said; the opportunities were in Northern Canada, the cold version of Hell on earth."

Lieberman smiled.

"Anyway, my parents settled in Edmonton and, as I said, years later my dad became terminally ill just as I was ordained. I'm glad he got to see that. One of his final comments was, 'one day you will be a bishop, son; I am sure'. I just laughed. 'But you will have to put on some weight. Bishops always travel business class; too many of them can't get their rear ends into regular seats, it seems.' Not that I am saying that Gloria or I ..."

Anne laughed out loud. "Wait until you are trying to fit in time for a trip to somewhere, for whatever reason, and have a boatload of work to get through as well. Don't rush to judgement about business class."

He nodded. "I suppose so. Now I have my chancellor quoting the Book of Matthew to me."

So, he had no problem in asking Anne for guidance after bringing her up to date on the events since the first call about Andrew Moore.

At the end of his summary he asked, "Should I bring Moore in for a serious discussion now, do you think?"

Anne crunched up her face a little, a sign that she wasn't in wholehearted agreement.

"Do you know what you want to ask him first, James? That's the thing. What's the purpose? Simply to know what went on between him and Aster is not, I feel, sufficient. What do you want to achieve?"

James responded. "Well... the obvious, for a start. Is

there an issue for us with the Roman Catholic Diocese of Greater North Bay? After all, I think Bishop Tremblay would like to know if his priest made a confession before dying, if he did that with Andrew. Not what the confession was; but was it a true confession, did the man die unconfessed or not? Also, if the RCMP or the OPP are involved now, what does that mean for our diocese? Will they interview Moore and what legal support might he need? What are our liabilities, in a sense?"

He stopped and started again almost immediately. "And I have a dangerous flaw; too often I rush in offering help before I know I can give it. I trust God's guidance that I can assist, but sometimes it turns out to be God's reminder for me to pull in my ego."

She smiled. "I've noticed. You do overcommit some-what, at times."

He pressed on. "I want to help Andrew Moore. During the memorial service I prayed for Duncan Aster, but I also thought how hard it must have been for Andrew, the joy of the Keswick Ministry contact, the shock of the death, the interviews with the police. On the drive there and back he avoided the subject like the plague, never asked for my help once. He even suggested –."

He stopped himself.

"He said people were waiting to know what my 'big issue' is. I thought I had made that clear already, unity within the diocese. Apparently not. What I mean is, the man would talk to me about anything other than his own problem."

He looked suspiciously at Anne.

She said, "On the last point, I think a lot of people are waiting to know that, actually; your 'big issue'. Most of us are happy to wait. We'll know when we see it, we always do. Regarding Reverend Moore, why don't I speak to him?

I'll just tell him that the diocese has been informed that there may be a follow up of some sort in Canada by the UK police, perhaps via the OPP. I'll let him know that he shouldn't worry about it, but if he is contacted, we are there to assist."

Azikiwe thought for a moment; it seemed a good path forward.

Lieberman added, "If he needs help, I'll have Jeremy do it. His practice is in Hamilton, and he lives in Stoney Creek. It would be easier for them to meet."

Jeremy Hinks was one of two assistant chancellors, both volunteers like Anne, who provided day-to-day legal guidance to the diocese.

By the time they had wrapped up that matter and another issue on their agenda, a land agreement, James thought it had been a productive meeting. If anyone knew how to handle any police follow-up of the UK inquiry it would be the Chancellor.

15 REFUSAL

James's rosy perspective on that point changed rapidly four days later as a result of a call from Anne Lieberman, who was clearly irritated.

"You'll have to talk directly to Reverend Moore, James. The conversation with him did not go well, I'm afraid."

She could hear the bishop sigh down the phone, but he said nothing.

"He was affronted that I called, and he refused to discuss the matter with me at all. He made a reference, more a slur, if truth be told, that I was not an ordained priest and that I had no right to know anything about his interaction with Aster. If he needed legal advice, he would get it himself, he said.

"I'm glad it was over the phone. If in person, I would have given him a piece of my mind and probably not part of my calm, legal mind, at that."

James had no doubt that 'a piece of her mind' would be elegant but argumentative; she was a lawyer first, not a conciliator. But he felt bad. The fact that one of his priests would show less than full respect for the Canon Chancellor was troubling. That would have to be brought up with the man, too.

He said, "I'll bring him in here; talk to him myself. Would it be helpful at all, do you think, for one of us to speak with the UK lawyer whom the Bishop of Carlisle's office organised for Moore; to get a read of how he found the interviews over there? Is that appropriate?"

Lieberman mused on the question. "He couldn't tell me anything that transpired which is covered by solicitor-client privilege. But he may be able to give me an overview of the issue - yes. First, I think it would be good for you to talk with Reverend Moore. If that clears the air, there may be no need to call the UK."

She added, "Just one more thing. Have you given any thought to the next steps if he refuses to talk to you? How far do you want to push him?"

Azikiwe pursed his lips. "Not really. I'm his bishop; he has a duty of obedience to me, and he knows I mean well, I am sure. He'll understand that I need enough insight to be able to speak again to Bishop Tremblay, at least."

She pressed the point. "It's just that... if he crosses a line; if you place him in a position where he has no recourse but to speak to you as he spoke to me. It's a matter of canon law; disobedience."

"I will certainly try to avoid that, if possible. But he is not an employee of a business firm; he is a priest, and I am his bishop. Now, while I have you, is there any development on the issue of the land severance at St. Winifred's; where are we up to?"

He wrote a brief action reminder as Anne brought him up to date with the thorny issue of the dispute in a different parish over a proposed sale of some land. The St. Winifred's issue was never going to be resolved, James thought. He glanced at his watch. In twenty minutes, he was to meet with Karen Davidson, in charge of the Youth Ministry Planning Strategy. It was very dear to him, how the churches fostered the opportunities for young people to grow within the Anglican community. But the Moore issue niggled. He would get Audrey to set up something with Moore as a priority in his calendar. Audrey had a way of fixing things.

Audrey Lille had been a member of the cathedral congregation since her childhood. For much of her life, her time there was limited to weekends. She had worked in Toronto, a long commute that left little time for evening activities - unless they were in Toronto. An administrative professional in a bank, she rose in the ranks by diligent hard work and skill, joining in her early forties the senior administrative staff for executive level officers.

Then the career bubble burst. In a wave of reorganisation and 'synergization' she found herself out on her ear with a package, supported by an outplacement service headquartered in Toronto with 'a convenient Hamilton branch office to work from as you call possible employers and contacts'. She felt she was in freefall, and the bottom had dropped out of her self-esteem.

It was her church community that helped the most, and the advice from a clergyman. "It's not an end, Audrey, but an opportunity. What about church administration? You have access to a re-training fund, a transition package, and a chance to think of something else. You are well-known in the Anglican community and the diocese. Think about it."

A year later, she applied for and was appointed to the job of personal assistant to Bishop Gloria. And one of the benefits of her new role was that it wasn't in an anonymous glass tower on Bay Street, it was based in her spiritual home.

When she saw the note to set up a meeting with Reverend Moore in the next few days, she just added it to the never-ending list of changes to the bishop's appointment schedule. Calls from the cathedral to a parish church were a little like those from her former boss's office at the bank; they got a rapid response at the branches.

Other than, in this case, from Reverend Moore at St. Matthew's.

~~

Two days later, Audrey popped in to see the bishop between two appointments. She wasn't looking happy. It had not been a good day so far for the bishop and her news wasn't going to change that.

"Bishop, your next appointment is here, waiting. However, I finally spoke with Bethany, the administrator at St. Matthew's. I couldn't reach Reverend Moore directly yesterday, my second call to him, but I left him a reminder voicemail simply to call you. Provisionally, Bethany and I have slotted him in to see you the day after tomorrow at 3.15 p.m. for a forty-five-minute session."

James nodded, looking at her face, seeing that more bad news was coming.

"Then she told me that a police officer came to see Reverend Moore yesterday, but she didn't know what it was about. He cancelled his activities for today at short notice, including a funeral of a long-time parishioner. He passed the service to his curate. One of the churchwardens was in the office at St. Matthew's as I spoke to her, and I think he pushed her a bit to tell me. They are concerned. Bethany said it is quite unlike Reverend Moore and it is currently causing a stir at the church. Something is wrong, she believes."

James looked down at his desk for a moment. "I'll call Reverend Moore myself, right now. I want to see him as a priority if you get a call back."

As the door closed, he pulled up the contact file on his computer. Within a minute, he, too, had reached Reverend Moore's voicemail. After leaving a message, he dialed another number, Andrew Moore's wife.

Five minutes later, he called Audrey back in. "Reverend Moore is nearby apparently, in Hamilton, at the offices of Goldstone & Unwin. It's a law firm, and he is meeting with Leo Unwin. Get on to them, please. Have them pass a message directly to Reverend Moore. I want him in here today and please cancel or re-arrange whatever you need to do to make it happen."

Azikiwe had had enough of this.

At 4.15.p.m. Dean Thomas Grieves was making a short presentation, thanking the new members now appointed to the Liturgy Guidance Committee for their support, while also apologising for the bishop being called away on other matters at short notice. And Reverend Moore was sitting in the bishop's outer office area, waiting for the door to open. Audrey thought he didn't look pleased to be there.

James opened it with a welcoming smile. "Andrew, I'm glad you could come in today. I think we need a talk."

Then the door closed behind them and, ever the administrative professional, Audrey just got on with her work.

Once seated, James began with, "I wanted to see you anyway, but Audrey told me you had changed your plans for today at short notice. We understand that a police officer came to the church yesterday to see you. Is it connected to the UK matter and if so, what is the problem?"

He was careful to sound measured and supportive, to leave it wide open to begin with; to give the man a chance.

Moore had sat down as invited, but was sitting stiffly, not at ease. Neither was he looking ready to talk, James saw.

"Well, it's really a personal matter, Bishop. The officer was following up on my visit to the UK and the unfort-unate matter of Father Aster, yes. She was asking me if I knew any more about the identity of a person in Canada that may be linked to the priest. I didn't, and I told her so."

Azikiwe replied, "And that necessitated an urgent appointment with a lawyer today?"

He had made it sound like it was a question, not a rebuttal, James hoped. But he didn't want to be fobbed off.

Moore's focus on the bishop didn't waiver, nor did he acknowledge the obvious inconsistency. He just replied, "I felt I needed my own legal advice."

He stopped. James waited, hoping the man would explain further, but it was clear that he wasn't going to say anything more until a further question was asked.

Azikiwe sighed visibly, deliberately and, despite a fleet-ing wave of annoyance with the man, smiled again, empathetically. He said softly, "Andrew, you say it is a personal matter. Well, it isn't. You know that, really. I think it is about time I knew something about what went on in England, and then I can try to help you sort this out. I want to do that, to help. So, open up a bit. Tell me what concerns you, both about your interactions with Father Aster and the events thereafter. You can take that as an offer or, if not, you can take it as an instruction from your Bishop. I need to know."

He waited. The man had no choice now. It was either

an offer from a mentor to a junior colleague, or an order from the Bishop of Hamilton-Brant to a priest whose ordination vows affirmed his obedience. In the silence that ensued James realised that he was already at the point where the Chancellor had hesitated during their earlier discussion. A line set by canon law was already looming up right in front of them.

What worried James most at this point was not what might be revealed, it was the expression on Andrew Moore's face. It wasn't fear, or stress, or a sign of a man with a dilemma. It was the same expression he had shown for most of the drive to North Bay and back. Now James thought he finally understood it; Andrew Moore was calculating, analysing exactly what to say or do.

James began to wonder what sort of priest this man really was.

Audrey had telephoned the bishop's next appointment, fortunately with a member of the cathedral staff.

"Bill, I think it is best if I call you when he is free, he may run a little behind. I'll give you a heads-up once I sense this meeting is finishing, so you don't have to sit around here and wait."

She thought she had it sorted out now, but then she heard Reverend Moore's voice raised, even through the door to the inner office. It flew open as the man stormed out without even seeing her, his face red with anger. She knew she had it completely wrong, so she quickly stood up from her desk and went to the open doorway. Bishop Azikiwe was still sitting at the table looking frozen; astonished. He turned to her.

"Audrey, can you get me the Chancellor on the phone as soon as she is available, please?"

"And the meeting with Bill?"

Give me a few minutes, I need to... gather myself, make some notes. Give me ten then call him in. But if you get Anne, put her through right away. I'll ask Bill to wait outside with you when I take the call."

As Azikiwe explained the new developments to the Chancellor she didn't interrupt. When he finished, she said, "Just a few questions. First, your language before the end, before his tantrum. You said, "You can take that as an offer or, if not, you can take it as an instruction from your bishop. That's correct?"

"Yes."

"Please ensure that is in your written notes of the meeting, if you would. Second, did he say who his legal counsel is at all?"

"No. Yes, Audrey mentioned the firm, 'something and Unwin'; he was seeing Unwin. But his family is well connected and..."

"I know Leo Unwin. Look, I am in Toronto in a meeting and can't get away from it for long, but this is pressing. I'll call Jeremy; I know he is around Hamilton today as he and I talked this morning. I will have him come over."

"I wish I'd got through to him. Andrew, I mean. I will leave it until this evening and give him a call, see–."

She interrupted him. "James, please don't do that – not now. Jeremy will explain. As much as you want to help him, you are the bishop; you chase after no-one within this diocese. And Moore is now dangerously close to being in breach of canon law. Once documented, he will be. And before we do that, I think Regional Dean Walters, as his Clericus lead, needs to meet with him."

Clericus was a regular set of area meetings of clergy in each part of the diocese to discuss problems and developments, a mutual support group for the area, usually led by a regional dean.

"Don Walters, why him?"

As I recall, but will check, he was present when Andrew Moore was ordained. If anyone can get through to him about his vow of obedience, it will be Don. And it is probably best that Jeremy should be there also – and by the sound of it–."

There was a knock and Audrey came in, closing the door firmly and looking anxious.

"One moment, Anne. I missed the last bit, Audrey came in with something urgent – and relevant, I hope."

His assistant was nodding. She whispered the message and James nodded, partly to say he had heard, partly to tell her he wanted privacy again.

"Anne, there is a call from Bishop Tremblay in North Bay. He would like to speak with me and my legal representative in Toronto as soon as possible, at the offices of a firm called Geller & Thomas. He will have his legal counsel with him. Preferably tomorrow or the day after, he asks."

Anne sighed. "Well, James, I don't know about your calendar, but mine is full. How about tomorrow early evening, not daytime? I'll host it here, in our offices; they aren't far away from the firm he mentioned. We two can meet a little earlier and have a snack to tide us over, per-haps, to get ready. Try that one, if it works?"

James thanked her. "It would certainly be better for me, if I could keep my appointments for most of tomorrow intact."

16 DECISION

6 August, 4.30 p.m. EDT

It had been quite some time since Azikiwe had travelled into Toronto on a GO Transit commuter train, he realised. Even in his free time he didn't go in much, despite the big city being only an hour and a quarter away by train, less by road if the traffic was co-operative. He suddenly remembered guiltily that he had promised his grandson a ride on one of these trains, and his promise was overdue.

Anne Lieberman met him in the lobby area of her offices in the RBC building, just across the road from Union Station. The Royal Bank building was one of the skyscraper towers in the downtown core. She led him to an elevator and, thirty floors higher, through to her own suite of offices.

"I had one of my team organize some soup and sandwiches here for us; I have coffee and tea for the meeting room and a young man called Jason, my intern, will look out for our guests. I have a suspicion that you aren't that hungry, given the developments, so I didn't want to push it."

James nodded. "No, I'm not feeling hungry, you are right. A light meal like that sounds good, thank you. This is all so… different."

Anne nodded but changed the subject. "Some good news. Dean Walters and Jeremy Hinks have an appointment with Reverend Moore tomorrow at his church. Don says he seemed quite calm when he called him and set it up."

James looked at her. "I've seen Andrew calm and I've seen him angry; I'm not sure which disturbs me the most at present."

She smiled understandingly. "Now, the Catholic visitors. You've met Bishop Tremblay – how do you find him?"

"In what way? When we met in North Bay, he was candid that Father Aster had a problem in his past, but didn't go into detail. He seemed to want a good relationship with me, though, as if he wondered if something might develop with the OPP asking questions. But that was about it."

Lieberman responded, "I've talked to one or two people about Simon Nugent at Geller & Thomas. He's been the legal guru for the Greater North Bay diocese for many years, apparently. He lives there. Checking his case history, he has been involved in everything; administrative law matters like me, but also at least one clergy abuse settlement. Whatever Father Aster was up to with this mysterious Susan, he may well have been their legal front man."

Forty minutes later, that proved to be the case. After gathering in the meeting room and making introductions, offering coffee and tea, they settled around one end of the long table. Simon Nugent was silver-haired, like Tremblay, and well-dressed, in a somewhat conservative and old-fashioned suit, Anne thought.

Tremblay began with, "It's good of you both to fit Simon and myself in at short notice. I know we are all busy people."

The young intern, who had been introduced as Jason, hovered, looking at Anne for guidance. She in turn asked Nugent, "Do we need notes of this meeting?"

"No," replied the man. "Just the four of us will be fine."

Anne thanked her intern and he left, closing the door firmly behind him. She then said, "To be clear, what we discuss here is covered by solicitor-client privilege on both sides, we take it. But the fact we are meeting at all is not. If asked by the police, we will tell them so if we are pressed on the point."

Nugent said quickly, "We understand that."

He looked to his bishop. Hugh Tremblay spoke up, giving what was clearly a prepared comment. "We were contacted by the OPP three days ago. Two local officers in North Bay came to see me. Apparently, they have received a report from the Cumbria Police in the UK; the police force that investigated Father Aster's death. It was passed along the chain there. One of the OPP officers who saw me is attached to the sexual abuse and vulnerable persons unit in the North Bay region."

Tremblay let it sink in.

Anne said, "To do with your priest, I take it?"

He nodded and, with a sweep of his hand, turned it over to his own legal adviser.

Simon Nugent added, "There is no active enquiry here, let us be clear on that. The incident involving Father Aster was with a young woman of legal age at the time and was a single incident, a single lapse. It was settled and is behind us all, we told him. I gave him the court file reference but no details; he understood why. What they do with that... I am not sure."

He looked at Bishop Hugh, who grimaced then sighed. "You need to be aware that we do know who this 'Susan' is and the circumstances, as Simon infers. We can say no more than that."

Anne responded, "Thank you; in fact, we would rather not know, anyway. But as I understand it, Bishop Tremblay, this is more or less the concern that you shared as a possibility with Bishop Azikiwe?"

He nodded, confirming it, then responded, "We expect that the OPP will also contact Reverend Moore to see if he had more information on the woman Susan, or the act that Aster talked to him about. From what you said to me, James, he is not talking about that?"

"No, not that I am aware. He hasn't mentioned even the name to me."

James was wondering how much to reveal of their own problem when Anne spoke up. "Is there more? I sense there is."

Simon Nugent said, "The OPP officer who asked the questions made it clear that his interest in us was related only to the issue regarding the person 'Susan'. The emphasis was clear; that the OPP or UK Police interest in Reverend Moore might be broader. That was not stated explicitly, but we both took it that way. He was sending a message, we believe. The officer is a member of our faith, I should add, and North Bay is not Metropolitan Toronto. And the second officer asked several questions. He clearly wasn't part of the same team."

He paused and looked at his boss. "Bishop Tremblay thought you should know that."

His own expression as he looked at Anne was that he didn't go along with it but had no choice.

She said, "The inference is that they are looking at

something else regarding Reverend Moore's activity or involvement while in the UK? Not only for information that Father Aster shared with him but… what? Not similar allegations, surely?"

James was wondering where this was going. The possibility that his priest was even more involved in the problem was chilling. As was the other possibility; that Moore had shared something with Aster that related to a similar act – or worse.

Reading Azikiwe's face, Nugent said, tersely, "My own view is that this interest is something to do with Father Aster's death. It was clear that the pair were doing 'double duty', following up on two lines of enquiry. At one point they particularly focused on Father Aster's bible. He had one with him that was found in a church there. Something about that is out of kilter for them."

James saw he was watching Anne carefully now.

She said sharply, "I'm getting the sense that this is about an act of omission related to the death, or worse? Am I right? Involvement in it, somehow?"

James gave a sharp exhalation as he caught on. He had just concluded that the OPP officers had been rather more open with Bishop Tremblay and his lawyer than they were currently conveying, but the word 'omission' grabbed him.

He said, "They think that Reverend Moore had some insight that Father Aster was suicidal, is that it? That he should have done something. Or in some way he contributed to Aster's decision to take his own life?"

Anne nodded, "It's what I am sensing."

Nugent nodded his agreement. "It was the impression we were left with. Why they are thinking that way, if they are, I don't know. We have no expertise in UK law."

James looked at Anne, who nodded, reading his mind. She said, "We need to update you also, I believe; Bishop?"

James said, "The OPP met with Reverend Moore two days ago, we understand."

Tremblay jumped in. "So, you already have that in hand. Good. Glad to hear that."

Anne shook her head and addressed her opposite number. "It's not that simple. Moore is not saying anything. Anything at all to me at least, and even to Bishop Azikiwe. He is seeking his own legal counsel. It's an issue, one we can't back away from. We are at the line."

She didn't explain further; she didn't have to.

The lawyer nodded slowly. "And, as I recall, your canon law is often as messy a process as ours on occasion. Good luck with that. Our preference is that Father Aster rests in peace, in whatever peace God feels he is entitled to. However, if it becomes a visible issue, we will refer to the secrecy agreement but otherwise be transparent and co-operative."

Bishop Tremblay reinforced the point. "There will be no cover up if it becomes public. Others will be hurt, and that grieves me even more than the impact on Duncan's reputation."

James suddenly became annoyed with the turn of events, and it took him a moment to work out what to say.

"We also will do whatever is both legal and right, I assure you. Reverend Moore is under some strain at present. I have seen that myself and I want to help him. He was on holiday in the UK, he talked to your priest, and now finds himself in a dilemma; perhaps a serious one. And perhaps a legal one. And there is a woman whose name may soon be bandied about who has rights, too. Are you talking with her, also?"

Anne said, "Bishop, they can't talk about that at all with us; there is a secrecy agreement in place. They are bound by it."

She looked at the two visitors. "We thank you for taking the time to share your thoughts, and I assure you we want to keep the lines of communication open. Simon – can I call you that? Why don't we do that directly, between us? I'm sure this is a weight on both Bishop Tremblay and Bishop Azikiwe; but we can perhaps carry some of that load professionally?"

Nugent smiled for the first time. "I would be pleased to do it that way."

He looked at his own bishop then at Azikiwe. "With your permission?"

Tremblay said "Of course," as Azikiwe added, "Yes, with thanks to you both."

What a mess, James was really thinking.

By prior arrangement, Anne drove James back to Hamilton. It was mid-evening and the highways had cleared a bit leaving the city. She could see that the bishop was troubled, lost in his thoughts.

"As I said earlier, James, I think you need to leave this stage to us. Hopefully we can get Andrew Moore to see sense and talk to you, then we can advise how to proceed both in his interests and those of the diocese."

James pursed his lips. "What troubles me most is the fact that a member of our clergy is under suspicion for involvement in some way in this man's death. What I didn't say earlier to you is that I find Andrew to be calculating, as if he measures every word, deciding just how little to give away. On the drive to North Bay, I didn't see it that way but in hindsight, it was."

He paused, thinking, then said, "But you are right, I need to leave this to Don, Jeremy and you at present."

As his cell phone rang.

Anne drove in silence. All she could make out was that

it was a female voice. The bishop made a comment, "Yes, Ginny, thank you for that bright spot; it has been a long day. Goodnight, God bless you."

He closed the call and sighed. 'Reverend Ginny Farmer at Park Royal. She is with the family of Benjamin Okafor, the young man killed recently."

Anne nodded. "The beating death. I recall."

"Yes, she is staying close to the family in their grief. She wanted me to know that the funeral will be at Park Royal. The daughter, the young man's sister, started going there with a friend some months ago. Now, in their need, we can help them at this terrible time."

Anne said softly, "Now that's a member of your clergy who isn't causing you problems."

James smiled. "She is a bright spot in our lives, as I said. And she told me the grandmother asked after me; I made a hit with her. I went there with Ginny a few days ago. She wanted someone who spoke Hausa, and how many Nigerian-speaking clergy do you think the Diocese of Hamilton-Brant has?"

He pointed at his chest. "I made the grandmother smile – unintentionally, I might add. My Hausa is only a boy's vocabulary. But I was glad to help."

Anne smiled. "At least she talks to you."

~~

7 August, 4.30 p.m. EDT
They had gathered around the table in a meeting room, the door firmly closed. Dean Donald Walters, Jeremy Hinks, Anne, and James. Walters was looking troubled.

James began, "So, what happened? All I heard was that he refused your request point-blank. At least he didn't lose his temper with you."

Jeremy responded quickly. "Not refused. Rejected any discussion of it. And in writing; in a letter to the Chancellor that we have with us, and I'll read. At present, it should be considered undelivered. Depending on our discussion, I will give it to you, Bishop, or to Anne. If the latter, it becomes a formal breach of Canon 4.7. I will add that I don't think he wrote it alone. He involved someone very familiar with legal language. Dean Walters should speak first, we decided."

Walters was a large, overweight man who was nearing retirement age.

"Andrew worries me, James. And it's not the first time, I am afraid. When we met him, he seemed welcoming, I thought, as did Jeremy. I later revised that; rather, he seemed confident. As we went through our preparatory statement Andrew waited until I came to the bit where I spoke of the need for him to take the tension out of this situation; the strain on him and on you. He needed to act for the good of the diocese, I said, and keep firmly in his mind his need as a priest to work closely with you, his bishop. He stopped me then."

Jeremy interjected, "What was disturbing from that point on was that Reverend Moore addressed only me; he simply ignored Don. He produced the letter I will read, saying he wanted it delivered to the Chancellor, but we should both be aware of the contents as it gave his position on the meeting we were having; it shouldn't be taking place, shouldn't have been initiated at all."

Walters was nodding. "It was very disappointing, to say the least."

Hinks pulled out the letter. "It is formally addressed to the Chancellor."

Dear Chancellor,

I hereby seek your formal decision on a matter of some priority and importance. Recently, while in England, I was interviewed by the police in relation to a sad event around the death of a person I met at a convention in Keswick. I fulfilled my obligations to the man there and with Bishop Azikiwe I attended the memorial service here. I consider the matter closed.

However, I have been approached on several occasions to reveal more of my discussion with the man, discussions that I consider privileged by my ordination vows. The matter is escalating and that concerns me. I have duties to perform in my parish and cannot continue under this pressure.

First, I question the definition of 'jurisdiction' in the context of events occurring during my holiday, when I was not performing any duties within the diocese and was not even in the country. As an ordained Anglican priest at the time of the discussions with Father Aster I was effectively within the jurisdiction of the Bishop of Cumbria.

Canon 3, clause 13, says that the vow of silence around confessions cannot be broken under any circumstances and it is my belief and understanding that the only person who can decide on the merit of that claim is I, as the priest hearing the confession. Yet I also have taken an oath of obedience to my bishop, who is pressing me to discuss the matter. It is a conflict for me.

I request in writing either a formal acceptance of my interpretation by you and the bishop affirming that this matter is closed or, failing that, an opportunity to present my case to a duly constituted hearing according to the pertinent diocesan canons. I recognize, of course, that only the bishop has the authority to convene a hearing of this nature, outside synod itself. I hope that you will discuss this with Bishop Azikiwe and you both will act in accordance with my wishes.

Yours sincerely,

Andrew Moore, M.Div., Rector.

Dean Walters spoke up. "Bishop, I believe he is not simply wanting this dropped; he knows it is not about Aster's confession, he's an intelligent man. He well understands that this is about his behaviour and the lengths he is going to... to deny that. It worries me, for a priest to be so hostile. What can have happened between those two men, I ask?"

James glanced quickly at Anne who seemed impassive. They couldn't comment on their recent discussions with Tremblay and Nugent.

Hinks continued, "His final comment on the matter to me was that he knows your question to him during your last meeting together was a formal instruction, but he rejects it at least temporarily and will continue to reject it until clarification of diocesan policy in this matter is reached."

James shook his head slowly, almost in a daze. He looked at each person in sequence, reading the faces.

"Anne, there must be a case precedent regarding this issue of his oath of obedience. Do you have an opinion?"

She said promptly. "There are precedents. Obedience is not limited by geographical boundaries. He is your priest, whether here or in the UK. Yet the underlying matter is one of the most sacred aspects of a priest's duties, the issue of confidentiality of a confession. He is looking to argue that has precedence, of course, but the core issue here is his refusal to meet your direct instruction, which was much broader than any aspect of a confession by Aster."

She took on a formal tone; she was Chancellor now; not Anne Lieberman. "Bishop, what do you wish us to do?"

James said slowly, "Chancellor, please accept the letter from Reverend Moore from my delegates whom I sent to him on the matter of my earlier instruction. You have my authority to convene a hearing in accordance with the canons of this diocese to resolve this matter. How you do that is your decision but for me, this is an issue of his wilful disobedience; relating to Canon 4, as Jeremy said. That must be the primary item addressed."

Having decided, he stood and spoke to Dean Walters and the Hamilton lawyer. "I thank you both for your efforts to bring a more sensible and loving solution to this matter, but if it is a formal canon court he wants, so be it."

As he left the meeting room to return to his office, he was hit by the weight of the moment. In all his time in the diocese as a priest, there had been canon courts held for a range of issues; dry, technical meetings around deliberations to do with property and land, some personnel issues to do with a retirement pension dispute, and one he was aware of, after which the priest resigned his post. But never, he recalled, one where a priest rejected the authority of the bishop so blatantly.

Word would get around. He was in no doubt that it would feed the dissension between the traditionalists and the liberals in the diocese that he had been working so hard to heal over the past year.

He changed his route and headed into the main cathedral worship space, sat down at a seat, and began to pray, oblivious to a warden giving a visiting group a brief history tour.

17 TRIERS

21 August 10.00 a.m. EDT

Over the last two weeks, Jeremy Hinks had prepared him for this meeting. Azikiwe was tense as Audrey popped in to say that the visitors had arrived and been settled in the meeting room.

He sighed, "Let's go, then."

This was an entirely new area for him. Audrey picked up a pad to take notes. She was there as the bishop's witness.

In the meeting room, the setting was formal. Bishop Azikiwe sat at the head of the rectangular table with Audrey next to him, at the corner. At the opposing end sat Anne Lieberman, as Chancellor. Either side, in the middle, sat the two opposing counsels, a Leo Unwin for Reverend Moore and Jeremy Hinks for the bishop. Next to Anne at the opposing corner to Audrey, to preserve the symmetry, James thought, was the young, smartly-dressed man called Jason he had last seen in Anne's office in Toronto. His first impulse was to go and meet him, but he sensed he was meant to sit down. So, he did.

Lieberman said formally, "Bishop, you know Jeremy and

me, obviously. This is Mr. Leo Unwin of the firm Gold-stone & Unwin, representing Reverend Moore, and Jason Muller, an intern at my offices."

Leo Unwin nodded to the bishop but said nothing. A well-dressed man in his middle years, his expression was neutral.

She continued, "Jason has agreed to act as the recorder throughout the proceedings today and the court hearing itself. He is a member of the Anglican congregation of the Cathedral of St. James in Toronto, so he is subject to his bishop as any member of our diocese is to you. In a legal sense he is more than suitably qualified for this task."

The man smiled at the bishop. In front of him was a sound recording device of some sort. Anne didn't pause, she just went straight on.

"We will now go on record."

Jason started the recorder and nodded at her.

Anne said, "This is the first pre-meeting of a hearing within the Court of Canon Law of the Diocese of Hamilton-Brant between the parties in the claim against Reverend Andrew Fitzgerald Moore, Rector of St. Matthew's Church in Stoney Creek. Bishop Azikiwe, you are here at this point in your capacity as the appointed leader of the diocese, not as the plaintive. In that regard, Mr. Hinks has already met with you and explained that all discussions of the charge with the court must now be conducted through him.

"On the agenda today we have three items, only one of which requires your presence. These are a) the number of members of the panel of triers, to use the correct canonical term; b) a discussion of the number of witnesses, whether a fact witness or an expert, and c), the schedule for the hearing.

"We may need additional pre-meetings, of course, prior

to the hearing itself to resolve some of these matters. It is my wish as Chancellor and I am sure I speak for all, that we maintain the dignity and tradition of the court; albeit I cannot recall a case of this precise nature in any diocese in Ontario in recent years. Are there any other items of business today?"

Unwin raised his hand. Anne said, "Mr. Unwin."

"I am a criminal lawyer, not a canon law expert. I have read the canons but had no time to delve further; I am a busy man. What about pre-trial and trial confidentiality. Will this be a public event? Should we discuss that today also?"

Lieberman nodded. "Let me deal with that directly, with the bishop present. A canon court is held at the request and under the authority of the bishop. It is normally a private affair of the parties and witnesses. There is no right of public access. Only persons invited by the bishop as observers can attend other than the parties, triers, staff, and witnesses. Observers have to be acceptable to the bishop alone, unless I, as Chancellor, say the presence of a particular person will be unduly prejudicial to the proceedings. Even then, it is still his decision, but it is expected that he would listen carefully to the guidance of the Canon Chancellor."

Unwin said, "So there will be no media coverage of the trial?"

"No. There will not be media coverage of this canon court hearing; and, Mr. Unwin, it is not a trial."

Lieberman's tone of voice made it clear that point was not debatable. She added, "One further preliminary item. As Chancellor, at this moment I confirm that I will have no direct dealings on this matter with Bishop Azikiwe or parties other than through their representing counsel until the court is concluded. In the interim, any meeting I have with the bishop on other diocesan legal matters will also be attended by Jason Muller, who has already sworn an oath of confidentiality applicable to such meetings. He may be called at court, if needed, to verify my claim. My role now is to ensure solely that the canons of the diocese are followed."

No one spoke, but Audrey thought that Unwin was looking more skeptical than impassive now.

Lieberman continued, "Let me move on to the only item requiring the bishop's presence, the number of triers, or panelists. The procedure is this; I will chair the court hearing according to the canons and established legal procedure. Panelists will be legal experts in Anglican canon law from outside this diocese selected from a list I alone will propose, but each person must be agreeable to both parties. The number of triers should be consistent with the complexity of the issue but normally their number is increased in pairs.

"This case focuses on a defined issue; the precedence of canon 4.7 regarding obedience and canon 3.13 regarding the vow of silence. Triers may or may not require per diem payments, depending on their declaration of service as *pro bono* or not. In any event, the diocese must pay their travel and accommodation expenses, so there are practical matters to consider."

"And the decision; by vote; it's a majority verdict?" interjected Unwin.

"Yes," replied Anne. "A declaration of unanimity or majority by the panel. In the event of a tie, I cast a vote."

Audrey had been writing her own notes as the meeting started. She had been thinking about this point. She was sure that Moore's lawyer would want a large panel of triers but couldn't rationalize why.

She was surprised when Unwin interjected again with,

"So, let's cut to the chase. A narrowly defined issue and the need to minimize costs. We propose a panel of two triers and the Chancellor."

Lieberman looked at Hinks. "Jeremy, your position?"

Hinks seemed to be caught by surprise at the rapidity of the development, but said, "I have no objection, but I was expecting a panel of five; yourself and four others."

He looked at the bishop, who said nothing.

Anne asked, "Is that acceptable, Bishop Azikiwe?"

Audrey looked at her boss. He took a moment, frowned, and then said, "It is."

Then Audrey realised the implication. A three-member panel including the Chancellor could only come to either a majority or a unanimous verdict. If a majority decision, the Chancellor must have voted for the bishop or Reverend Moore. Whichever way it went, the voting would be transparent to everyone.

The Chancellor nodded and said, 'Thank you, Bishop, for your attendance. You may leave other details for us to resolve. Is there anything you wish to say?"

Before leaving us, she was politely inferring.

James took a moment to compose his thoughts. "Thank you, Chancellor. There is just one thing. I understand that the hearing itself will begin and close each day with a prayer?"

She smiled. "That is correct, it is a church proceeding."

James looked down at the table. "So is this. May I say a prayer for guidance for us all before I leave?"

"You may, of course; in your capacity as leader of the diocese, not the plaintive, I might add."

It was Unwin who looked ill at ease now, Audrey saw, as her boss said an impromptu prayer for guidance before wishing them well and leaving the room, with Audrey following close behind.

Back in his office, as Audrey asked him if he would like some coffee, he nodded, thanking her and saying, "It's not sitting well, this; the whole thing. Reverend Moore choosing a criminal lawyer as his representative, a man who hasn't a clue about canon law process... I worry what will go on under this roof."

Audrey didn't know what to say; she had felt the same misgivings, watching the defense lawyer in action.

They found out the first hints of that the following day. The Hamilton Spectator, the local newspaper, contacted the diocese for an interview or statement. They were preparing an article based on a recent interview with Sylvia Moore. She was concerned that her husband was now being 'tried by a church court'. Would the bishop be available for an interview with their reporter and if not, could they speak to him now for a comment?

Then the phones started ringing.

18 NIGHT OWLS

Susan Carson was working on her laptop in the lounge when Ute, a resident in her second week at Haydn House, came downstairs with her hands deep inside the pockets of her hoodie. She was using it as a cover over her pyjamas.

"I can't sleep. It's hard having a roommate. Not that she snores badly or anything, it's just... I am not used to it."

Susan closed the laptop and said, "Do you want a hot drink? I'll put the kettle on."

Ute nodded and smiled. "Some of that apple stuff. What are you working on?"

Susan said, "My course. I have a diploma in Addiction Studies, but I want a Master's degree. It's taking time; the course is expensive."

She filled the kettle and switched it on. What would it be with Ute, she thought? Would she spill out revelations about her past catastrophes, perhaps? They always seemed to bother the guests in the wee small hours.

The two women sipped their respective drinks. Ute

asked, "How often do you have to stay up all night?"

"It's a week in every eight. The responsibility rotates among the counsellors. There has to be someone on duty overnight, but in the summer months the schedule gets a bit messy."

"To chat to the night owls like me, I suppose?"

Susan smiled. "Sometimes; there are lots of reasons. I do rounds; check that the rooms are quiet, that people are actually sleeping; take the incoming telephone calls to Haydn House, things like that. And some of the best one-on-one counselling goes on at night, on occasion, as well."

There, she thought; what will she do with that?

Ute thought for a moment. ""I'm having trouble with this God thing, the third step, turning my will over to some God. I'm not religious. It's keeping me awake. I worry that I won't make it here."

Susan responded, "It's not a religious thing; it's a growth issue, about breaking your isolation. God's just a word; don't let that stop you. At this stage it's about finding anything that makes you feel that you aren't alone in your journey of recovery, still trying to run the show by yourself; that you are starting to open up to receiving help. That's partly why you are here, right?"

Ute said, "And I want to see if I can save my job, that's why I'm here, really. If I show my boss…" she petered off.

Susan said confidently, "Then you have already asked for help. You are on your way."

Ute didn't look convinced.

Susan asked, "Who was your best friend from way back? Someone you lost touch with completely. We all lose touch with people as we spiral down."

The woman smiled and replied straight off. "Hayley Roberts. She was eight, I was seven when we first met; I so missed her when her parents moved, when I was fourteen.

After that…"

Susan said, "Then don't use the word God. Call it Hayley; think of her when you ask for help. Thank her each night for a day during which you were able to stay clean. Share your fears with the Hayley in your memory. Ask Hayley for guidance each morning. Try that for a few days, as a beginning – see how it goes."

Ute replied, partly in black humour, "Wherefore art thou, Hayley? Good question."

Susan laughed softly. "Stay clean, you may get to find out one day. You'd be surprised."

Ute reflected on it for a bit, then she yawned.

"Back to bed?" asked Susan.

The resident nodded. Susan stood. "I'll deal with the cups; you head back. Breakfast is at seven fifteen."

The corridor door opened; they could both hear it. Fire doors were closed overnight and Diane, a new arrival that day, came in. She was shaking rather than shivering.

She blurted out, "I really need something. I tried. I am so stressed out that…"

Susan assessed her quickly, checking if she needed to wake up the duty nurse.

"Wait here, both of you."

She unlocked the office and went in, leaving the two women talking. She checked Diane's file and the notes Beverley had left. She then relocked the room and entered and locked the medical office door behind her. Beverley's notes were clear, and the nurse had been on the go; Susan didn't want to wake her unless it was really necessary.

Susan unlocked the 'counsellor access only' medical cabinet, separate from the dispensary used by the nurses and doctor. She shook out one lorazepam tablet from a bottle, putting the tiny pill in a disposable dispensing cup, then locked up and returned to the lounge.

She said to Diane, "Under your tongue, with a sip of water; you know the drill. And then we wait fifteen minutes or so while I watch you. Then back to bed or, if I have to, I'll call the nurse."

Women admitted to Hayden were meant to be seventy-two hours clear of alcohol or drug withdrawal. It didn't always happen. She, too, had been an exception to that rule years ago.

The grateful woman did as she was told as Ute watched intently. She said, "I thought we couldn't have anything here."

"You can't without medical approval. It was in Beverley's notes for Diane, with Dr. Hartley's approval. It's not a rehab centre, it's a recovery house."

Susan declined to explain further but the newcomer said, "It's for my stress, to stop another seizure. Dr. Hartley put me on them, but only if I feel the weight of the world descending. And only for three days; if I need it after that I have to go back to rehab. I got through the last two nights before coming here without anything at all. It's just so different here, it stresses me."

She lay back in the armchair and took a deep breath, closing her eyes. She asked, "What are you talking about?"

Ute responded, "The God thing; the God of my Understanding in Step Two and Three is now called Hayley." She smiled.

Diane opened her eyes and gave her a derisory look then moderated it as she thought about it, nodding. "At least it's female. Not a 'him'."

Susan looked at her, knowing Diane's background now, read in her admission file earlier. A 'him' had hurt the woman a lot. She could relate.

"Off you go," she reminded Ute, looking at Diane. Ute

took the message and said goodnight and left.

Susan watched the woman sprawled in the easy chair with her eyes closed again, but she said nothing. Suddenly Diane said, "I'm a long way from thinking about any god thing. I just need to get through this night. I really want to make it here."

"Well, once the newness wears off and you have a good night's sleep and make a friend or two, it will help. You've been through a lot. You can heal here."

She saw that the new resident was already responding to the medication; the tremors were diminishing, and her arms were now still. Only her knees were jittery. She checked the time for her report.

After another fifteen minutes watching Diane in silence, she said, "Let's get you back to bed, you can sleep there now. I'll go up with you."

Diane nodded and stood up but said nothing. Newcomers were often monosyllabic or withdrawn. The two women headed out of the lounge for the stairs.

Janeca Slowovitz had a security support and facility maintenance role at Haydn House, and started work at 7.00 a.m. She always brought in the morning papers as she arrived. As a habit, Susan scanned them quickly, waiting for her shift to end before they were passed out to the residents. The women were up, dressed or getting dressed and heading to breakfast, most of them. The latecomers would be scurrying through soon.

It was an article in the Globe and Mail that caught her eye, in part because it was an issue in Hamilton, a city where she had studied. The wife of an Anglican priest had blown her top to a reporter from the local paper about her husband being in trouble. The Globe had a short pick-up on it. The words, 'while on holiday in the Lake District' had caught Susan's attention. And the dates; they were the same period as when Duncan Aster was over there, in the same location. She thought back to her discussion with her mother after the memorial mass; the comment that two Anglican clergy had attended.

Janeca said, "Was it a hard night? You look worn out. I see Iris arriving; I'm sure she can cover the breakfast session."

Iris was her day shift replacement this week.

"Yes, it was all go last night, so I need to rest. I'll talk to Iris, see if she agrees."

But her mind was on getting a copy of the full article and talking with her sponsor.

19 COMMUNICATION

27 August, 9.00 a.m. EDT

Reverend Jean Ames looked surprisingly young for her position on the diocesan staff; she was the Director of Media Communications. Prior to Bishop James's installation, that role had been combined with another communications role. She was James's first staff appointment, and a surprise – she came out of nowhere; or not quite.

A curacy in a rural parish, followed by only two years with a large church as Assistant Rector, she had served in the farming country. It should have been years before she became visible, people 'in the know' at the centre of things thought.

Nine years earlier, Ames was a reporter working as part of a Hamilton-based TV crew. She had driven around the city and outlying areas to one news scene after another, the adrenalin and excitement of being at the centre of events always with her. Over time she saw the impact of the media arriving; the coverage, the departure afterwards; a sea of sound bites crashing across real life. It disturbed her enough that she started going back to her family church, trying to make some sense of it all.

It was a slow news day when it happened. They were hanging around waiting for something; anything. The six o'clock lead slot was a total void. Then Cody, their crew lead, came over. "Let's go; thank God we got something; a roll-over near the exit 289 black spot with two fatalities. It just fits, if we move it."

The cameraman said 'Yes!', happy to be moving as they headed for their van. It was Jean's tipping point. A week later she went to talk to a priest called Azikiwe. A year later she was studying to be one herself.

James hadn't forgotten her.

Her introduction to the diocesan deans had its impact, too. It was made at the second monthly meeting of the deans with Bishop Azikiwe after his appointment, in preparation for their own Regional Clericus meetings.

In introducing Reverend Ames in her new role, James said, "I promised you at synod that I would work towards the harmony of the diocese. The first step of doing so will be that the clergy will deal directly and openly with me, you, and each other on our differences in theology and direction for the diocese. The days of polite smiles and silence in meetings when differences need to be discussed are over with; because sometimes at present they are voiced externally, showing only dissent. The media love it, and it reflects poorly on us, as servants of Christ."

It was Dean Walters who asked, "But we can't muzzle the clergy on such matters, Bishop; surely? These are important, deeply held matters of conscience."

James smiled. "Muzzle; no. Deal honestly and trans-parently, yes. Our internal meetings, whether big events such as synod or the smallest gatherings, have been held largely with respect and the impression of goodwill to all. But outside? Let's hear from Jean."

Within ten minutes, Jean Ames presented the distillation of anger, disappointment, intolerance, and the occasional vindictive phrase pulled from the media analysis over the last thirty-six months. It brought the room to silence.

The priest finished with, "Young people are bombarded with information like this via the internet, moreso than others. Much of it is peripheral, but leaves an impression; indeed, that is the core principle of marketing. If you were my age, with a young family seeking a spiritual truth and with no prior religious experience, would you choose an Anglican church in this region over another choice, with that subliminal background?"

Dean Lowden countered, "We get new congregants all the time."

In dribs and drabs in many churches, thought James. As the mean age of our population rises. Jean Ames looked at her bishop to respond because they knew this would come up. Jean's brother was now a pastor in one of the new, Southern Baptist affiliates springing up across Canada. People in search of God in their lives were attending those churches in droves.

James said, "Nevertheless, I will be issuing a letter to all clergy saying we are one voice on external communications around issues of diocesan policy. On other matters there is no restriction, but if a policy is agreed at synod, it is the position all clergy will accept externally. Inside, they can voice their differences to me, to you, and to other priests - but face-to-face, honestly, hopefully with less invective than we have just heard in Jean's summary. And perhaps, eyeball to eyeball, it could be presented in a more constructive and healing manner with options for a path forward."

The Deans looked at each other and at Bishop James. The letter would be the bishop's first instruction to them. And it was going to make their monthly clericus meetings less social and more combative; they understood this.

James smiled at them, seeing their collective unease. "Clericus meetings will take more time, more effort, more love, and more prayer. You can decide whether that means more or less of the exotic tea selections or fine sherry."

One regional dean flinched slightly. Her clericus meetings had a reputation for being a regular tasting party of each year's finest amontillados – at least, ones available at a decent price.

~~

For most of the morning after the Hamilton Spectator article broke, Jean Ames and Audrey were engaged in screening and answering calls. Jean insisted that the bishop should not make a statement at this time or accept any interviews. Within an hour of the Spectator's first call, she had a short press statement issued under the aegis of the Chancellor. It read, 'Canons are the set of rules which govern our diocese within the Anglican Church of Canada. Canon court hearings are internal business matters of the diocese and, as such, are confidential. We are not at liberty to comment further.'

"Whatever the question; that is the answer. Nothing else. It's not about answering their questions but about giving them something to quote."

Anne Lieberman was happy with it; in her work life, dealing with the press was a regular experience. For the bishop, it was a harbinger of his worries about the whole issue.

Early in the afternoon, Jeremy Hinks called the bishop.

"It's a standard criminal law defense tactic, Bishop, I am afraid; to use a relative as the vehicle for the defense case. Moore's lawyer is playing hardball."

From the sources of the calls and their tone, Jean Ames saw it a little differently. "Reverend Moore is rallying the traditionalist troops, I think, from the messages, both at St. Matthew's and other churches. He's casting you as being not on their side; not necessarily for other camps but not with them, it seems. He talked with you on the matter on a road trip recently, one person let slip."

Now James regretted his discussion with Moore on the drive back from North Bay, concerned about what the priest might have his wife quote next. It made him think of Hugh Tremblay. He decided he owed the man a call – and an update.

20 GRANGE-IN-BORROWDALE

30 August, 10.30 a.m. BST

John Trent sat listening to Harriet Calder as she led the service in the little Methodist church in Grange-in-Borrowdale, located at the southern tip of Derwent Water, south of Keswick. It was the following Sunday morning.

He was from Penrith, he told the people who greeted him on his arrival, but he was visiting today to hear Mrs. Calder preach and have lunch with her afterwards.

The older person, a woman, said bluntly, "That's miles away. You aren't here to assess her, are you? Sounding her out to recruit her for your church? She's well-loved in our circuit; a fine preacher. She's here about every four weeks. We wouldn't want to lose her."

Her co-greeter smiled. "It's none of our business, even if Mr. Trent is here for that. We normally have coffee after the service; you are very welcome to join us. There aren't many of us, but we are friendly; well, some of us are."

He mockingly glowered at his colleague as they turned to greet a regular attendee.

I'm not here to recruit her for my church, thought John.

Not that.

Trent recalled the last time he had heard Harriet preach, in Penrith; in that case, as a visitor, she was there to give the sermon. She had spoken well; it had taken him a moment to connect with the fact she was the police officer who had once been with MIU. But this time, as he saw her lead the service for the small gathering from beginning to end, he was struck by how Calder seemed to have two lives; one in uniform where she was indistinguishable from other police officers, and here as a spiritual leader.

He was taken back to his youth, to the chapel his parents attended. It had a visiting minister but most weeks the service was led by one local preacher or another. The Eucharist was not a weekly event for Methodists. Somehow it seemed more intimate, the entire service belonging to the congregation.

It was in a pub restaurant back in Keswick that John Trent got to talk in private with Harriet, at a place called The Pleas. Its full name, ironically given their profession, was the Chief Justice of the Common Pleas. Over the promised lunch Trent said, "I had better get it on the table why I asked to meet you today."

"Not to hear me speak again then, sir?" There was a taunt in there somewhere.

"John, please. Here at least. Today it seems strange for me to be pulling rank, don't you think?"

Harriet smiled; the sort of smile that meant that she would live with it but didn't necessarily agree. She rebutted him by saying softly, "It's about work, though, isn't it?"

He couldn't argue with that.

"It's the Aster case. I met on Thursday with Tim Hutton again over at CPS. Sammie said she told you at the service at St. Anselm's about the Aster case not being closed yet."

Harriet replied, "That you had talked to CPS and also to the Ontario Police; yes, she mentioned it."

He asked, "How up to speed are you with IICSA developments?"

Acronyms, she thought; the Crown Prosecution Service; the Independent Inquiry into Child Sexual Abuse.

"The Child Abuse enquiry? Well, I read about it in the media. I saw a couple of sessions about the different churches live on the internet, just to get a feel. That's about it."

"Why those?" he asked, his interest piqued.

She thought a moment. "I have reservations about the moves to bring the Methodists and the Church of England into the same fold, to be honest. I wanted to see how the Anglicans dealt with the IICSA issue, particularly. Other than Archbishop Welby's testimony, I wasn't impressed, overall."

Trent nodded, reflecting. "The proposed union is more a matter of economic survival for both churches, to join forces and have a common future strategy rather than a desire to bring doctrine together. They both have too many buildings to care for."

She smiled. "My grandfather was a Methodist preacher. I think of him more now I am one, too. He used that quote a lot about the Anglicans; 'The Tory party at prayer'. It was how I discovered the meaning of the word Tory. Our family was working class."

She sighed. "At the heart of it, I'm concerned how it will affect local preachers like me in the future. I know my grandad's path; I know mine. I don't want that to disappear in their frippery and bureaucracy. I don't want the intimacy between a preacher and the congregation replaced by that... that 'loving distance' I call it."

He raised an eyebrow in question and immediately

answered it himself. "Loving distance; that 'arm's length' gap between the clergy and the laity?"

She nodded. "You could call it that, too. But the Aster case; is that a fit? Are you looking at it in an IICSA context now?"

Trent was still focused on her earlier point. "Listening to you again today the church is a very important part of your life, I realise."

She nodded but declined to expand further in response to his opening. Instead, he changed back to the business at hand.

"It came up in discussion of 'next steps', that's all. IICSA is looking into institutional failure to protect children from sexual abuse and part of that is the appropriateness or not of police engagement and action over the years. We live in different times, people say. Well, Hutton and I live in a time when Cumbria Police must be diligent in the investigation of allegations of any such abuse. The superintendent and others higher up agree, and so does DCI Fenton with the Safeguarding Unit."

She paused before responding, while working out the connection. "Sammie told me that the Canadians have been informed about the man's comment, the reference to a 'Susan'. Isn't that over with, or over to them?"

"I hope so. The problem is that Aster was a regular visitor to the UK for holidays, from his border entry records. And while this girl Susan Clapham at the Keswick site says there was not a problem, that they just exchanged conversation and smiles, Hutton is concerned there might be others in the past. Perhaps Aster was grooming Clapham but hadn't got very far."

Harriet pursed her lips, thinking. "I recall it was an issue of confusion for Reverend Moore, mixing up the two. But it might not be the full extent of it, you think?"

He shrugged. "Hutton is concerned about dotting the 'i's on that aspect. My worry bead is the quality and thoroughness of our own investigation about the bible element; how Aster's bible got into St. Anselm's and whether I should have done more? I've re-familiarised myself the file. The Ontario Provincial Police are telling us that the Anglican Church diocese is now holding some sort of formal examination of Reverend Moore over his refusal to talk with his bishop about whatever happened here. Apparently, he has asked for a ruling by their canon chancellor on whether he has to tell anything at all about it to his bishop–."

Harriet interjected, "He's an ordained priest; he has no choice but to obey his bishop in everything but breach of the confessional seal. That's surprising."

He nodded and picked up where he left off. "And the bishop has arranged an expert hearing to decide that. It will be held – when I am not quite sure – but soon. I want us to have observer status there, and I want that observer to be you. I have funds for it now after the discussion with Superintendent Jackson and Tim Hutton."

She sat back, hit by the suddenness of the proposal. "Why? No. Shouldn't someone from the Safeguarding Unit deal with this now?"

Kent knew this would come up. "Hutton and I talked through that. He made the point that a safeguarding issue with Aster is speculative; the issue of the bible's route to St. Anselm's isn't. He's also wondering if we have a 'duty of care' case with Moore, rather than worry solely about Aster. Bluntly, did Moore contribute to Aster's death?"

Harriet eyes widened. "That's a big stretch. That he should have intervened? That he had a sufficient basis to do so? A moral duty is one thing…"

She paused, seeing the other side, suddenly. "But Moore

is a priest; there are duty of care provisions for doctor-client relationships and the like, which are similar. I'm starting to get it."

"You see the scenario. I am not convinced one way or another yet. Something relevant may emerge in this hearing and that aspect of the investigation stays with MIU. At least we can say we made the effort."

She sat analysing the development as he continued. "And why you? You are well qualified and better versed in church affairs to participate than most, I think. It'll be a one or two-day church hearing in the guise of some sort of court process, I gather; not a drawn-out trial."

He smiled. "The OPP may take you to Niagara Falls, perhaps; it's not that far away from Hamilton, I gather."

Harriet looked at him seriously, skipping the inferred bait. "And both times in the interviews with Andrew Moore, my questions disturbed him; wound him up. That had crossed your mind, no doubt?"

Trent smiled. "It did. He would certainly notice you being there and... who knows? But you won't get to interview him in Canada unless something breaks. You'll just sit in the room and take notes, assuming the Anglicans agree to it. I gather their hearings are private, but they accept *bona fide* observers. It wouldn't look good if they turned us down, would it?"

Harriet looked away, thinking. Her mind went back to seeing Aster in the water, her prayers there.

She said, "John, you aren't using this as a lure, are you? Trying to get me into MIU; to re-awaken my interest there?"

She was half-smiling, half-worried, he thought. He shook his head. "No. If you are interested, then that's another thing. But I thought you weren't, that it wasn't your sort of policing any more, your file said. That's what

Murray told me, too. But time has passed; are you interested?"

Murray Cassidy, Trent's predecessor.

She pursed her lips then smiled, more at ease. "No, it hadn't crossed my mind. I balance my life - the church and the work I do in Keswick as a local officer."

She paused. "Did Murray tell you why I left MIU?"

"Your husband; he was terminally ill, I gather. That's what he said."

He looked at her steadily. She didn't become emotional when she responded, he noted. Time had passed, as he had said.

"My husband Ian was a land surveyor, a very active, fit man. It was out of the blue, the tests, the news. In almost no time I was on a leave of absence at home, looking after him. His dad helped a lot; his mum couldn't cope, really. It's the other way round more often. In the middle, at the worst part, it turned out I... found this, 'my other calling' his dad says. And in the end, for both Ian and me, it was as good as it could be, I think. I couldn't give up this life now."

She took a breath and seemed to re-focus on the issue at hand. "I am glad you are not really chasing me for MIU again. By the way, I think Sammie is a good addition; she brought back memories of my own time there..."

She's mulling it over, he realised, as she explained. He sat it out.

She stopped, looked out the window then back at him. "I'll do it, subject to line approval. I assume you have that informally, just to approach me?"

He nodded.

"I need as much notice as I can get, with my church commitments, but... I'm with you on your reason for wanting someone to be there. A dead clergyman and another who went out of his way to be unhelpful. It doesn't sit well. And there is the development with the man who found the body, Colin Kavanagh. Did you hear?"

Trent shook his head. "What?"

"Someone I know at St. Anselm's keeps in touch with the Maywood family – the guesthouse where the Kavanagh family stay. Apparently, he is not doing well, a reaction to the shock of it all, I gather. Funny; I mean, funny-strange. He seemed alright at the time, compared with others I've met in similar situations."

Trent grimaced. "It's not easy to tell, though, is it? Physical shock, we can react to that. Sometimes people just brood on these experiences; it gets into their minds."

She nodded, finally accepting the logic of her involvement. "Perhaps I will find out more to help us and him."

Then she smiled. "And I'll get to see Niagara Falls. I wonder when it gets really cold over there; hopefully this hearing is before that."

21 GRACE

Reverend Jean Ames entered the bishop's office just before noon with the iPad that seemed inseparable from her these days. On the iPad were all the media position statements and press releases of the diocese on issues, ready for any media call. The Moore canon hearing topped the list these days.

After the Hamilton Spectator article appeared, Azikiwe's twice-weekly communication briefings had been changed to morning and afternoon updates.

Reverend Moore had steadfastly refused any media interviews on the subject. His wife and several of his parishioners had not. But Moore's photos in the media articles; at St. Matthew's with his congregation in his robes, and one of him in jeans and a clerical shirt and collar at some social event, seemed to accompany each print or online article. There had been half a dozen or so articles in various media since the news had leaked that the diocese would hold a canon court hearing.

"I wish I could get a set of photos of you to use like this,

Bishop. It's a great media strategy that Reverend Moore and his team have developed, I'm sorry to say."

James smiled ruefully. "I'm too busy for photo sessions; and I don't wear jeans and cowboy boots, despite being an Albertan. And I'm not naturally photogenic."

Jean shook her head. "Yes, you are, Bishop, on the last point. We are going to have to work on you a bit. But to the matter in hand; the communication strategy for this afternoon. I think we should hold our ground and use the same key message, if pressed; the matter is an internal review within the diocese."

James had been ambushed twice at public events in the last three weeks on the issue. He was officiating later today at a memorial service of a local councillor, so he needed to be prepared. He just nodded.

Jean continued, "There is a new factor, though. You said you have agreed to allow a UK police officer to observe the hearing. It's not out there yet and we wouldn't want to make it so, but if that comes up?"

James thought about it a moment. "We will say nothing on that, either. I doubt Reverend Moore's people will raise it. They have already said it relates to an event that occurred while he was on holiday in the UK, but not explicitly provided the link to Father Aster, thank goodness. Flagging a police interest will infer that there may well be other reasons for Andrew's reluctance to speak about his visit to Keswick."

Ames nodded in agreement. "And if it comes up as, 'If a foreign police officer is allowed to attend the hearing, will you now also open it to the media?' I suggest we reiterate that the hearing will be held in private. We are, however co-operating with pertinent authorities in the UK and Canada which have a *bona fide* interest and their own confidentiality provisions. The rights of privacy need to be respected."

James nodded. The sooner this hearing was over with, the better; whatever the outcome.

~~

In Toronto at Haydn House, Susan Carlson had just dealt with a regular complaint while she was supervising the lunch break. As with everything else at Haydn House, meals had their process and expectations of residents; that they would be on time, behave civilly, and unless they had pre-declared allergies, eat the meal provided. Too many of them during their addiction had ignored food as a priority in their lives. Good nutrition was a component of recovery, as much as getting used to a well-structured day. After lunch, they would divide the duties, cleaning up afterwards and loading the dishwashers before the afternoon group sessions.

A woman called Irene had just said in an outburst, "There is no way I am saying grace; it's meaningless; it's fucking meaningless. This is not a bloody nunnery. I won't have religion thrust down my throat every morning, noon, and night."

Irene had been admitted three days ago: a twenty-four-year-old from Kingston. This was her third treatment centre. Her family paid each time; they were wealthy. Every counsellor read the admission profile of each guest and, as far as Susan could recall, nothing about religion had been a factor in Irene's. Perhaps it would come out in individual counselling sessions during her stay.

She said softly, "Irene, in here you were told you would do things that you wouldn't normally do, like getting up at a set time, being at sessions, and eating meals at a set time. Saying grace is one of those things. It is simply a way of getting you into the habit of expressing gratitude; nothing else. And you will do it loudly, silently, or just stand when the others do – or you will talk to the director; that's the rule."

Irene just let out a breath, a sigh of frustration, "I hate this place. I do. I said to my mom I wanted to go back to the one in Montreal."

It was a younger woman still, Meagan, nineteen, sitting next to her at the table who suddenly reached out and held her hand. "It was nicer, you told me?"

"Yes, it was!" said Irene, with a vengeance.

"Teaching controlled drinking strategy, right? Had nice gardens?"

Suspicious now, Irene said more quietly, "Yes."

Meagan nodded. "When I shared with the group in the session this morning that I used to finish anyone's drinks, including the stale party leftovers of people I didn't even know, you smiled. You weren't appalled or disgusted like Sarah over there."

She looked at the next table. Sarah gave a shudder at the reminder. "Sorry; it's–."

"Disgusting," said Meagan, matter-of-factly. She looked into the eyes of her neighbour at the table. "Do you really think people like us can say, 'Oh, half a glass of wine was fine, thank you, I have a control strategy to follow'? I don't."

She gave Irene's hand a quick squeeze then let go.

Susan was watching the interaction carefully, seeing how well Meagan had interjected herself and had handled her input. She was doing very well, she thought. She was monitoring Irene's reaction when the comment from behind her came as a surprise.

"Is someone having trouble with the grace?"

Consuela Ramiro, the director of Haydn House, had just walked into the dining room with another counsellor. She was still in her outdoor coat and was carrying a briefcase. She didn't wait for an answer, "Irene, just do it. It's not about religion; it's about getting from breakfast to now without a fix or puking your guts. Be grateful for that. Fake it 'til you make it. You wanted to see me?"

Her last question was to Susan, who nodded.

"Let's go; Wendy will cover the start of lunch."

With that she was out of the room, followed by Susan. As Wendy called them to say grace, Irene stood with the others.

By thirty-five years of age, Consuela Ramiro had been a hot shot in the Toronto Stock Exchange. By forty she was on the streets of Vancouver, a broken addict. Her first substance of choice had been red wine, by Vancouver it was mainline cocaine. Her story, told in the tradition of Alcoholics Anonymous about her decline, the point she sought help, and her recovery, was shared with the assembled guests at Haydn once every three weeks in an evening session. Every guest heard it at least once.

In recovery, by age fifty-three she had retired wealthy, having also completed a degree in addiction counselling while working for an investment firm. When she was subsequently hired at Haydn House, she insisted that her salary as executive director should be paid only once a year by the chairman of the board, a substantial lump sum cheque and a yellow rose. The cheque was donated back, the rose was retained. Only guests got to hear the reason for the rose and its role in her recovery. She had been in charge at Haydn House for twelve years now and had no wish to retire again, she claimed.

To say she was driven was an understatement. Much of

her time now was spent in external matters; in fund-raising for Haydn; in a network dealing with the growing addiction issues in Toronto; and, more recently, she had been appointed to a federal committee established by the Deputy Minister of Health.

Susan knew better than dither around. In her boss's office, as Consuela removed her coat and got settled, she said, "My sponsor said I should talk to you. I am offering to be a witness at a church hearing, in support of a priest."

Consuela looked at her. "This relates to your recovery, I take it?" She knew Susan's story as well as that of any staff member at Haydn.

"Yes. It's something I need to do. Initially I offered to talk with the priest, then his lawyer asked me to speak at his trial. But they may ask me about what I do here. Miriam said I should run it by you. Lawyers are 'amoral rats', she said. I think that was the kindest thing she said about them."

Consuela smiled. "She's still doing OK then, by the sound of it?"

Susan said, "Mentally she's fine. Physically, she's having difficulties, but she still gets to meetings one way or another, all weathers."

Consuela thought for a moment. "Well, you know the rules. About Haydn's purpose, there is no problem. My role is externally visible if a name is needed. But nothing at all about any other employee or guest, past or present."

"I know. But to say I work at Haydn House... that's OK?"

Consuela nodded. "They do like to peel away, though, lawyers. It's a church hearing, you say?"

"Yes, an Anglican one, what they call a canon court."

"Be careful. It will sound like something official, but it

is really an internal matter of the church. It has no legal standing. If you don't like the way it is going, just stand up, thank them for listening to you and walk out. And don't take Miriam with you. She dislikes priests almost as much as lawyers."

Susan laughed. "No, I wasn't going to do that, anyway. And rabbis, don't forget rabbis. She says all of them get in the way of a person finding a faith in God because they are too busy stuffing their own potted version down your throat."

Consuela smiled. "She hasn't changed then."

Susan replied, "Thanks for the clarification on this hearing thing. I'll give the man I want to talk to a call, then I will get back to the lunch. I have the Step Four group at two o'clock."

As she turned, Consuela said, "And keep an eye on Irene; she's not settling yet. It is only two days until her first assessment review."

"I will."

"And give Miriam a hug from me, next time you see her. You know, I still recall her turning up in my office that morning with you. It's a joy of a memory. You looked absolutely wrecked."

Susan smiled. "You have said that to me previously. Watch it; I will tell her you are doing well physically, but I am not sure about your mind…"

Consuela laughed. "Get out before I give you something else to do. Now, what's next?"

~~

In Hamilton that afternoon, Jean Ames had her hands full. She and a Roman Catholic nun, a young woman who was also a natural and trained communicator, shared a thirty-minute spot each week on a local radio station. It was a segment called 'Wows & Vows' by the station, but now more usually referred to as the 'Jean and Jo Show'. They answered questions live from listeners, about what it was like as young people with a religious vocation to be in their roles; what was ordinary, what was not. It had been running six months and was quite popular. One of the first segments aired had ended up focusing on a questioner's strange interest in, 'do priests clean bathrooms, do normal stuff?' Somehow the pair survived that with honesty and humour. It had been the start of a good relationship between them and the development of a following.

But this last show had almost exclusively focused on the Anglican canon court issue. Jean explained how they worked but pointed out her difficulty in dealing with this in any specific way because of confidentiality issues. The questioners had persisted until Sister Jo had joined in.

"They are more common than you think in most churches. They sound alarming, but it's not like being hauled up before a real judge. That's far more frightening, I know, from personal experience. But these are internal meetings, just as any organisation may hold; mostly boring facts about decisions on church property or dealing with people's jobs, just like you being sent to Human Resources to talk about a performance review. It's the language and terminology which makes it feel different, but that's the church for you! We've talked about that aspect before on other shows, haven't we, Jean?"

The questioners moved on to Jo's experience before the court; an act of civil disobedience during the G20 meeting held near Toronto some years earlier. By the time the broadcast slot finished, Jo had conveyed that, through her faith and new role as a nun, she had found a more peaceful and effective vehicle for her mission.

Afterwards, off-air, Jean said, "Thanks for that, Jo. Taking the hit."

Jo smiled. "You needed a break, I could see. You are welcome. I'm just glad that Father Aster's diocese and yours are in good communication, you told me. It would be ten times worse if they were at each other's throats."

Natalia, the program editor came over to them and said, "You two are gems! Do you know that? You are really getting through to people. That was a great session."

Jo smiled. "Our churches have a lot of gems; it's just that most of them are in absolute terror of sitting in front of a mike, listening to the countdown to go live on air."

22 WITNESSES

27 September, 2.15 p.m. EDT
It was the Monday following, after James had returned
from another visit with his friend Rabbi Simmons, that he
took a call from Jeremy Hinks. Unlike Anne, who knew
James well, Jeremy was always formal, a little less at ease
with his bishop.

"I had a call from Leo Unwin, Reverend Moore's lawyer,
Bishop. They have declared that a Susan Carlson will be a
witness in support of Moore."

"A character witness? The witness list was limited, we
agreed."

"They offered that we could add a witness, too, if we
wish. Can I come to see you? There are other complications."

This was the third time that he had needed to fit Jeremy
in at short notice. The lawyer, too, had a busy schedule,
and James was acutely aware that this case was *pro bono*
service work for the diocese.

"Yes, of course; when? So that I can ask Audrey to adjust
my schedule accordingly. But what complication?"

"It will be early December for the hearing now, not early November."

James could feel his blood pressure rising; another month of this issue dragging out. Thankfully, the initial round of calls from concerned parishioners and the media had declined to a trickle, but it was a looming threat for his efforts to create harmony in the diocese, largely around 'misinformation flows'.

"Let's do this today."

In Azikiwe's office, Jeremy explained. "It's legitimate. Their expert is a canon lawyer from England. We had quite a tussle over who would pay his costs and that the diocese would not reimburse these expenses, even if we lost the case.

"Now the man has developed a medical problem and he can't travel abroad. Unwin and Moore have agreed on a university theologian from the USA, a Roman Catholic. He has impeccable credentials and acts as an expert witness a lot, despite his teaching load."

Given the number of church dioceses in court cases, it must be a thriving business, expert witness work, thought James. But he stayed silent.

Hinks continued, "It's the scheduling of the man with our own expert and the panelists. We were lucky to keep it within this year. We have a window of two days, and all have agreed to it. Hopefully we can complete it in less."

"And our expert, this Dr. Loomis?"

"Hilary Loomis is fine with the change. She's in Toronto and more flexible, so it's less of a problem."

James moved on. "And this new witness they are calling, what's her role?"

Jeremy looked surprised. "Susan Carlson; that Susan; the one in Aster's email."

James had missed it completely. He had assumed this person was either a member of Andrew Moore's loyal followers at St. Matthew's who wanted to speak to the character of the man, or another expert.

James said nothing for a moment.

"Why?" he then asked, feeling a little foolish, followed by a growing sense of alarm. It hit him that as much as he wanted to know what, if any, role his own priest had in the events leading up to Father Aster's death, he didn't want the Catholic priest's past brought up in court. This was not going to be an exposé around Aster's wrongdoings, whatever they were. His mind went back to the first meeting with Bishop Tremblay.

He brought himself back, concentrating on Hinks's explanation.

Jeremey had just said, "I think it is retaliatory, to be honest. I know Unwin was not happy at all with your decision to allow the UK police officer to have access as an observer, but he also has a good point. While Reverend Moore is unwilling to divulge anything Aster said to him, if another person involved wishes to speak to the gravity of the matter in support of Moore's position, he wants the panel to hear it."

"But to go to the lengths to track down this Susan – what was her last name again? That's a bit extreme, don't you think?"

Jeremy responded. "Carlson. I explored that with Unwin for exactly that reason. Apparently, she contacted Moore directly, asking for more details about Aster's death. She told him that she knew Father Aster when she lived in North Bay. Reverend Moore picked up on the link but didn't speak to that, Unwin claims. He told her nothing that wasn't in the UK papers; that he had met Father Aster at the conference, they had got along well, and he was as shocked as anyone by the turn of events. Unwin said that her response to Moore was that she was shocked too but that, in a way, she understood. She offered her support to him."

The bishop asked, "Isn't there some sort of preliminary information exchange? What's it called – disclosure? Wouldn't that determine relevance?"

"In a civil case, yes. In a canon court hearing, if it was a document of significance in an estate issue, for example, yes, we'd share it in advance. But in this case, no. I hardly think it is material to the issue, to be honest. I would prefer to leave it for the panel to decide. We are not trying to establish any facts about Father Aster; just that Reverend Moore is failing in his duty to obey you. If anyone else would be called as a witness by us, I would want it to be the UK police officer. She could speak to Moore's refusal to comply with their enquiry. It would be consistent with his stance with you."

"I'd rather not; I don't want this to be an attack on Andrew; all we are doing is defending our position. He, in fact, requested this hearing, not me."

"That may be so, Bishop, but we are the 'prosecutor', in a sense. It is your court."

It was later, after mulling it over, that Azikiwe decided to have a quiet conversation with Hugh Tremblay. The Roman Catholic bishop listened to the update on developments without any questions.

"Thank you for keeping me informed, James."

The Anglican wasn't sure what to say next, other than sign off. Then Tremblay said, "Would it be acceptable, may I ask, if Mr. Nugent, whom you have met, observes the hearing also? My thoughts are only for Father Aster and Susan Carlson, I should add; now you know her identity. I don't want to interfere in any way. As I mentioned, there is a secrecy agreement between the diocese and the Carlson family. No-one would want her to fall foul of the law. It would not be us who would act, I assure you of that, but the court could see it as a breach. It was a civil settlement; there are penalties in law, you see."

I don't, thought James. I don't see anything about this, really, other than a secrecy agreement that doesn't sit well.

James responded, "Well, I will ask the Chancellor, in case there are aspects I don't fully understand yet. I've not been through one of these hearings before. But I don't see why not, myself; after all, it does have a bearing on the matter of Father Aster's unfortunate death, and if anything is said there, I would rather that you hear it directly from your own representative. I'll call back with an answer tomorrow."

Hugh Tremblay said, almost paternally, "I'm not familiar with Anglican process, but just remember that the hearing is in your court; you have direct responsibility for it, and are the final arbiter of your canons outside a resolution of your synod. And... if my experience is anything to go by, you won't be there at all, I suspect. It's best that way."

PART 3

COURT

(b) The parties to the DCA shall be the Bishop
and the Respondent.

(d) The DCA shall hold an oral hearing at which time the
parties may be represented by counsel or other
representative, may call and examine witnesses and may
present submissions to the arbitration board.

(g) The decision of the majority is the decision of the
DCA, but if there is no majority, the decision
of the chair governs.

*From procedures for a Diocesan Court of Arbitration, Canons of
the Diocese of Toronto, 2017.*

23 HOOPER

December 6th, 2.30 p.m. EST

As the aircraft crossed the coast of Canada and they left the vast expanse of ocean behind, Harriet looked out of the window at the white, frozen landscape of Northern Labrador. She was glad that, on encouragement from a friend, she had forked out personally the surcharge for a window seat with the extra legroom. Her long legs weren't cramped, just a little cold now, protected by a blanket. Her eyes went from the view outside to the map on the entertainment system.

She had no interest in any of the movies, but the map was wonderful. The friend had said, "Book it out and back. You will get to see something, and on the return flight you have a little more space to sleep."

It was her first visit to North America. Neither the United States nor Canada were on her travel list. Her holidays since Ian's death had changed focus; his death had changed everything, really. Part of her leave time each year now was given over to assisting at a wilderness campsite with the local girlguiding organisation in Keswick.

For two years after Ian's death, she holidayed with a recently divorced friend from her schooldays and her two children. They went to France, to a holiday home the family still time-shared.

After the summer trips to France, the following year she went off alone, joining an organized spring tour to Italy, one that didn't pan out too well, other than she came across a retreat near Assisi run by some very modern Catholic nuns. Somehow, the people and the area called her back. Since then, she and another Methodist friend called Frances, an unmarried local government employee, had visited there every other year. With a little rental car, they toured Umbria, ate well, relaxed and, if truth be told, prayed and meditated in peace.

So, she had given no thought to travelling across the Atlantic.

If it's like this now, she thought, taking in the desolate view beneath the aircraft, what's it like in February, in the heart of winter?

On landing, the customs and immigration line snaked out in front of her, and the tiredness began to hit. It had already been a long day. It was as she exited the security area with her bag that the reality of her reason for being here returned. At the barrier was a female police officer in Ontario Provincial Police uniform with a sign saying simply 'Calder'.

After Harriet introduced herself, the officer, a Cindy Hooper, led her directly outside to an OPP-marked vehicle. "I'm to take you to Hamilton, to the Sheraton hotel downtown, and brief you about our interviews with Reverend Moore and Bishop Tremblay. I suspect you will want to rest up afterwards. Was it a good flight?"

"Flights; yes, they were," replied Harriet. "I came via

Reykjavik but didn't get to see it other than the airport. But I can say now that I have been to Iceland as well as Canada."

Hooper was assessing her. "We'll do the briefing at the hotel, if you agree. I don't want to do it while I drive. Are you OK with that; not ready to crash yet?"

"I'm fine. That sounds like a good idea. In my hotel room would be best, I suppose."

They were police officers; they understood the need for privacy.

The hour-long drive along the highways to Hamilton went by in light conversation about their respective travel experiences and work. Cindy commented on the places they were passing. Hooper was attached to the OPP Sexual Crimes Unit and based in the detachment in Hamilton.

"It's a decentralized team; mine is a liaison role largely with other units and the city police counterparts around here. Hamilton and Toronto have their own police forces. Still others are serviced by regional authorities like Halton Regional Police. It's a bit complicated; there are government layers. Everything in Canada is one layer on another; city, region, province, and feds. Is it simpler in the UK? You are a lot smaller, geographically."

"Hardly," replied Harriet, thinking of the various police jurisdictions back home.

Just before they left the highway for downtown Hamilton, she saw a huge church or cathedral on a hill.

"Is that –," she stopped. It looked too ornate, too Catholic in style, she thought.

"No, that's the other cathedral here; the Roman Catholic one called Christ the King. The one you are going to be at is Christ's Church; it's about ten minutes' walk from your hotel. We'll route past it."

"That's easy then; I can walk."

Cindy responded with a smile in her voice. "It's not the distance, it's the wind. Make sure you wrap up warm and wear gloves."

They drove into central Hamilton, entering a one-way street system. Harriet knew immediately she was in an industrial town. She'd read up on it, but there was still that feel, just like the steel and coal towns in the UK. They may seek a new image, but they never lost the grit, the feel of the past, one now faded. But she didn't comment.

Cindy drove past the hotel first, then turned into James Street North to show Harriet the location of the cathedral. As they stopped momentarily to see the façade, Harriet took in the grey stone, the Gothic revival style, and the arched doorways facing the road. Her immediate thought was that the architecture should be viewed from a distance, but it is squeezed in here on a plot almost hidden until you are on top of it.

Cindy smiled. "Your courthouse for the next day or so. Enjoy."

She waited a moment, flashed her lights and siren briefly to warn the traffic then did a U-turn to take them back to the hotel.

On the way from the front desk to the hotel room, Hooper picked up two coffees in paper cups from a self-serve machine in the lobby. Calder had her case and a small backpack to handle. Once inside Harriet's room it was all business.

Cindy opened her own folio case. "I have print copies of the two interviews; one with Moore – I did that one – the other with Aster's boss; Bishop Tremblay. If this develops, we will transmit them officially. But don't bet on it. The bottom line is my boss doesn't think we have anything here for us. Have a read; I'll check in."

With that, she pulled out her cellphone and made a call as Harriet scanned each report, knowing she would go through them again much more slowly later.

As Hooper finished her call, Harriet looked up and waited. Hooper put her phone away and took a sip of her coffee. "In my interview, Andrew Moore was dissembling – you'll see it in the notes – and hiding something, I thought. I didn't get much from him or push it at this point; it was a preliminary interview. I made it sound a boring, routine follow-up."

Harriet smiled. "Which it probably was, for you."

Hooper returned the smile but didn't comment.

"My team member Ray Krantz and a colleague of his in the North Bay detachment did the interview with Bishop Tremblay, accompanied by his lawyer, a man called Nugent. Tremblay's lawyer is a sharp one. There is a civil file, a secrecy agreement. It's sealed. Ray did some background work on the timing. This Susan is a Susan Carlson. From her DOB and timing of the agreement, the best Ray can put it, without starting something active, is that she was between seventeen and nineteen at the time the agreement was signed.

"Sixteen is now the age of general consent for sexual acts in Canada since 2008. Here, no consent means it's a criminal act at any age and someone under sixteen can't be deemed to have given consent unless the other person is within two years of their own age; even then it's a judicial decision.

Harriet butted in, "Same in the UK; no consent means it is a sexual assault."

Cindy puffed her cheeks. "With a priest? It's a clear breach of trust and that's different. Leaving aside the church's own rules, the age of legal consent criminally in such cases is eighteen here, generally; but again, a court would need to decide. A lot would depend on the incident timing and detail, and we have none at present.

"Our boss believes that the church would never have got a civil secrecy agreement outcome if Carlson had even hinted at an assault or no consent. Ray got the vibes that the diocese had its ducks in a row. And we know from the RCMP analysts that the Diocese of Greater North Bay is one of the better ones nationally; not just Catholic, I mean, I don't distinguish about that. There are a lot more churches, of all stripes, that have been running interference on us for years, blocking action, despite fine words from the top. Under the bishop there, it hasn't been like that, at least under his watch. This one associated with the Greater North Bay diocese is out of the blue, a surprise really.

"But I shouldn't go there. I was told to tread carefully with you being a visitor. And some sort of church deacon, or something. No offence meant."

Harriet smiled. "It's no problem; none taken. I am not ordained, a priest or a deacon. I am a lay person. It's the way my church works."

Hooper nodded and seemed to want to drop it but couldn't stop from asking, "You aren't assigned to safeguarding? Your term for our team, I believe?"

"Yes, we have a safeguarding unit in the Cumbria Constabulary with similar duties, but I am not with them, no. The first thing I do with every priest is mentally remove their clerical collar then I look at the person, their actions and words and assess why they wear that collar. Sometimes, I must admit, I don't like what I see at times."

She stopped herself. "But then some of them don't have much time for me, either."

"Because you are a cop?"

"No. Because I don't fit properly the Anglican or

Catholic templates around communion, particularly. I know some wonderful priests, but I believe all people are equal before God and that Jesus calls each of us to carry his message. If we meet in common prayer, then I believe Christ is present with us and that is enough; he will bless the communion and be with us. We don't need a priest for that, I feel. As a Methodist, I respect my church's position and stick by its rules but that's the way I feel personally. And I don't hide it."

She stopped. Cindy was smiling. "Well, that's clear. You could get into some arguments on that one, I am sure. You should have some fun the next day or so with the bunch at the cathedral, if my experience with Moore is anything to go by. Now I see why they sent you."

"I'm glad you do. I'm beginning to wonder myself."

Hooper stood up, picked up her folio case and her partly drunk cup of coffee, making sure that the lid was still tight. "I am to convey that if you need anything, call me and we will do our best to assist. I guess we are sisters-in-arms on this one for the next couple of days."

She smiled. "And you don't even carry a duty firearm, do you?"

"No," replied Harriet.

As she thanked her for the ride and the support, Hooper responded, tongue-in-cheek, "Mind you, if you get arrested for ripping dog collars off priests in a Hamilton cathedral, the OPP will probably deny all knowledge of you. It will be the city police who haul you off to Barton Street Jail."

~~

Later, as Harriet settled into her room in the hotel, enjoying a hot shower to freshen up, she wondered about tomorrow. It was the first of possibly two days of this strange hearing. She had become accustomed to courts; it went with the life of a police officer. But this one was different, being held in a cathedral, a canon court of church law. If her time change issues didn't mean she was struggling to stay awake, she thought it might prove interesting.

Refreshed, she decided to go for a walk, to experience first-hand this Canadian cold she had heard about. After her brief exposure between the car and the hotel, she wanted to get a better feel for the place.

Outside, she decided that the weather would be called 'fresh' at home. Orienting herself, she set out in the changing light as the sun dropped further. She had asked Cindy about street safety.

"Between here and the cathedral? Fine. Your biggest risk is crossing the road looking the wrong way. It happens to Brits over here."

"Funny that," responded Harriet, "It happens to Americans and Canadians on my patch, too."

As she turned on to James Street North, it wasn't the temperature; it was the wind that was icy, as Cindy had warned. It was like being up on the moors at home. She took in the shop windows as she walked, and the people passing her. There were some boutique stores and older businesses, and a shopping mall of some sort, called Jackson Square. Some bars or bistros with fancy names caught her attention; she was thinking she may eat at one on the way back. The people were a mix of office workers, shoppers, and locals; including some street people, bundled up.

A flash of hands; an expression of pleasure on one face, a watchful cynicism on another. Her practiced eye took in a doorway drug deal several yards away down a side street, the satisfied client walking away into the main street as the dealer, a man with a tattoo on his smoking hand, gave Harriet a hard stare. Perhaps a dealer can always spot a cop, even one from another country, passed through her mind. She stared him out but didn't break step. And he didn't follow her; she checked for that.

She spotted some mittens in a store window of a place called Morgenstern's; they were brightly-coloured with a maple leaf emblem. Somehow the shop struck her as a local fixture rather than a chain store. Harriet entered and looked around. Eventually, on a whim, she bought a pair of mittens to wear over her thinner leather gloves, and a second pair in a smaller size as a present for her niece, pleased with the find.

When she arrived at Christ's Church Cathedral, she saw again how it was set back from the road a little, as she entered its forecourt. Its three main arched wooden doors facing the road were closed, to keep the cold out, if nothing else. People are still in the offices, she thought, probably somewhere around the back, but she had no plans to find out. The walk had done her good, to freshen her up. A bowl of soup or something and a glass of a Canadian wine in somewhere warm on the way back, and she'd be ready for an early night after a long day.

In the declining light, she was reading a large plaque describing the history of the cathedral when a woman in a quilted coat carrying a small daypack came along the path by the side of the building.

She smiled at Harriet. "Hello. They have leaflets inside if you want to know more about the cathedral."

"I'm just visiting and getting my bearings, having a look around the area," replied Harriet. "I only arrived in Canada this afternoon."

It was the expression on the local woman's face that gave it away. Recognition. The woman said, "You are

English! You wouldn't by any chance be Sergeant Calder, would you?"

Harriet confirmed it, as the woman continued, "I'm Audrey Lille, the bishop's assistant. I know about your visit. The bishop is away in a meeting, or I would take you in and introduce you. But... do you want to look inside? There's no regular meeting scheduled in here now until the family yoga group arrives later, but they will be in the hall, not the main cathedral."

Harriet was hesitant, so Audrey persisted. "Come on. Just a minute or two. You aren't intimidated by churches, are you? Some people are. It'll get you out of the cold for a minute, to warm up. You could do with a hat that keeps your ears warm, I suspect, rather than that beret?"

Harriet laughed out loud. "Thanks, I will. I just didn't want to put you to any trouble and no, I'm not intimidated by churches. I'm a Methodist."

By then Audrey had led her to a smaller side entrance and let Harriet enter first. "Methodists; they became the United Church here."

"I've been reading up on it, Methodist history here," replied Harriet.

Inside the cathedral, with its high vaulted ceiling and rows of dark pews, Harriet was instantly reminded of several churches back home, her mind not that far from Cumbria in time. It was as she started to take in the detail it struck her that this was about Canadian lives and history, from the carvings to the decoration and displays.

Audrey sensibly let her guest absorb the sight and the atmosphere, in no rush, it seemed, to hurry her through or talk. As Harriet moved closer to the choir stalls, she asked about the organ and Audrey started to give her some of the history of the Casavant brothers' instrument.

An internal door at one side opened as they talked, and several people came into the aisle of the nave. One was an older woman, Harriet saw; two were men in suits and the third, also in a suit but with a clerical collar, was Reverend Moore. Both Moore and the man with him were carrying topcoats. As Moore saw the bishop's assistant standing with the visitor, he recognized Calder and stiffened.

Audrey said in a whisper, "A meeting with the Diocesan Chancellor, Mrs. Lieberman, to go through the final preparations for tomorrow, for when the panelists are here."

Harriet looked at Moore for a moment then she turned away, taking in one of the stained-glass windows that Audrey had been talking about. So, a moment or two later it was a surprise to hear Andrew Moore speak quite loudly to her from a distance as he approached. The Chancellor stood by the doorway with one of the men as the other followed behind Moore. He was his lawyer, Harriet quickly concluded. Lawyers like to keep their clients in check.

"Sergeant Calder, welcome to Canada. You are not in uniform this time."

He smiled, the smile forced, Harriet thought. She was still in her travel clothes; casual pants looking crumpled now and a little incongruous alongside her best winter coat. She was glad she had put on a fresh top before going for the walk, she thought, for some reason; it had a nice collar. But she was conscious of the mix of clothes, not to mention the newly acquired mittens.

"I've just arrived, Reverend Moore," she responded. "I took a walk and found the cathedral. Audrey is kindly showing me around. It is beautiful."

The man behind Moore smiled briefly at her and said, "Andy, I think we had better –."

He looked at the door. Harriet thought he didn't want any complications.

Moore turned to him. "Sergeant Calder is a Methodist, Leo. One of their 'Miriam'."

The comment hit Harriet hard, caught unawares by the jet lag and the surroundings. Miriam, the sister of Moses, had been a prophetess. The comparison was inappropriate, to say the least, and a little sacrilegious. It was certainly an inappropriate taunt from a stranger in, of all places, a cathedral setting. Moore was smiling but, being closer together now, Harriet saw that there was no humour in it.

She looked down, saying nothing, then at Audrey who, she saw, was not amused at all. Harriet said to her, "I think I should be going; it's been a long day... and thank you for the welcome and showing me inside the cathedral."

As she turned around to leave, she saw Audrey giving Moore a sharp, accusatory look then she followed her.

Outside, Audrey spoke up. "Sergeant Calder, I'm sorry. I don't know why he said that–". She stopped speaking as Harriet turned round, seeing the disquiet in the woman.

Harriet responded, "I'm also a Methodist lay preacher, as well as a police officer. That's what he was referring to, I think. It's OK. Thank you again."

Audrey responded sharply, "A lay preacher is not a prophetess and certainly not someone accused of slander."

Although Miriam had watched over Moses in the bulrushes, she was later to find herself accused of slander against him, and cursed.

Harriet smiled. "I'm glad to see you know your bible so well."

Lille had gone straight to the point that so disconcerted Harriet. Was Moore trying to be clever, inferring that in their interviews in Keswick, and now in her attendance here, they were slandering him in some way? She wasn't sure. Worse, in a sense, was he being rude and dismissive of her role as a preacher simply because she wasn't ordained?

She turned away heading back to the hotel, thankful that the wind was behind her, not in her face now. She was sorting out her thoughts. The preacher in her was affronted. The police officer was thinking about the case they had, and that Andrew Moore may regret those words. In the end she skipped the idea of a bar or bistro; she ate at the hotel and sent an email to John Trent.

~~

It was later the same evening that James Azikiwe phoned his assistant.

"Thank you for the impromptu welcome for our UK visitor, but Jeremy tells me that there was an unpleasant exchange between her and Reverend Moore. Can you tell me about it?"

"Not an exchange, Bishop. Sergeant Calder said nothing in response. It turns out that she is a Methodist, one of their part-time circuit preachers."

She explained what had taken place. At the end, the bishop was silent for a moment.

"Thank you. In our cathedral, of all places."

As he closed the call, Audrey knew her boss was going to stew on it. The plan agreed with the Chancellor was that the bishop was not going to make any appearance during the hearing. Audrey had been instructed to attend, as his eyes and ears. She had the feeling he wouldn't hold to that, but she couldn't say why.

24 LIAISON

Sammie Livermore was working her way through her notes in a case where a young teenager had been pushed off a first-floor balcony by his sister's boyfriend. The kid had broken both ankles and a wrist. She was due to give evidence at the trial that afternoon.

John Trent walked up carrying a coffee cup and said softly, "I need you for a minute or two, if you would."

By the time she stood, he was going through the door of his office. She grabbed her notepad and followed him in.

"Take a seat. But close the door first. I've several things to cover. First the good news; you are promoted to detective sergeant in a permanent position here effective tomorrow. The paperwork is arriving on it soon. I'll be announcing it tomorrow at the briefing, so keep quiet and don't smile too much – yet."

Sammie beamed. Her hard work and performance while filling in for other team members this last summer had paid off. Plus, the slog for the sergeant's exam, of course. But she understood that the promotions board results for the

212

last batch of applicants wasn't due until next week, so the timing was a surprise.

"Thank you, sir. I'll do my level best."

He smiled back. "I know you will. And you deserve it. It was going to happen within a week, but I worked it through sooner because there is also some bad news. And I wanted you to know that your promotion was happening anyway, but there will be some other changes. DI Green is leaving us very soon, for health reasons. Some tests he had recently gave him the worst answer. He wants to be very private about it and will speak to it himself tomorrow at the briefing, then he will be off. He'll be in Cumberland Infirmary in a day or so for surgery."

"Neil... I can't believe it. He's like the rock that doesn't move. He's been here since..."

She was lost for words and the tears flowed as Trent pushed over the box of tissues. After a few moments of wiping her eyes and blowing her nose, she apologized.

He dismissed it. "We have a hard job, Sammie, and see a lot of hurt; but when it's our own, we are no different from anyone else. I told him I was telling you and why, and he agreed. Pop into his office and see him after this. He's not going out anywhere today."

She nodded. "I'd like to do that; talk to him, I mean."

"He'll be very abrupt on it, so that you know. He will get straight into work transfer, that sort of thing.

"I have two more jobs to give you, as well. You'll be Neil's key liaison here after tomorrow, if we need to pick his brains about on-going or past cases. You'll be on the phone to him and visit him at the hospital or at home. I don't want every Tom, Dick or Harry calling him. You'll do it right, I know.

"I'm bringing in a new inspector from outside to replace him, but I can't say more at present. You will be the new person's DS, so will be pivotal in making the team work smoothly. We will be doing some shuffling of people. Again, more tomorrow.

"Finally, you have yet another little job today. Recall the Aster file?"

"It's not that long ago, yes. Right. It's that hearing you lined up Harriet Calder to babysit this week. I'd totally forgotten it."

Trent said, "She's hoping to get Moore's fingerprints, but not officially; nothing we could use in court. The OPP will help, she said, and if she is successful, they'll get them here – to you directly, I told her. I've already been on to forensics; they will be processed and checked against that bible we pulled from St. Anselm's Church. But I want this done fast, so we know the result while Calder is still in Canada. Run with it."

Sammie nodded. "I will. And thanks again, for giving me the chance."

As she moved to open the door, she asked, "It's probably not my place, but Harriet Calder has team leadership experience, and I don't think she's forgotten anything about this team's work. Is she…?"

"The new DI? No. Let me scotch that one, straight off. It's a good thought. In fact, I talked to her speculatively about coming back to MIU when I asked her to attend the hearing. It would bugger up her other life, we both accepted, and she didn't want that. And I didn't want my wife giving me heck if she had said yes."

He smiled. "It's the right approach though, looking for talent."

Then he turned serious. "Off you go. Talk with Neil. He'll appreciate it, I hope; he is struggling today, as you might expect. But get over the hump of it. And turn off your phone before you go in; don't get distracted. Take the time it needs and follow your instincts, not procedure. If he wants to get out of here, go for a coffee or something, go with it. I'll cover for you. Tomorrow, after the morning briefing, it will be easier. He'll get a lot of support."

As she left his office, he watched her cross the open area. It was a tough start for her in her new role, he knew. But she was also the right one to bridge between Neil Green and the new DI, who he had just found in the National Crime Agency.

The reference to Calder made him wonder how she was doing. He had responded positively to her little plan and wondered if it would yield anything.

25 HEARING

Anne Lieberman surveyed the room as she and her co-panelists entered and seated themselves in the reserved places, in the middle of one side of a long table.

The room had been laid out in a courtroom fashion, with their long, rectangular table and its three seats facing into the room, with a view of the entrance doors. A church-warden sat at a small table outside the room. He and other volunteers would ensure people did not enter for the two days of the hearing.

The lawyers and Reverend Moore were at a matching facing table, with a view of the panelists and the windows behind; they were positioned about eight feet away. Their table had a divide created by an absence of chairs at the centre, separating the camps of plaintiff and defendant at each end.

To the left of Anne, on one side of these two tables, was a small square table and one chair, to be used by the witnesses, in sequence. Further back in the room were two rows of five chairs each, at this point with only three visitors and the Dean of the cathedral, all of them now seated.

Anne saw the tall woman she had observed at a distance yesterday, Sergeant Calder, now in a dark suit, sitting in the front row of the observer seats. Simon Nugent had taken the end seat in the back row. Both seemed to be at ease. Everyone else present did not appear to be; their faces showed their tension and uneasiness.

She didn't pause. "Good morning. I am Anne Lieberman, the Chancellor of the Diocese of Hamilton-Brant. I'd like to welcome everyone here today. This is a disciplinary hearing in accordance with the canons of the diocese, held under the authority of its bishop, The Most Reverend James Azikiwe. The panel will examine an allegation of an act of disobedience by Reverend Andrew Moore contrary to the said canons.

"I will confirm for the record at the outset that the instigator of this hearing was Reverend Moore himself, to clarify a diocesan position relating to Canon 4.7 and Canon 3.13, in order to give guidance to both him and the Bishop as to how to proceed on the charge of disobedience.

"This is an internal matter of this diocese according to its own rules. If this was a dispute within a private or public corporation, it would be regarded as an internal matter conducted in the language of the business world. However, tradition and precedence derived from the Anglican Communion, and particularly the practices of the Church of England where similar proceedings are, in fact, a matter of state law, mean that the process we follow is similar to that of a court of law.

"I say this so that you understand that in one sense, it is an internal matter of the church. However, this hearing touches on several aspects of statute law in both Canada and the United Kingdom material to our deliberations. I don't want there to be any confusion simply because of our structure here. First, it relates to information associated with the unfortunate and untimely death of a priest of the Roman Catholic Church in Ontario while he was in the United Kingdom. That matter is still under examination by the coroner there.

"Secondly, it also relates to a ruling in civil law within the province of Ontario regarding a secrecy agreement involving a witness to be presented by the defendant; that secrecy agreement must be respected. Finally, as a disciplinary hearing of an employee of the diocese, it has relevant aspects of employment law in the province of Ontario. My co-panelists and I will be attentive to all these elements.

"With the concurrence of the Bishop, I have agreed to allow several observers to be present representing interests just enumerated, but I make it clear that this hearing is still a private matter and observers cannot address the court unless called by me to do so. Breach of the confid-ence of the court will result in the removal of the person from the room and a report to the bishop.

"We have allowed two days for this hearing but are hopeful that it may be concluded in one. The panelists, the triers in our parlance, are lawyers with expertise in canon law. Mr. Hollis Carter is from Kingston, Ontario, and Mrs. Roberta Steinfeld is from London, Ontario. Both have kindly given us their time on this matter. According to our canons, they will be the primary arbiters. My job is to ensure that this meeting is conducted in accordance with our rules. I will render an opinion only if there is an irresolvable disagreement.

She smiled. "However, I want to begin with a prayer for guidance. I have asked the Rector and Dean of the cathedral to lead us in that prayer. Dean Grieves?"

Thomas Grieves stood. As the prayer began, Harriet,

having readied herself with her police training for the event, found her two worlds gently bumping up against each other.

Hinks began his opening statement in a calm and matter-of-fact manner.

"Chancellor, members of the panel, I am Jeremy Hinks, a vice-chancellor of this diocese and I speak for the Bishop.

"There is no dispute by either party that Reverend Moore refused a direct instruction of his bishop, contrary to Canon 4.7 and his oath of obedience, part of his ordination vows. The question before this court is two-fold. First, what constitutes the boundary around the seal of confession between a priest of the Anglican Church of Canada and a penitent? The penitent was neither a member of the Anglican Communion nor a parishioner; is that relevant, we ask? When is a conversation, albeit of a personal or intimate nature, simply that?

"Secondly, given the sanctity of ordination vows and affirmation of obedience between Reverend Moore and Bishop Azikiwe upon his installation, can all aspects of a conversation between a priest and another person be withheld from his bishop solely on the decision of the priest alone, by using Canon 3.13 as justification, as Reverend Moore has averred? We think not. The bishop's question which gave rise to this hearing was about the state of mind and actions of Reverend Moore, not of Father Aster. It was posed primarily from the bishop's concern for his own priest and his professional interest in the performance of Reverend Moore as a member of his diocesan clergy.

"As such, we will present expert evidence that the stance of Reverend Moore is contrary to both the canon law of this diocese and of the Anglican Communion in general.

We ask that the panel rule on this and find in favour of the bishop. Thank you."

Short and sweet, thought Harriet.

The lawyer at the other end of the table sitting with Moore spoke up.

"Chancellor, panel members; I am Leo Unwin, a partner in the law firm of Goldstone & Unwin, and I speak for Reverend Andrew Moore.

"The entitlement to secrecy between a person and a priest is sacred and absolute. From the earliest times, every priest has felt such an obligation; has been trained to meet this duty and, in the cases where it has been broken, has faced condemnation and discipline. It is right that every priest takes such vows seriously, sacredly, and places the vow of silence above all others.

"Even in modern times with the evolution of civil and criminal law and issues surrounding the protection of children and other vulnerable members of our society, as much as there is legal redress against a priest for failure to reveal information, it is recognized that this is a burdensome obligation. Failure of this nature is decided ultimately by a court of criminal law – and some priests have protected this vow above their own freedom."

"If it were simply a matter of principle, it would be easier; but it is not. The specific case we are considering has complications; complications which I contend are a clear illustration of the reasons why my client acted as he did.

"We will call a recognized expert on the issue of the vow of silence. We will also call a witness who will confirm, as best as she can given other restrictions in civil law, that the matter on which Reverend Moore refuses to speak is entirely and appropriately within that seal of confession.

We consider that Reverend Moore, and only he as a trained and properly ordained confessor, can determine the boundary of that privilege.

"We ask that the panel find in favour of the paramount right of a priest to protect information he or she considers within the vow of silence around confessional matters, and that the said priest, in this case my client, is the only person with the right to make that decision. Thank you for your attention."

Now to the meat, thought Harriet.

An elderly woman, Hilary Loomis, a retired administrative law judge from Ottawa, who now taught a course in canon law at Trinity College in Toronto, was called forward. She sat in the chair set for the witnesses as she placed on the table a large binder extricated from her briefcase.

Within ten minutes, Harriet knew they were in for the long haul today. This witness would take time up to the break and perhaps well beyond, she thought. After establishing her credentials, the opening questions were on the absolute nature of the confidence between a priest and a penitent. It led the expert back to the Book of Common Prayer of 1662. She was making her way forward, in steps, with reference to key decisions taken in other canon courts in the past.

Harriet found herself studying Moore, watching his facial response to various questions and answers, assessing his state of mind. He was still the calculating individual she remembered. He glanced at her once, recognized her, she saw; then he looked away.

At about 10.00 a.m., Harriet heard the door to the room open and a blonde woman carrying a small bag entered.

She was wearing black dress slacks and a smart cream top, accented by a cream and coffee-brown scarf. Following the directions given, she came and sat in the same row as Harriet, about two seats away.

A junior aide to Unwin sitting at the defense side of the table saw her and came across to speak. He was so quiet that Harriet didn't get a sense of it. Clearly the person was one of the two defense witnesses and intuitively, she thought, this wasn't their 'recognized expert'. One of the men in the back row was that person, she had gathered earlier. An American by his accent, she guessed, as he had smiled and said hello to her. He, like her, had been there from the outset. She took a quick glance; this was the mysterious Susan Carlson.

The woman looked a little ill at ease, then suddenly put her hands together and looked down at the floor in front of her. It took a moment for Harriet to realise that Carlson was praying. Almost as quickly as it started, she finished and looked up. The look of unease had disappeared.

It was the summary question put to the prosecution expert forty minutes later that was most useful, Harriet thought. At the end, Hinks had taken a stab at reprising the main points, the core component of her testimony, and had asked the expert if that was correct.

Loomis responded, "That is the essence of it, yes. If a priest determines that the content of a discussion with another meets the criteria of confession, he or she must maintain absolute secrecy, even from a bishop. The priest may make his own confession to the bishop on issues of his or her own conscience, if he or she chooses, but in doing so must maintain the secrecy of the confession of the original penitent.

"Nevertheless, the priest has a duty of obedience to his

or her bishop. Questions surrounding the act of confession such as the state of mind of the priest are legitimate questions. Similarly, for the bishop to question the basis under which a priest is sure that the penitent has understood the role and purpose of confession is fair game. Failure of the priest to answer questions like those is a failure of duty."

Hinks wanted to make sure it was explicitly clear.

"So, Bishop Azikiwe's question to Reverend Moore was, 'Tell me what is concerning you, both about your interactions with Father Aster and the events thereafter'. He must answer – yes?"

"Yes. Reverend Moore has the duty to answer, but in doing so, he must not reveal information covered by confessional secrecy, even by allusion."

Hinks thanked the expert. Unwin spoke up instantly.

"Dr. Loomis, if Reverend Moore found no way to answer that last question without revealing the causal element of the confession, his refusal to answer would be consistent with your interpretation, would it not? The paramount obligation to protect the inviolable seal of confession."

The expert smiled. "That is a failure of a different sort, I think. A parallel is the dilemma of a witness in a civil or criminal court asked a question, one which would implicate a third party whom he is not allowed to reveal. The witness has the right to ask for guidance from the court on how to answer before answering. It is the duty of the judge to guide the witness accordingly. Reverend Moore could have asked his bishop to clarify that aspect, or even asked for the opportunity to seek guidance from the Chancellor, before responding to Bishop Azikiwe. He did not. He should have done one or the other, I suggest, rather than refuse to answer at all."

Unwin looked at her then said, coolly, "I have no further questions."

Harriet thought that Unwin could see he would get nowhere by chipping away at Loomis. She was a solid expert. Time for a mid-morning break, Harriet hoped. With no significant cross-examination of this first witness, they were moving quite fast now. She began to wonder whether John Trent would, in hindsight, consider his decision to send her here to be something of a wild goose chase.

26 CARLSON

December 7, 10.40 a.m. EST

A cathedral is the seat of a bishop, but Christ's Church Cathedral was also a community church; a very active church at that. The Dean and Rector, Thomas Grieves, left the meeting room at the start of the proceedings, immediately after the prayer requested by Chancellor Lieberman.

At 10.40 a.m., at the start of the break, he walked into the refreshment room set up across from the committee meeting room. He was holding the door for his own visitor, a woman in a light grey suit and bright floral blouse.

Inside, as people realised that the Dean had returned and some smiled at him, others present looked surprised, including the Chancellor. But Grieves focused only on Audrey, as she directed him to the tall woman standing near the latecomer to the morning session. They weren't talking to each other, he noticed, just each one drinking coffee. Having been briefed regularly by the bishop, he concluded that this other person standing near the police officer must be the additional defense witness.

He walked over to the two women and, born of

experience in many gatherings, ensured he stopped in the right place. This time he had Andrew Moore and his cluster having coffee across the room also in his sights as he spoke.

"Sergeant Calder, I'm Tom Grieves, the Rector here. This is my good friend Reverend Gladys Marshall from Knox United Church. Bishop Azikiwe told us you were here, and we want to welcome you properly, both to Hamilton and our cathedral."

"And hopefully to Knox, too," added Marshall, shaking her hand.

Harriet was surprised. Her research on the United Church here, into which the Methodist Church in Canada had amalgamated many years ago, had brought up the name of the church and the woman. But Harriet's visit was so short and so focused on her police role, she had made no contact with the community here.

Gladys Marshall immediately took up the reins. "If I had known that you were visiting, I would have asked you to make time, if possible, to join one of our services. I have visited your own circuit during a holiday there in 2008… and a visiting Methodist preacher from the UK is always most welcome here."

Susan Carlson followed the sudden arrival and intervention, moving slightly aside as Marshall had moved closer to the woman now identified as a police officer. The newcomers seemed oblivious that others were now watching them, but they weren't, Susan knew. Clergy in their position were crowd animals; they were always aware of others in gatherings. And, as the female visitor spoke to the English woman, the Rector's gaze was firmly on Reverend Moore. He's sending a message for some reason, she concluded. She wondered what had provoked this display.

The Dean turned slightly to face her. "Hello, I'm Tom

Grieves."

"Susan Carlson."

"Miss Carlson, you are very welcome here also, I assure you. But I had better be going before the Chancellor says the coffee break is over and hauls people back into the session. I'm an interloper really. Gladys, thank you for making the time..."

With that he was out of the door, shaking hands only once, with a young curate assisting during the serving of refreshments. Susan watched him give a look, almost an apologetic *mea culpa* across to Chancellor Lieberman, and then he was gone.

Susan headed off to the washrooms. As she reappeared later, she saw the second visitor just leaving the refreshment room as the UK police officer and preacher, she now gathered, walked back into the room set up for the hearing. She hurriedly did the same; she was the next witness, she had been told after she arrived, not questioned this afternoon, as she thought might happen. A clerk assisting the Chancellor, a young man, was waiting there looking out for her.

Inside the meeting room Harriet was smiling to herself, at both the welcome from Gladys Marshall and the ploy that, she assumed, Audrey Lille had organized. Conscious of the limited timing window, she reached into her bag and pulled out a small, well-used bible. In the minute or so people were still talking, taking their places, and sorting themselves out, she walked across to Reverend Moore and his colleagues, getting directly in front of him and right in his face.

Harriet had already opened the bible at the page with the ribbon bookmark and held it out for him to see. She said earnestly, "Reverend Moore, is this the reference to 'Miriam' that you made yesterday? In the book of

Numbers? I was a little confused, to be honest."

She made it sound a biblical question from a lay person to an expert, she hoped, adding a tinge of anxiety for good measure. As the priest automatically took the bible, he swiftly scrutinized the text on the page Calder pointed to, seeing the reference to Miriam's act being slanderous and undermining Moses, resulting in God's retribution on her, a 'leprous' skin.

Moore sucked in his breath then said rapidly, "Goodness me, no! Nothing so deep at all. Simply that you were a Methodist preacher, that's all. I remembered you telling me that. I was a bit awkward; I'm sorry about that. It was a poor attempt at lightness with you. My apologies."

His expression was more one of dismissal; that he was being bothered by a trivial matter at such an important time as this; his hearing.

"Thank you," she said. "It was an unusual phrase, so I just wanted to know. I wasn't sure whether it was jet lag or that which disturbed my sleep the most. I appreciate knowing that it wasn't meant that way."

She took the open bible back and, in facing him, held it by the opposite edge. She gave him a brief, forced smile, and returned to her seat.

As she sat down and returned the book to her purse, no one saw that it was placed still open directly into a plastic bag, which she then sealed. She wrote something in her notebook, then concentrated on the session now starting.

She saw that Susan Carlson had been invited over to sit in the chair for the witness and was about to take the oath.

Unwin was pleasant, supportive in his expression and tone of voice as he began his questions.

"Please state your full name."

"Susan Maja Carlson. M-a-j-a."

"Miss Carlson, you are currently employed as an addiction counsellor in a treatment centre called Haydn House in Toronto. Is that correct?"

"Yes."

Unwin asked in a steady voice, "Can you confirm that the requirements for a position of that nature with the facility are as follows: the counsellor is required to have both an academic qualification in psychology, addiction therapy or a related field, and also have direct experience of addiction recovery themselves?"

Harriet saw that the question caught Carlson by surprise.

Carlson looked at him. "I thought you were going to ask about Duncan?"

Unwin responded, "I will, but first could you answer the question I just posed, please?" He was looking at her intently.

She gave him an irritated look and said, "Yes."

He continued, "So, without any question of detail, you have recovered from an addiction as well as gained an academic qualification in the field?"

Harriet saw that if this was Moore's witness, Unwin hadn't prepared her for this. And it was getting very personal. She looked at the head of the panel, the Chancellor, and saw she hadn't missed the point either and was poised to speak.

Susan sighed, then said simply, "Yes. I am an alcoholic, by my definition a recovered alcoholic. I don't drink, and now I help others dealing with similar challenges with alcohol and other drugs."

She looked around the room at people, searching out, it seemed, anyone who took issue with that.

Unwin said, "You are no longer an alcoholic then, if you are recovered?"

Susan looked at him almost as dismissively as the first

witness in her earlier rebuttal of his cross-examination. "Yes, I still am. Like most people in my line of work, I believe that alcoholism is a disease. By recovery, I mean that I no longer suffer from the symptoms and conditions of that disease. But these can return if I drink alcohol or otherwise lose my sobriety."

Unwin nodded, accepting the correction. Harriet was impressed with the woman; after showing her surprise at the opening line of questioning, she had recovered and spoke clearly and without embarrassment.

The lawyer continued. "You grew up in North Bay and attended St. Paul's Roman Catholic Church, I believe?"

"Yes. My family is Roman Catholic, and I attended that church."

"But you now live in Toronto. Do you attend a Roman Catholic church there?"

From her face, Harriet put it together. The lawyer and the witness were now on ground they had covered before.

"No. I am not a member of that faith now."

For some reason, Harriet noted, Carlson glanced at the silver-haired man sitting in the back row of observer seats. He, too, looked like a lawyer.

Unwin just nodded. "You knew Father Aster at St. Paul's, did you not?"

"Yes, he was a priest there. Our family knew the priests there."

Unwin looked at his notes and then at the panel. "I draw your attention to Exhibit 1, an index of court records of the Ontario Court of Justice, Central Ontario Division. The highlighted item is a record title of a settlement between the parties of the Roman Catholic diocese of Greater North Bay and Susan Carlson, Victor Carlson, and Elena Carlson. You will note that the record is sealed. If the witness could be shown a copy, please?"

Jason passed over a copy of the document to Susan Carlson, who looked at it briefly then looked up at Unwin.

He asked, "The date of that agreement is just under ten years ago. Were you a member of the church at that time?

'Of St. Paul's? No. My parents attended the cathedral regularly by then; the Pro-Cathedral, I mean."

"Did you talk at any time with Father Duncan Aster after you left St. Paul's Church?"

Susan answered carefully. "Only once, this summer in Toronto. We met by chance in Toronto airport. He, I gather, was on his way to England. I was returning from a funeral in Sarnia."

"Not a funeral of a relative, I understand?"

"No. Of a former resident, as we term a patient at the treatment facility I work at. Not everyone in recovery makes it back to a sober and clean life. She died some months after leaving Haydn House. I was asked to represent our facility, as I had worked closely with the woman. Her family had been – and still is – very supportive of our activities."

"Your interaction with Father Aster in the airport was brief, I understand. Can you tell us what was said, respecting, of course, the secrecy agreement provisions placed on you by the court?"

Susan nodded matter-of-factly but glanced at the silver-haired man again. She knew him, thought Harriet, but not as a friend, more a foe. She clued in; he must be from the Roman Catholic Church here, policing the agreement, perhaps. Given his age, he may have been the lawyer who represented them at the time.

"I was surprised, taken unawares, as was he. But he recovered faster. 'Hello Susan,' he said. 'I am off on holiday – and you?' I replied, 'Returning home'."

"Go on, please."

Harriet could see the apprehension building in the woman.

"There was a gap, a pause. Then I said, 'I forgive you'. And I added, 'I ask that you forgive me, too'. He replied that I had done nothing that he needed to forgive me for. We said goodbye and that was it."

She took a deep breath, as if some threshold had been crossed.

Unwin nodded, supportive.

"Thank you. Now, you are a trained and experienced counsellor, dealing with people with addictions. I wanted to establish that at the beginning. The conversation you just described sounds like a very simple exchange. Yet you came forward and offered to support Reverend Moore. Why did you do that?"

"It was Father Aster's expression as he responded before he turned away. I had seen it in others. It didn't matter that I had forgiven him; he had not forgiven himself, I saw."

"So he ran into you by chance and then he left for the UK shortly thereafter?"

"Yes. The encounter was totally by chance. Neither of us intended to talk to each other."

"And you offered to tell us this; why?"

"In my professional opinion, he was very troubled by the meeting and by me forgiving him. It brought back – things I can't speak about. But I have seen similar reactions in others. In a sense, it was my error."

"How was it your error?"

"In my own program of recovery, we try to live by the twelve steps of Alcoholics Anonymous. Step Nine is the stage where we make amends to people we harmed, but only when it does not injure them or others. The encounter was so sudden... I didn't think it through fully."

Unwin nodded and addressed the panel.

"We accepted Ms. Carlson's offer to appear today simply to establish the state of mind of Father Aster as he set off for the UK. While Reverend Moore cannot speak to the discussions he had with Father Aster only a few days later, it is clear this event both surprised and bothered him. It supports the fact that Reverend Moore is duly observant of his vows in not speaking at all about his discussion with Aster to Bishop Azikiwe."

"Ms. Carlson, I have no more questions, but my colleague here, Mr. Hinks, represents the bishop. He may have some for you."

As Hinks began, Harriet immediately got the impression that the bishop's lawyer was improvising; this was not a good sign at the outset of a cross-examination, she knew.

Hinks spoke up. "Miss Carlson, good morning. You said just now, 'in your professional opinion'; did you really mean that? Can you be so sure of that interpretation?"

The witness responded firmly, "I can't be sure of anything; I can only give my opinion. Alcoholics and addicts are habitual liars; the disease makes them so. I'm used to that, to reading people's faces and behaviors as much as their words. That's why I said 'professional'. Not that I am saying Father Aster was lying to me; I was just reading his face and body language."

The lawyer nodded. "I see. I understand from your answers earlier why Mr. Unwin might want you to be here and speak. But it's not clear to me why you would want to do so. This hearing is about Reverend Moore, not Father Aster, as I said in the beginning. Is it fair to say that you may harbour some resentment to Father Aster for events in the past? Is that really why you agreed to be here?"

Susan Carlson looked at Hinks and frowned. Then she

turned slightly to face directly the panel chair.

"Look, do I have to answer all these bitty questions, or can I just say something? I thought this was a hearing of some sort, not a trial. That's what Mr. Unwin told me."

Lieberman smiled at her. "It is. You must forgive the way in which a canon court functions, Ms. Carlson. Yes, you may speak – provided it is pertinent – and hopefully you will address Mr. Hinks' last question in doing so. Go ahead, please."

Susan looked at her for a moment then said, "Thank you. I feel like just getting up and walking out after a question like that."

She turned to face the lawyer and said firmly, "I don't hold resentments very long when I have them. I can't, with my disease. They will burn away at me, be a reason to drink again. I'm better equipped for dealing with those than most 'normal' people, in my experience."

Her hands had moved up, making the sign of quotation marks as she said 'normal'.

"I forgave Duncan Aster a long time ago even though we could have no contact. I wrote him a letter, sealed it up, and my sponsor and I prayed as I tore it up. It was a very... healing process. I did what I could.

"But running into him - I couldn't stop myself. As I said, I forgave him to his face, and I saw his expression. And now he is dead, and I don't know why. In my job I talk to people, counsel people who may get their lives back together wonderfully or may not."

For some reason, Susan's eyes fell on the first witness, Dr. Loomis, who, she thought, had pontificated so much on penitents, secrecy and 'God's purpose'.

"It is my primary purpose in my own recovery, given to me by the God of my Understanding, you see, to help people with addictions try to recover. But I know they may not make it; they may die the next month or year and I can't second guess everything I say."

She turned her head to look at Reverend Moore. "When I heard about this hearing, I thought of you. I know how it feels to speak with someone one day who is dead shortly afterwards. I thought it might help you and, in doing so, help me also, for the reason I gave earlier. When Mr. Unwin contacted me and asked me to appear, I thought it might also be useful to tell others as well, not only you."

She swung her gaze back to the panel. "That's it."

Anne Lieberman nodded and waited a moment before addressing Hinks. "Any further questions, Mr. Hinks?"

Hinks nodded, a little mollified, it seemed to Harriet. It appeared almost an afterthought question, as if he had run out of his brief line of questioning. "Was Father Aster a good priest, would you say?"

He's still trying to show that the witness has a personal agenda in being here, thought Harriet. She saw that the question brought another sharp look from the Chancellor, but she didn't intervene.

Carlson turned slightly, looking at the silver-haired man again, addressing him directly. "He was a human being, like you and like me. But if you want one simple descriptor for Duncan, he was a good and dedicated priest. I'm sorry I spoke to him at all in Toronto, that's all."

Hinks seemed surprised by the answer. Carlson simply looked down, waiting for the next question.

"I have no more questions."

Anne Lieberman kept her face impassive as she quickly checked each trier to see if they were ready to move on. She knew Jeremy had decided to just run with Carlson as a witness. Analytically, she thought that he might have done more preparation; Carlson's testimony had been inform-ative and somewhat surprising but added nothing to address the primary charge. But she was the chair; she couldn't say that.

Across the room, Harriet was working out the interplays as best as she could. Although Susan Carlson had offered to support Moore, and in doing so had given her surprising insight to pass on to DCI Trent, Carlson's appearance here today was hardly justified by the evidence she presented. That it gave a reason why Aster was in the Lake District worried about whatever haunted his past was interesting. So was her comment on the man. It appeared that she held no resentment and actually respected the priest, in a sense.

She had also seen a transient frown on Lieberman's face immediately after Susan Carlson mentioned that Unwin had asked her to appear; Harriet knew that tell-tale. Defense lawyers often say that a witness had come forward voluntarily when, in fact, there had been some persuasion and, in the worst cases, coercion. The Chancellor clearly hadn't missed that one and wasn't happy with it.

Her final thought as she jotted down her notes was that Carlson may be right in perceiving that Aster's conversation with Moore had burdened the Anglican priest, but that wasn't the man's primary problem. She recalled Moore's interviews and had been watching him closely today. Harriet was now convinced more than ever that Reverend Moore's primary issue was about the concealment of his own role.

The final witness on the slate was Reverend Moore's expert on the sanctity boundaries of the seal of confession, a Brother Jerry Rinaldo, Distinguished Professor of Theology and Ethics at St. Bonaventure University in the State of New York. He took the witness seat and swore an oath on his own bible, Harriet noticed.

In the interchange between the Chancellor and Leo

Unwin before the questions started, it became clear that the defense lawyer wanted only to do the scene-setting with the expert before lunch; to present his qualifications, experience, and suitability as an expert witness. That seemed to satisfy the Chancellor.

As Unwin led the questions, it became apparent to Harriet that Moore and his lawyer had chosen a Roman Catholic academic, a Franciscan monk. It took, she noted, almost ten minutes for the man to give his qualifications and relevant experience, carefully led along by Unwin. From her experience in law courts, she sensed that this would carry on well into the afternoon. His binder was as least as big as the prosecution expert's. But he didn't get far.

At 11.55 a.m., Lieberman finessed the lunch break explaining that it would be a little longer than planned; one of the panel members regretfully had to participate in a conflicting conference call from noon until 1.15 p.m. They would reconvene at 1.45 p.m.

The Chancellor had her cellphone turned on in seconds, which was something of a giveaway.

Harriet had seen Susan Carlson return to her seat and collect her belongings left there. She thought the woman might leave, but she didn't. She sat silent, presumably reflecting on her role as witness.

At the close of the morning session, as snacks and beverages had been provided at the morning break, Harriet half-hoped that a light lunch of some sort might be available in the other room. But it wasn't the case. As the gavel dropped, she saw Audrey disappear quickly, presumably in the direction of her boss's office. Others present clustered into little groups.

She noticed that Moore and his legal people huddled

together. She was a little surprised that no one came over to thank Carlson for her appearance. Even in criminal courts, that happened fairly often in the UK.

But the first expert witness, Loomis, and the one now on the stand, Professor Rinaldo, had got together and were treating each other like old friends. The woman from Trinity College didn't realise that while talking, her voice level had gone up. She had her back now to the rows of chairs for observers and Harriet clearly heard the phrase from her, "It's the language of Alcoholics Anonymous, the 'God of her Understanding' term." They were talking about Carlson's testimony, she gathered, or perhaps her comments on her loss of the Catholic faith.

At the time, the New York lecturer was giving Carlson a look that was somewhere between curiosity and a wish to talk further. Returning the stare, Carlson made him look away after he had smiled at her. With one hand pointing, he gently steered Loomis a little further away still.

Carlson said suddenly to Harriet Calder, "Is it you or me that has the plague, do you think?"

Harriet smiled. "Perhaps they don't like police officers. You were a good witness; you spoke very well, I thought."

"Thank you. My friend told me it would be like this."

Carlson was now looking at Moore, Unwin and the junior counsel as the young man glanced in her direction, smiled, but then concentrated again on Leo Unwin's comments.

"I was warned that lawyers would talk to me on the stand and not remember my name if they ran over me in the car park afterwards."

She picked up her bag. "Do you fancy having lunch together, by any chance?"

Now there's an opportunity, thought Harriet.

As they left the meeting room, Carlson was approached by the silver-haired man who had sat on the rear row. He glanced at Calder first, then said, "Susan, could we have a word?"

She shook her head. "I'm going to lunch, Mr. Nugent. I'd rather not, if you don't mind."

He nodded. "I just wanted to say that you did very well. Thank you."

She seemed surprised. "It was OK with you, what I said?"

He nodded, obviously not wanting to say anything in front of the stranger. "I wish you well, Susan. I really do. Goodbye."

With that he turned around and left the building. Harriet looked at Carlson, who was focused on the man walking away. Then she smiled at Harriet. "I know a bistro, if it's still there. It's not the sort of place this lot would go to; OK?"

'Fine with me," replied Harriet.

27 BISTRO

"Is it Mrs. Calder, Reverend Calder, or Sergeant?"

Susan had seen the wedding ring.

"It's Harriet. Or Sergeant Calder, as I am here for work purposes."

As they walked along James Street North, Susan Carlson matched her pace to Harriet's longer stride. "I realised at the break you are a visiting police officer and British and... I wondered if you were part of the investigation into Father Aster's death."

"I am, yes."

"Are you a witness, then?"

"No, I'm not."

Harriet chose not to expand on that, instead she just waited.

Carlson asked, "Can we talk as we eat? I'd like to know more, if possible and–."

Harriet held up her hand a little, to stop her, and stopped walking. "I can't discuss any UK investigation whether active or not. It's procedure. Sorry."

240

Susan Carlson's eyes filled with tears; she appeared not to hear the last bit. "Did he suffer? Did you see him?"

Harriet paused, assessing her. She said quietly, "Father Aster drowned, so it's hard to say. He looked peaceful. I was the first police officer on the scene after the call, so I can say that much, at least. He looked at peace, but I don't want to mislead you; bodies in water do that, the muscles relax and… that was the way I saw him. I did what I needed to do then; I prayed for him, as I couldn't touch or move him until the forensic people got there. For a little while before others came it was very quiet. The location is a beautiful lake by a church he had visited only a day earlier. For a few moments it was just about peace and prayer for his soul. I don't think I can say more than that."

The tears were starting to brim over Susan's eyelids, so Harriet pulled out a pack of tissues and offered them. "Shall we go for lunch now?" she asked, not wanting to stand still in this cold. She had left her fancy but bright mittens in the hotel room and was now wondering what she, in turn, could ask this woman as they set off, their pace a little slower now.

In the nearby bistro they ordered salads and Harriet added a half-sandwich, then baulked at the size of what was delivered. "I'm not sure what time my body's on, and I was hungry; but not that hungry; it's huge!"

Susan smiled. "Welcome to Canada. Sandwiches in this restaurant are quite a size, I recall. But Europeans say our meals are big, anyway."

They had indulged in similar small talk while walking to the place that Susan remembered. It was still a bistro, but now had a different name. On arrival she said, "It's still here, at least. I studied in Hamilton; I did a course in Addiction Studies here."

Once seated, though, Harriet became more serious.

"You have a hard job, I think. I'm a community police officer, so I know a little more than the average person about people with addictions and the troubles they get into; it's good to see places like the one you work at that can help. Some of them at least; we also tend to be there with the ones who don't make it, too."

Susan replied, "We have a pretty good relationship with the Toronto Police. They are really supportive of Haydn House."

She paused, then said, "That discussion at the break was confusing. I thought you were a member of the clergy. But it started out as sergeant so…"

Harriet explained. Susan listened to the English woman talk about the two roles in her life and how she fitted them together. Harriet finished with, "Some of my Cumbria Police colleagues are a bit leery about it, but that's OK. I'm not evangelically rabid, and don't push it with them."

Susan responded, "I prayed silently just before I went to sit down at the witness table."

Harriet responded politely, just before ominously regarding the thickness of her sandwich and the impending prospect of getting it into her mouth, "I saw. That's good. Prayer always helps, for me, at least."

She didn't mean it to sound as trite or offhand as it came out, but she saw it was the way the Toronto woman interpreted the comment. She'd seen the expression before during the session; irritation. Then Carlson smiled, as if she had reined herself in.

Susan said firmly, "It's not 'good'. For me and people like me it's vital. It's at the heart of my ability to live sober and it's a key component of my work; to help those struggling with booze or drugs break through their spiritual isolation and find a conscious contact with God. Your Methodist god, the Cathedral's god, my former Catholic god, or even just the CN Tower, if they want. It doesn't matter to me. Anyone's will do if a person can open their heart and mind to accept help."

As she finished her mini-lecture, she immediately looked away at the window. Harriet thought that Carlson was now wondering if she had been too forthright with someone who was a stranger.

Harriet had to wait while she finished her mouthful of sandwich before speaking again.

"I'm sorry; I made it sound too... I don't want to sound like the academic dog collar set we heard this morning. It's not like that for me."

It was a second's pause, then something in her made her say, "I'm a widow. When my husband became terminally ill, I was so angry and heartbroken and... I took time off work, focused only on him and his declining health. People were good, very supportive; they sent flowers and brought us meals. I couldn't do anything but think of Ian and me, changing from a police officer to a home caregiver.

"Then one of Ian's work colleagues came round, Gord and his wife Barbara. I didn't know them. They brought themselves, not a pie or flowers and a quick visit. Gord insisted on staying with Ian for the afternoon and Barbara took me out; for afternoon tea, she said. She didn't say where, but she took me to Bassenthwaite Methodist Church. I thought we would be going to Keswick or Penrith, to a tearoom or a café. There were just the two of us, the place was empty. She made tea there and she had brought some homemade cakes with her. It all sounds so mundane, doesn't it?"

"No," said Susan quickly, not wanting to stop the woman's flow.

"Barbara said I needed some time to be me. She didn't push anything other than she insisted we take our tea and plates into the church proper and not stay in the kitchen, which seemed strange at first. I worried about crumbs on the floor. Just the two of us. Nothing happened, no bolt of lightning. No one interrupted us, talking. Then we prayed. I enjoyed it, being normal for an hour or two.

"We did that every Thursday afternoon after that. It was the start of my finding inner peace and regaining the faith I had as a child. So, I do know, you see, about prayer and a conscious contact with God. I wasn't being trite."

They looked at each other, recognizing that, for some reason, each of them had been more open than they had intended to be when they agreed to lunch together.

Susan said, "I thought, being a police officer, you would be grilling me about Duncan. You aren't doing that."

Harriet shook her head. "There's a court order; I can't. You surprised me with both your forgiveness and your candour in that room. I think it was… I was going to say impressive, but that's another trite thing to say. I think, in a theological squabble like this, it was simply exemplary that you chose to speak up that way. At the heart of it, that was why I wanted to have lunch with you."

After a moment, Susan asked, "What are you doing this evening? Can I ask?"

"Well, I have an open invitation to something going on at Knox United Church, but I have also agreed to go to a meeting there tomorrow if this finishes in time, which it should if the man from New York doesn't go on forever. Why?"

"The other reason I am staying around here for the rest of today is that I am speaking at a recovery meeting tonight in Burlington, a little east of here, towards Toronto. I accepted the invitation when I knew I would be in Hamilton today. It's an open meeting so anyone can attend. Would you like to come with me?"

Harriet was surprised and had mixed feelings suddenly, so she temporized. "I don't know… is it far?"

Susan responded, "Not too far. I need to head back to Toronto afterwards, but we can fix up a taxi, or a ride with someone coming this way. We can get you back to your hotel, one way or another, I am sure."

It was Carlson's expression that made Harriet decide. If she was the speaker, it would be about her story of alcoholism and her recovery. She wondered if that related to Aster in some way; was this the reason for the invitation?

"I'd really like to be there. And don't worry about me getting back; I can fix something."

She'd call Cindy; she was sure that someone in the OPP could look after her or find a safe taxi driver for her to get back to the hotel. To hear more about Aster and this woman, possibly, was a golden opportunity.

Susan was nodding to herself, as if in making the invitation she hadn't been completely sure of doing so, but somehow now it felt right. She added, "There's just one thing; it is Alcoholics Anonymous."

Harriet smiled. "It's confidential, I know. People don't give full names or break their anonymity."

Susan added, "Or share with others what they hear there. I was thinking that with you being a preacher and police officer, which is first? Isn't that why we are here now talking like this, in a sense? I don't want you either repeating what I say there, or to put you in a difficult situation with your job."

Harriet had no hesitation. "At the meeting today, I am Sergeant Calder. Tonight, I will be just Harriet. I guarantee that."

She meant it. If Trent or others prodded her on it too much, she could handle it.

Susan gave a small smile. "Well, you should be happy

there anyway; it's in a church; a United Church, to boot. We just have to go in the back door to the church hall and be quiet for the first bit. Choir practice won't have finished in the church yet, I was told."

Not quite what Gladys was thinking about, thought Harriet; but it would be interesting.

Harriet looked at her watch and checked a text. "I really need to get back, though. I have to meet someone outside the cathedral. But I would love to come tonight. The rest of this sandwich is going to have to stay here untouched, I'm afraid."

~~

The big man in an OPP uniform and a black and white cruiser came to a halt just outside the cathedral.

"Are you Sergeant Calder?" he asked as he powered down the nearside window and held out a hand across the passenger seat loaded with equipment.

"Yes, thanks for coming." She leaned in and shook his hand and then pulled the sealed bag out of her purse. "I don't have your paperwork, but Cindy is looking after that, she said."

"Already covered," he answered, opening his own evidence bag into which she dropped hers. He sealed it up and tore off an edge, pealed a section and stuck it on a form. He gave the back copy of the set of sheets to Harriet.

"There, the chain of custody is intact. You want this back later, she said, to the hotel reception. Someone will text you. It shouldn't be too long. Lifting prints from leather is rarely the problem if they are there. Reading them is. But you know that."

"There are people back in the UK doing that once Cindy sends them through. But thanks for helping us out."

The reconvened hearing continued with the Roman Catholic expert. Harriet was really feeling the effects of the time change now and had to concentrate hard, fighting off occasional waves of tiredness. Every police officer has bouts of fatigue; it goes with the job and its hours. She began to realise that the effect of jet lag was different.

It was the final set of questions from Hinks during the cross-questioning that made her more alert, as if suddenly there was a lawyer in the room rather than a doting fan of the erudite expert, as Unwin had been.

"So that I am clear, Professor Rinaldo, your consideration of – to use your term – the extended influence of God's guidance on a priest, the intuitive point about which they know they can or cannot speak about a priest-penitent relationship, cannot be judged by civil law or canon law, you assert."

"Indeed."

"But, if I am right, you said, 'not criminal law, because a priest can be found at fault, to be in breach of criminal law'."

Rinaldo nodded and added, "But not morally wrong, even then. A priest may go to jail for disobeying the criminal law in a country but cannot be found wanting by his own bishop, or at fault by the canons of the diocese he belongs to, or of those canons in the diocese in which the act occurred. I believe I was clear on that."

He was smiling.

Excruciatingly so, thought Harriet. You took far too long to tell us that; don't start again, please.

"If the bishop asks Reverend Moore whether he gave Father Aster a cup of coffee, for example; he would need to answer that; right?"

The question was so trivial the witness smiled again. "Yes."

"If he asked him if he was sad or happy after his encounter with Father Aster, he would need to answer that, as well. Correct?"

"Well, yes; but he couldn't be pressed to explain what Father Aster revealed that led to such emotions, you see?"

"I do. But if Reverend Moore had a cold, the bishop could ask how he feels. Is he up to leading a service, say? He could expect to find out the man's condition without Reverend Moore having to say explicitly he had a cold and he caught it from his niece a few days ago. Just that he feels a little low or has a sore throat. He should respond to such questions, should he not?"

"Well, that's not about the seal of confession, so yes."

Now the Roman Catholic cleric was more thoughtful, finally seeing the trap.

Hinks said, "The precise words used, according to the bishop, and not disputed by Reverend Moore, were, "Tell me what is concerning you, both about your interactions with Father Aster and the events thereafter." Is that not the same? He is not asking what these interactions were. He is asking what concerns Reverend Moore about his interactions and his feelings after the sad events that unfolded, is he not?"

Brother Rinaldo squinted, his eyes concentrating. Hinks waited on him, looking ready to pounce. This is more like it, thought Harriet.

The witness took a deep sigh. "On the surface, the answer would appear to be 'yes he should'. But in his introspection, in the depths of his moral dilemma, as it is not about a head cold but about a confession, it is much harder to judge and only Reverent Moore can decide."

He smiled again, hoping a smile would bolster the response he had just given.

Hinks just said, tersely, "Thank you. 'Yes, he should'. I

have no further questions."

The wrap-up was brief; there were no closing arguments as in a civil or criminal trial. The Chancellor thanked everyone for attending and for 'maintaining the dignity of the court', whatever that meant, thought Harriet. She suspected that it related to the preparatory meetings Lieberman had held with the legal counsels, one of which she had caught the tail end of yesterday. She wasn't too sure that Susan Carlson would agree to that statement, but she avoided checking her facial reaction.

Lieberman reiterated her role, that of the expert on process. Judgement would be rendered by the two invited panelists, the 'triers' in the parlance of the canons, she declared. She would only cast a deciding vote if they did not agree. The decision would therefore be 'unanimous' or 'a majority'. They would meet 'shortly' and consider their ruling. No date was given as to when that would be reached or communicated and, strangely enough to Harriet, no-one asked.

Harriet had seen a hand signal sent earlier to Audrey by the person acting as a recorder, just as the Chancellor started her wrap up. Audrey had sent a text in response, she noticed. The Chancellor's final comments were, "Before we close, Bishop Azikiwe wishes to join us and lead a closing prayer. He should be here shortly."

Her timing couldn't have been closer. Within a few seconds, the meeting room door opened; the Bishop, the Dean and a young female priest carrying an iPad entered, and the bishop went forward to be greeted by the Chancellor as she stood and moved from her chair.

He has 'presence', Harriett noted, as they all stood for the prayer and the bishop made some similar comments of appreciation for all their efforts. His full African features, the flashing eyes, the sense of energy coming from the man all contributed to the effect. And, of course, the bright purple front of his shirt beneath the white clerical collar.

His voice in prayer pleased her; she always listened to the tone of prayers as much as to the words spoken. The majesty of his office disappeared; it was simply a prayer for guidance in tones humble and sincere. That he prayed for the meeting and its decision to be restorative and supportive of all struck her. But he didn't drag it out; it was over with as soon as it had begun, she felt.

Then, as people prepared their exit, he made a beeline over to Audrey and, in doing so, Harriet realised belatedly, to her and Susan Carlson.

"Sergeant Calder, Ms. Carlson; would you both be so kind as to spare me just a few minutes together now, for some tea, perhaps? I won't keep you long, but I would very much appreciate it if you could."

As they each said yes, somewhat surprised, they found themselves being led out of the gathering by the bishop, Audrey, and the younger priest, with the eyes of others now on the little party as they left.

The tea was already made and cups and saucers, not mugs, were laid out with a plate of cookies in the centre, as they settled themselves around the bishop's meeting table.

Without preamble, as Audrey served them, Bishop Azikiwe said. "I owe each of you an apology."

Harriet glanced at Susan; again; they seemed equally surprised. She saw that the way the table was set out and Audrey's delivery of the cups that she was also going to join them. The younger priest had stayed outside and simply closed the door on them as they entered.

He continued, "This cathedral is a very special place. To me, at least. I was deeply disturbed by certain events over the last day or so. May I call you by your first names?"

Susan replied, "I'd prefer it," as Harriet simply said, 'yes'."

"Harriet, you are here in an official capacity as a police officer. I did not know you are also a minister in the Methodist Church–."

"Local preacher, bishop," interjected Harriet quickly.

"It doesn't matter. For your ministry to be subject to a slight in our cathedral is completely unacceptable. I'm sorry it happened."

He turned to Susan. "I am so deeply sorry about whatever happened to you; that it did happen, and even more impressed that you still came forward today. And I know you can't talk about it. But I want you to know that I appreciate your courage in doing so."

Carlson gave a nod, and looked down, not responding, her face impassive.

He continued, "Audrey was also quite disturbed by one of the questions posed to you this morning. Again, that shouldn't have happened here, I feel, although I understand the rationale. This hearing was simply a matter of canon law. I know you volunteered to assist Reverend Moore, but your life is private. Your work with others who suffer from addictions is wonderful; but your personal information should not have had to be revealed here to all. It is a house of God."

Harriet saw Susan bridle at the words. "Bishop – can I call you James if you call me Susan?"

"By all means."

"James, I still have difficulty saying 'father' and 'priest' and 'bishop'. It doesn't sit well. At one point, words like that gave me nausea. But I have no problem sharing that I am an alcoholic if it helps others, I assure you. Compared with other things, it's no problem at all. Did I appear bothered?"

The last point was to Audrey, who replied, "No, but I was."

Susan said quite forcefully to the bishop, "You may have a monopoly on your doctrine, but not on God. There is more than one path to bring our higher power into people's lives, and I take my direction from mine as I can best understand it. I didn't even use 'him' or 'her' this morning; to me, God is above gender. But I know I was meant to be here today, so I was OK; I was in God's care."

Harriet saw the bishop nodding in agreement, and smile. It seemed to irritate rather than placate Carlson, and that seemed to make the bishop's smile broaden even more.

He said softly, "Oh, you so remind me of a man called Eddy, Eddy R., that I knew once."

Susan looked surprised. "You mean Eddy R. from here? He's dead. I have a recording of him speaking in Toronto at the AA World Conference in 2005. You knew him?"

He nodded. "When I had a parish, yes. I told him once he should be lecturing to seminarians on the true meaning of pastoral care; he was so eloquent and passionate."

Susan was all smiles now, too, Harriet saw. "Not for him, a job like that. He worked down in the trenches. He had forty-two years of sobriety when he died. Some called him 'Fast Eddy', you know, because -."

The bishop intervened. "No newcomer would get out of the hall before he took their hand and offered his help. I know. I was at his funeral; it was a massive gathering."

Susan suddenly sat back in the chair, placing her cup on the table instead of in the saucer, a little surprised. "Fancy that, a bishop knowing Eddy R."

James Azikiwe just gave a laugh. "People caring for others in the Hamilton community get to know each other over time."

Audrey gave a look at her boss. Harriet has seen and

heard the signs; a noise in his outer office; Lille's prior glance at the door. The bishop's next appointment was due, no doubt. She glanced at Susan and stood, moving away from the table leaving a third of her cup of tea undrunk, closely followed by Susan, Audrey, and the bishop.

Bishop Azikiwe's final words were, "I don't want to delay you; I just wanted you both to know Christ's Church is a welcoming place and will treat all people who come here with dignity and love."

As they left the office, they saw the Chancellor and the two panelists waiting to enter, talking with the younger priest who was apparently on unofficial guard duty. Harriet could hear Audrey moving cups away and bringing fresh ones. She realised then that the set-up was actually for the meeting between the bishop, the Chancellor and the panel of triers to close out the hearing; probably a personal 'thank you' session at this stage. Bishop Azikiwe had chosen to bump them in first.

As they left, she whispered to Susan, "He's a surprising man."

Susan nodded and smiled, "James didn't imply I was some sort of AA weirdo, at least. Fancy that. Eddy R."

In the cathedral entrance, Harriet asked Susan, "What time is this meeting later?"

"At 7.00 p.m. It'll finish at eight or thereabouts. We should leave here around six, as it will still be the rush hour and I like to be at meetings well before the start. My friend, actually my AA sponsor, is coming, too. She doesn't drive anymore; she's got a ride there from Toronto with someone, but I will take her home."

"Oh, right. What's her name?"

"Miriam – she's Jewish; well, sort of, but don't go there

with her. She likes to hear me speak."

She looked at Harriet, who had burst out laughing.

The Englishwoman said, "It's not the name, it's just a coincidence. I was called that name myself here recently. Why don't we walk back to my hotel, have something there rather than go through the issue of you having to re-park? Besides, I checked my phone, I have a text. I have to pick something up from the front desk. It was dropped off and I don't want to lose it. It's mine."

Harriet was wondering when the prints lifted from her bible would be processed in the UK. John Trent had said he would get the analysis expedited over there.

"Let's see what comes up while you are still over there," had been his comment.

28 GUELPH LINE

December 7, 7.10 p.m. EST

"Good evening, everyone. I am an alcoholic and my name is Susan."

Harriet thought Susan's opening words were upbeat and warm, as if they were a badge of honour. The loud response welcoming her was the ritual that Harriet had heard about. She was in a row about half-way back and estimated that there were perhaps a hundred seats set up in the church hall. It was pretty full.

"Bob said I would share my story when he introduced me, but what I share is my experience, my strength, and my hope. And Gary, is it? Welcome."

She smiled at one person in the audience. The apparent newcomer sat there looking uncomfortable, his hands in his lap visibly trembling as he nodded. Susan lifted her sights to another person.

"And Melissa; that's your mom with you, right? Welcome, too, both of you. There may be others here, new, or coming back. Welcome also. If what I say makes no sense to you, go to another meeting, or talk to someone;

someone here this evening, I suggest. For my experience may not be yours, but you can see recovery in this room and that can be yours, too."

Susan smiled at the older woman on the front row.

"I'd like to thank Alice for inviting me tonight, to such a big turnout to celebrate her thirty-eight years of sobriety. It is always a privilege to be asked to speak, but to do so for a person who has done so much for others at her anniversary celebration, I am humbled. Alice is a rock in our turbulent world – and Gary, Melissa, she will tell you she stays sober one day at a time, just as you will be told. That is both the mystery and the blessing of this program."

Harriet peered at the elderly celebrant in the front row. Next to her was a young woman who was turning sideways, also smiling at Alice. Harriet recognized the marks on the young woman's neck above the line of her T-shirt; a prison tattoo similar to ones she had seen before.

Susan raised her head, took in the audience. "The most important thing I can say to any newcomer is that I suffer from a disease called alcoholism. It doesn't matter why I drank. If I think enough about it, I can talk myself into a drink. 'Am I happy? Let's celebrate!' 'Is the day a disaster? Let's have a drink'. And if I have one drink of alcohol, I cannot stop. That drinking behaviour is the visible core of it. If you are new, that's what you need to know if you are like me.

"My problem is not that I am weak-willed, nor is it about any moral failure; I have a disease. Here we can learn how to live with it, and in doing so, have a better life than any of us could ever imagine. Remember that as I speak. My reason for being here, my journey, is how I got to these doors; but I drank the way I did because I am simply an alcoholic; and that's more about how I think and how I feel. That is the invisible part of the disease.

"It took only months for me to get here after I started drinking, so I was fortunate. For others well... it takes years, many years. But it doesn't matter how long it was before you started to drink this way; in these rooms we are all the same."

"My strength; let's deal with that up front. My strength is you, with your warm welcome, your lack of judgement of me when I told you of my worst behaviours, and your offer of a helping hand whenever I needed it; anywhere, anytime. There was a time I couldn't look you in the face and still you smiled and told me it would get better."

She looked up the room at the woman sitting next to Harriett.

"My strength is my friend, my sponsor who keeps me honest. My strength is a relationship with my Higher Power, a loving God of My Understanding that you told me about, that I found because of you in, of all places, a park in Toronto in the eyes of an old police officer who intervened to stop me freezing to death. From that moment, I have never felt alone."

Miriam leaned over to Harriet and whispered, "She's good, isn't she? That's why I have to knock her down a peg or two every now and again."

Harriet just sat there, absorbed both by Susan C. at the podium and the experience of the last few minutes in this church hall.

They had driven in heavy traffic along the Queen Elizabeth Way, exiting north in Burlington at a road called Guelph Line. It had started snowing lightly, but didn't, as yet, seemed to be sticking. The church was located in a residential area in the north of the city, Susan had told her.

Harriet said, "If we stayed on the QEW, it would take us directly to Toronto. I think?"

"Yes, right downtown. Toronto, where I call home now. This area is the Golden Horseshoe, the busiest part of Canada."

After turning a few times on built-up roads, they passed the front of a church with a large welcoming sign and a small steeple. Harriet said, "It looks very nice; I love the stained glass, all illuminated in the snowfall."

Susan replied, "We are around the back."

She parked in the car park at the rear of the building. As they got out in relative darkness, with only a streetlight at some distance, three hard-looking men standing smoking in the gloom waved. Susan waved back and pointed at some plain doors near several large plastic bins in blue and green markings. She stopped for a moment, then pointed at one door. "This one. And mind the icy bits under the new snow, they are lethal."

As they approached, Harriet saw a beat-up temporary sign on the door, an AA symbol, hanging on a cord almost evenly, but not quite. She felt as if she was on street patrol, going around the back of shops, checking for a break-in rather than about to enter a church.

Inside the hall and kitchen area three people were waiting, smiling, holding out their hands, two men and a woman acting as greeters. As she worked her way through the people gathered inside, talking, it struck Harriet that this reminded her of a Methodist church meeting, the warmth, the welcome.

Susan said, "There's Miriam; I told her about you. You can sit with her. She'll protect you." There was a whimsical smile on her face as she said it.

"From what?"

"From the people who think you are a newcomer needing help. Too late."

An old man was smiling at Harriet, holding out a half a

cup of coffee, black, in a paper cup. He said, "Would you like some coffee? It has sugar in it; it's good for you."

Facially, he reminded her of an old wino she knew in Keswick. But this one didn't smell. Uncharitably, she wondered if he was offering his own partly consumed coffee.

"Well, thank you–."

The older woman said, "She's not one of us, Arthur. She's Susan's guest. But that young fella coming in looks like …"

Arthur turned and looked. "He does, doesn't he?" He wandered over.

Susan said, "This is Miriam, the other Miriam. The coffee cup is only half-full because he was worried your hands would be shaking and you'd spill it."

Harriet smiled. "I know. We do that too at the station with the–."

She stopped herself. Miriam said, "Best just stick to being Harriett, a visitor, don't you think? Susan, go pee; you always need to innumerable times just before you speak; you'd better get started."

"Nerves," explained Susan.

I didn't see those today in you, thought Harriet.

As the young woman headed for a washroom, Harriet thought it might be a good idea to do the same, but Miriam asked her, "Did she do alright today? She said she did. I was a bit worried about her, but she wouldn't have me there."

Harriet smiled. "She did wonderfully, I thought. Both at the hearing, and later with the bishop. It was really good of her to invite me tonight."

Miriam said enigmatically, "She suddenly decided she wanted you to come, to listen between the lines of her story, I gather. But I also hear you are a church preacher but aren't ordained; you are an ordinary person."

"Yes."

"Glad to hear that; there's hope for you yet. Let's take seats where I can see her clearly, but not be too close. She's meant to focus on others, the newcomers, if we can keep her out of the bathroom."

Susan continued speaking, moving the microphone a little. "Through this fellowship, the help of others and that higher power I call God, I have not needed a drink to live life each day for just over nine years, a day at a time."

She took a sip from the bottle of water placed for her on the podium.

"I am going to focus tonight mainly on the issue of isolation. Alcoholism is a disease of isolation and if you are a newcomer, this is something you will understand but probably recoil from addressing; I know I did. You think others don't know about it, but in these rooms we do. We have been there."

Harriet was surveilling the room and it suddenly struck her that week after week, one of these people stood there, told their story to others for half an hour or more with no training, no liturgy guide or written-out sermon notes.

"I had a normal upbringing in a northern Ontario community. My parents had the occasional glass of wine but nothing regular, nothing heavy. There was no history of our disease in our family, as far as I know. I didn't drink in my teens at all; in fact, I was the churchy goody two shoes sort of girl; my friends and I stayed away from kids who partied hard; they scared me, really."

She paused. Harriet thought she was working out how to phrase something, but suddenly she focused on her, looking directly at her.

"Four months before my eighteenth birthday I had my

first real sexual experience. It wasn't a violent rape, nothing like that, but it was sudden and unexpected. Put a shrinking violet of a seventeen-year-old girl inquisitive about romance and sex with a man she has adored and admired for several years and… a lot is going to rest on that man, I assure you.

"I don't think it was planned, certainly not by me; it just happened. If that experience had been the whole of it, that he made it clear it was a 'one-off', a mistake or something that I had misread, it would have been bad enough, but perhaps I would have got over it easier."

She sipped from her water bottle again and her eyes started moving, taking in the audience.

"But the man was in a position where he should have stopped it happening. That was the first part of the damage to me, the breach of trust. It took me a long time to realise that. He was a person with influence; let's leave it at that. It was the steps taken afterwards, the way in which he and others went to great lengths to conceal what happened. The initial disappointment and embarrassment grew rapidly into an all-pervasive sense of shame and self-doubt. It made me feel dirty, used."

Another sip.

"That is the way I thought of it then. Now I know different; it was an abuse, on a number of levels. But in those few days I mentally left my home, my friends, my community, and my town. I was isolated inside me, and I hadn't even taken my first drink.

"I didn't become a rebel or a runaway, I suspect, because I saw an easier escape. A university in Toronto had already accepted my application. So, I didn't go off the rails, I finished school and did well. Suddenly it wasn't just the thought of going to the big city; it was the sense of being far away from where I grew up. My parents had no idea what I was thinking then; they thought it was depression. They were really good to me.

"On my first night in college, once my parents had gone, driven home, I got drunk. The whole works, the puking, the hangover, the lot. But I felt a wonderful release, as if the whole weight had lifted. Three days later I did the same. Then I found someone who had other substances that aren't an issue here. And out of the mess of that time, I decided to appear a normal student but get out of my own head as often and as completely as possible.

"That lasted no time, it turned out. Soon I was only concerned about not sobering up; the attempt to be a normal student didn't matter anymore. About half-way through the first term, I collapsed. Not a long drinking career really, but pretty different, nonetheless. I don't remember ever having the desire for just one drink!

"By November I was known as a problem student. Now the 'goody two shoes' I knew stayed away from me. Student counsellors were brought in, and then my parents. I was eventually sent to a treatment centre in Ottawa, where I stayed for nearly a month, including the Christmas holiday. Some Christmas, I tell you! Me, defiant, bitter, and desperate for a drink or a fix, and no chance of getting one."

She sipped her water again, clearly recalling the time.

"The plan was to let me finish my school year and not drop behind; I'd do some catch-up courses in the summer. I was clever, you see? They thought I could make it; I didn't. But I was clever enough to pick up the language and mechanics of recovery in Ottawa; how to say the right thing back in Toronto. But I didn't recover."

She paused a few seconds, thinking.

"What happened, I am supposed to tell you. Nothing too dramatic. On return to Toronto, to university, I went to AA meetings as I had been told, and I gave the impression of trying again. But it was a sham. I really felt uncomfortable in them. And it was totally, totally exhausting, the sense of failure, the craving for booze, and the bitterness. Nothing could move it."

She took a sip of water. "I need to stop this; I'll need the bathroom again."

She put the bottle down on the podium.

"Four weeks after I returned, on a really cold night in late February, I walked out of my student residence dressed in a long, thin fall raincoat, a really thin cotton dress, underwear and boots; nothing else. I had a bottle of vodka in my bag, sleeping pills, and a plan. I walked along Bloor to Christie Pits Park and sat on a bench well back in the park as it went dark. I was shivering, but I started pulling at my bottle to get the hit, my last buzz, to kill the cold and any other feelings. My plan was simply that before I felt at that point – you know what I mean – I would take the pills. They would find me in the morning, I thought."

Her eyes suddenly became wet with tears, her voice tightened a little. "Someone called the police; I never found out who, but there was a street guy there, minding his own business, I thought. He wasn't taking any notice of me; but it could have been him.

"The officers who responded were an older man with a young female officer. I was really blurry by then but I heard them talking; they were processing me; getting an ambulance, taking me to hospital, the works. I hadn't even had the time to take the pills and pass out properly; they got there just as I had thought, 'Do it now'. But the older one, the man, crouched down and looked me in the face and asked, 'Do you know where you need to go; have you got somewhere or someone?' A strange phrase really, I thought afterwards.

"But his face… God, I recall his face, his eyes. So caring."

She smiled, lost in the memory, it seemed.

"I pulled a card out of my pocket and gave it to him. I'd been given it sometime earlier at a meeting off Dundas Street; the meeting that is now my home group by the woman who is my sponsor today. The man telephoned Miriam. By the time my head cleared in ER, and they said I had been lucky, and that I had somehow escaped any serious frostbite, she was at the hospital waiting. She stayed with me overnight there, wouldn't let me be alone. She even talked to my parents when I couldn't bring myself to."

She smiled at her sponsor.

"I didn't get put in the psych ward. Instead, I arrived at Haydn House the following day in my thin coat and wrapped in a blanket, wearing underneath a Value Village reused hoodie and someone else's tube socks sticking out of my boots. I had nothing else with me other than absolute despair and guilt, tinged by a bewildering confusion brought about by the eyes of that policeman and the love and kindness shown by this woman. I didn't understand how or why then, but between them they had somehow provided the beginnings of hope. I'd gone as low as I could go.

"In the months at college I'd used people terribly, for money or for a good time. I had butchered each relationship maliciously. My parents were in anguish. But in the Dundas Street meeting, Miriam had told me that I had to stop fighting and accept help, as she pressed that card into my hand. I thought I had thrown it away once she was out of sight, but it was in my pocket when I needed it."

She picked up the water bottle and took another sip then drew out a tissue from her pocket and dabbed her eyes.

"I went to her, and the beginning of my isolation

fractured; first, just a chink, which became a crevasse, which led to me today.

"I didn't need Haydn House for very long compared with some; they could see I was ready this time. They were tough at times, particularly when I ranted on about God. You are not alone, they said; get used to it and, when I recalled that policeman's eyes, I did. And it grew and enveloped me, as it does today. In doing so, I suddenly realised that I wasn't craving booze because I couldn't get it while I was there; it was because I didn't need it anymore; the craving had been lifted from me. I had received such grace, the wonderful gift of sobriety.

"I changed my options at college when I finally got back. I lost a year in the process, but I switched to a degree in sociology and a minor in psychology. When I graduated, I transferred to Hamilton University, to do a diploma course in addiction studies.

"In my early recovery I went to an AA meeting almost every day; an NA meeting three times a week. I've never stopped going to meetings regularly. I've never been without a sponsor, and I am blessed that my sponsor is still the woman who loved me at that meeting when I couldn't love myself. And once I started in sobriety, Miriam never let up. She put me to work on my own recovery and, later on, with helping others.

"And today; my life today? It's great, really. Not perfect, there are some lousy days; try this morning, for instance. But a day at a time, I can handle the good and the bad without booze, which for me is a miracle.

"All through my studies I had been going back to Haydn House as a volunteer helper. Once I qualified, they gave me my biggest gift other than my sobriety; a full-time job there as a counsellor. Now it's my work, my world.

"The joy of my sobriety is that I can help others; help

the women that come into Haydn, young and old, to break that terrible isolation – and in doing so I help myself. I have found something I hold on to dearly; the grace of a loving God I can relate to, and my friends in these rooms who understand and love me."

She paused.

"I think I am about done. Today was a hard day for me, but I was looking forward to being here this evening. I have ups and downs, I have my flaws, my difficulties, but help is always there if I ask for it; if I don't isolate."

She paused, thinking of what to say next. She looked at the newcomer, Melissa. "Here, as we do the twelve steps of recovery, we have women work with women, men with men. It's best that way, particularly for the newcomer. Remember that.

"Strangely enough, I am now in a fairly rare situation. Recently I was asked to work with a man, a person I have only ever known in his sobriety and he in mine. He drank because, like me, he is an alcoholic. He asked me to be his sponsor because his story is like mine, exactly like mine, down to what happened in his teens and what happened in mine."

Susan swallowed hard. It was unplanned, and she's not sure she should have started this, thought Harriet.

"You see, he works professionally with people like us two, people who had similar experiences. In some cases, people who haven't drunk, or found a syringe, or a pill bottle. They haven't found you or our solution. They carry with them the guilt, remorse, and shame I mentioned earlier. He is, I feel, a braver person than I can be. I am still not all there; I know my limits now. But I can help him to keep his sobriety, he says, and it is a privilege for me to do so. In helping him, I am helping others.

"That's my experience and my strength. My hope? It's

quite simple."

She looked at Gary, his back bent forward now, his face looking at his feet, it seemed. He had pulled his hoodie so it was covering his head, hiding his face. To Harriet, further back, it was a familiar sight, a drunk in the agony of withdrawal.

"That each of us may find God's grace of recovery, or failing that, simply the hand of someone who understands, so we don't need to take a drink in the next twenty-four hours. Thank you, everyone, for allowing me to speak tonight and Alice, happy birthday once again."

In the applause, as she stopped speaking, and as the chairperson moved back to the podium, Susan moved forward and hugged Alice. Over the woman's shoulder she saw Miriam say something to the police officer then Calder burst into tears. It must be jet lag, she thought.

As Susan's story of recovery unfolded, Harriet felt something she hadn't expected; a sense of shame tinging the tiredness and slight nausea she now felt from the effects of the time change. She was a Methodist preacher, a good one, she knew, from people's reaction; but she had never paid much attention to meetings like this, other than think it was a good thing for churches to let twelve-step recovery groups use their facilities. She was touched by Susan's freshness around her spiritual strength; her dedication to helping others and, she realised, the honesty and simplicity of her message.

Then, for some reason, she thought of her own revelation at lunch, and recalled a comment to Barbara long ago in Bassenthwaite Methodist Church, just the two of them there. She was telling her about how angry she was at God for Ian's illness; how hard it was to bear, and Barbara saying softly that perhaps Harriet should just pray on it silently. She would help, she said, she would pray with her. Barbara had been her sponsor in a way, she realised, her guide. She suddenly felt that for different reasons and with different outcomes, her life had paralleled somewhat that of Carlson.

As Miriam leaned in and said over the applause, "She did well," Harriet found herself saying, "Yes she did," as she suddenly started crying.

The older woman took her hand and didn't say anything, but neither did she let go. No-one else fussed over them as the chairperson led the meeting to its close.

As the meeting wrapped up, people broke into groups. Some started stacking chairs and others hurriedly left. Susan eventually freed herself from people who had approached to thank her for speaking and came over to Harriet and Miriam.

"OK now?"

"Yes, you spoke so well! I'm really glad I came, not just for your story."

Susan said, "There's a guy – he's OK – going into Hamilton. I just need to know if you want a ride with him. Do you want to meet him first, then let me know? He's hanging on."

Harriet shook her head, "Thank you, but no. I arranged a ride back with a – person I met."

Susan called across to the man. "Thanks Frank, but it's not needed."

She looked at Harriet, still assessing her. "Should we stay in touch? I'm not sure whether we should?"

"I'd like that; I was just thinking the same thing."

Susan smiled. "I'll give you my Haydn House business card; I'll press it in your palm. Then I'll get Miriam home."

Miriam had been listening to them, watching and

smiling. "It's about time, too. It's nice to meet you, Harriet. God bless you. You have had a long and tiring day."

Harriet nodded. "A good one, though. And God bless you both."

Miriam said simply, "He did; he does; we are miracles of his healing, both of us."

It was ten minutes later in the car park at the front of the church. The English visitor who came with the speaker was seen getting into an SUV with OPP markings and driven away by a female officer. Two of the AA members leaving after clearing up the hall saw her get in the vehicle.

"I wonder what she's done?" said one.

"Nothing; she climbed into the front passenger seat. I saw that. It's you and me who used to get the joy of the back seat, behind the grill."

29 ENVOY

December 8, 9.30 a.m. EST
"Sergeant Calder, Bishop."

Audrey had squeezed her into the bishop's schedule at 9.30 the following morning.

For Calder, it was a relief. Her other alternative, John Trent had told her at 6.45 a.m. local time, 11.45 a.m. for him, was to call the OPP in and have an officer make time today with the bishop, whether he had it available or not. The fingerprint results from the bible were back and unequivocal; some were Moore's prints, some were from a person with a smaller hand, perhaps a female; and they both overlapped those of Aster in places. Trent was annoyed with himself for not doing more while Andrew Moore was in the UK and could be brought in to explain that, but he was still cautious about the next steps. So, he outlined what he wanted her to do.

James Azikiwe was welcoming, but a little reserved at the sudden appearance of the UK police officer, as he stood up from his desk and invited her to sit at the meeting table.

He said, as he sat down, "Before we begin, as we are

alone, can I ask you what you think caused Reverend Moore to make the comment to you, the day before yesterday?"

The insult was still bothering him, thought Harriet.

"It's not an issue, Bishop, but I thank you for thinking about it. The hostility? I don't know, other than I can say I was part of the interview team for Reverend Moore. He did not take kindly to some of the questions."

The bishop nodded, at last understanding. She gained the impression that he, too, had experienced Reverend Moore's outbursts.

She had clued in overnight about the morning break yesterday. "I take you know Reverend Gladys at Knox?"

"Very well indeed, a wonderful person. I am glad you got to meet her."

Harriet smiled but brought it back to business.

"We don't have much time, I gather. I am here on behalf of the Cumbria Police, Bishop, to say that our investigation into the death of Duncan Aster is still on-going. There is a complication. We have reason to believe that Father Aster's bible, which was discovered in the church near where he died, was not left there by him as we first thought. We think it appeared there afterwards; after his death."

She paused, giving him time to think it through.

The bishop said, "And you are telling me that because it may involve Reverend Moore, perhaps. Is that it?"

"We cannot say. All I am asked to pass on is that our investigation is on-going. Reverend Moore is the last known contact with Father Aster, and we have a witness now to their final meeting in Keswick. Reverend Moore had already told us he met Father Aster, but we now have more detail about that final meeting."

Again, she waited a moment.

"Detective Chief Inspector Trent asked me to come

here to observe these proceedings. He understands the outcome of yesterday's hearing will be in your hands once the panel has reached a decision. That our own investigation is on a different timeline, well; he wanted you to be aware of that."

James thought it through. "I take it he would not want me to reach a decision that could subsequently embarrass the diocese. I see that."

She nodded. He'd got it.

She added, "One personal observation also; perhaps one I shouldn't make, as I have no direct basis in evidence. It may be an extrapolation and perhaps an unfair one, I admit. Our bible is the source of love and inspiration but in the hands of some at times it can be a weapon."

James didn't respond to the point directly, but his face confirmed his understanding. A barb about a prophetess was the obvious inference but the Englishwoman wasn't being self-serving, he knew. Her allusion, he thought, was to her thoughts on the unknown discussions between Andrew Moore and Duncan Aster. It bothered him, too.

After a moment's silence, he said, "Thank you. And please thank Chief Inspector Trent. I do appreciate the consideration being shown."

He paused. "Did you find the visit helpful? It's a long way to come."

She smiled. "It was work, but was useful for us, yes, the testimony yesterday. I have never been to Canada before, so it's a new experience. And thank you for finessing the contact with Gladys; I am having dinner with her and another person from Knox this evening."

There was a small knock at the door and Audrey opening it slightly. "Bishop, the delegation has arrived."

Harriet started to move but he held his hand up and said to Audrey, "Just two more minutes."

She closed the door firmly.

"An unrelated question, if I may. What do you think about the efforts to bring the Church of England and the Methodist Church together?"

It was so blunt a question and out of the blue, Harriet said, "I'm not sure; I have misgivings, serious ones. No offence, I hope. But for people like me, lay preachers are a cornerstone of our faith delivery. I worry what will happen with our church if it is inside the Anglican Communion."

Azikiwe nodded. "I understand. Thank you."

"And you, Bishop; what do you think? I am a bit surprised you asked that, to be honest."

She heard the noise level beyond the door rising.

He smiled briefly then looked pained. "Somedays I wonder. I was just reading an email I received regarding next year's Lambeth Conference in the UK, that I will attend. My friend Karen Plowright, the Bishop of Fundy, will be there but without her partner, I suspect; at least officially. Apparently partners of same-sex unions will probably not be invited because of concerns raised by African bishops and others. I am sure it was a difficult decision made with a heavy heart, but I have to go home and tell my wife Dorothy this news. It pains me terribly. Lambeth is a gathering of church leaders held only once every ten years, as I am sure you know. Are we leaders, I ask?

"John Wesley was always an Anglican, but today I wonder whether the church he was ordained in or the one he helped establish is more effectively living Christ's message? But we do what we can."

He stood and held out his hand. As she took it, he said, "I will pray for your ministry, sister."

"And I will pray for yours, Bishop." Looking into his eyes, she meant it. His must be an awfully difficult job.

"You go back when?"

"Tomorrow, in the evening. I'm visiting Niagara Falls today, now the hearing has finished and… I have a feeling that Knox will be taking some of my time. And I have a report to write."

As he opened the door to let her pass, he said, "Talk about our respective churches with Gladys; I do. You are having dinner together, you said. She'll like that; she's a good person, as I said, and a clear thinker."

With the presence of people outside now looking in, waiting to enter, she just said, "Thank you."

With that she was out the door passing five or six people, several in clerical collars and bright, different coloured shirt fronts, collectively creating the atmosphere that their homes were further away from Canada than even hers.

What she had wanted to say, but hadn't with others there, was that she thought that James Azikiwe was a good person, too.

As she passed through the side aisles of the cathedral on her way to the exit, she took a last look at the architecture and furnishings, to hold them in her mind; the mix of experiences she had undergone here in such a short time. Reflecting on them, she saw the door open, and a stranger enter holding it for her, sensing she was leaving.

Harriet smiled and said 'thank you' as she walked out. She had no desire to return. She was looking forward to 'The Little Bus', as the bellman had characterized the tour bus to Niagara Falls, which would call at her hotel. And later, to the meeting at Knox and the dinner with Gladys Marshall. And tomorrow afternoon she would be on her way to the airport, glad to be going home.

But first she had to call DCI Trent, to confirm that the meeting with the bishop had gone as planned.

PART 4

VERDICT

30 PITY

December 19, 11.00 a.m. EST

The atmosphere in the cathedral offices was tense all morning; everyone on the diocesan staff could feel it. That Reverend Moore was coming into the cathedral was part of it; that he insisted that his legal representative be there also was troubling. This was not, they thought, going to be a healing meeting, moving forward from the strange event of the canon court hearing.

The only person who seemed completely at ease with the situation was the bishop's assistant, Audrey. But she was tight-lipped as ever about anything to do with her boss.

Eight days after the hearing, the panel had come back with a unanimous written verdict. Reverend Moore was in violation of Canon 4.7. He must keep silent about the content of Father Aster's discussion with him that was solely of a confessional nature. He could not keep from his bishop any aspects that were not, including his own state of mind or any actions he took during the period in question.

At 11.00 a.m., Andrew Moore and Leo Unwin appeared

and were shown directly into the bishop's office. The Chancellor was already there, they knew; she had appeared half an hour earlier. The door was closed, and people appeared to get on with the work of the day.

They sat either side of the meeting table. There was no offer of refreshments; it was a business meeting, and there were sides taken.

James began evenly, calmly. "Reverend Moore, do you have anything to say? Have you reflected on the findings of the panel?"

There was that calculating look again, he thought. Moore had worked out exactly how far he would go.

The priest took a moment to decide how to phrase his response. "I have, Bishop. I have prayed on it. I am firm in my resolve to hold confidential the conversation in question; I must protect Aster. The decision allows for that. I will answer your questions about myself, as directed by the court, if you insist. I do it out of obedience, not any wish to do so. It is in your hands. Both I and my congregation are praying that this matter will end now and be put behind us."

His voice was soft, appealing for calm and peace, it seemed. His eyes, though, were not.

James said, "Thank you. One moment, please."

He stood up unexpectedly, went out of the inner office and spoke only one phrase to Audrey then returned and firmly closed the door.

As he sat down again, he said, "The first and most important issue now is not the conversation between you and Father Aster; we are beyond that. Duncan Aster is beyond your protection or anyone else's.

"In the spiritually uplifting environment of the Keswick event he shared his deepest fear and shame with you. And you have hidden what happened next behind the seal of confession. Within hours the man is dead and, although the coroner hasn't issued a final rule, it very much looks like it was by his own hand. This is about you. What guidance did you give? What comfort did you bring?

"My only issue is how well you functioned as a priest once Aster spoke to you. If you may recall, that was the focus of our very first meeting; you and the burden you carried. Now I would like to know that. So, speak to me."

They had reached a watershed, they all realised.

Leo Unwin interjected, "I have counselled my client not to–."

Anne Lieberman spoke up. "To incriminate himself? Mr. Unwin, you are here at Reverend Moore's request, but this is a meeting between a priest, his bishop, and the diocesan chancellor. It is not a court of law, canon law or otherwise. I insist that you remain silent or leave. This is solely a church matter."

Unwin stopped, surprised, and looked at his client, who seemed to have realised he was at the end of the road.

Moore said suddenly, "There is a second issue, I take it?"

Azikiwe responded just as fast. "After the last months; how could there not be? The campaign – and I will call it that – against me in the press, through parishioners and others. It has hurt me, Andrew, I tell you. But worse, it has undermined the work we do in this diocese. I have to address that issue at this meeting."

Moore suddenly realised. "You went out once you knew that I wasn't going to cave in completely and spoke to Audrey. What was that about? It is to do with me, I believe."

His voice was even but there was the challenge in his eyes.

Azikiwe looked at him and waited a moment. "You are

removed as Rector of St. Matthew's effective this morning. Our most experienced priest in transitional ministry, Reverend Knowles, is postponing his retirement for a while at my request. He is now on the way to St. Matthew's. I will not have you in your parish acting as if nothing has happened, rallying them to take sides. They are your parishioners, Reverend Moore, not your pawns in the sorry battleground we have just experienced."

Moore looked shocked. "But… but it's Christmas; we have three services on Christmas Eve and…"

James said, "St. Matthew's has three services on Christmas Eve. Other clergy will lead them. What happens next will depend on your answer to my earlier question. What did you do?"

He sat back in his chair and put his hands together, composed; a signal he was waiting.

Anne looked at Moore and saw the anger rising above the shock of the bishop's decision. He will walk out; there will be another tantrum. It is as well that we prepared for this, she thought. In the file in front of her was a sealed letter, dated today. By the authority of its bishop, the diocese was prepared to remove Andrew Moore's 'Permission to Officiate', his right to perform as a priest in the most crucial role, the Eucharist. He would effectively be fired.

James had signed it reluctantly, she knew. He wanted Moore transferred to the cathedral, under the direct authority of the Dean. 'Tom will help him', had been the Bishop's remark. She had her doubts about that working; one needed to want and accept help, and she saw no sign of that in Reverend Moore.

But somehow the anger peak passed as Moore reached into his inside pocket and brought out a sealed envelope of his own.

"Bishop Azikiwe, I resign my position as Rector of St. Matthew's Church, Stoney Creek, and my employment with the Diocese effective immediately."

Azikiwe looked impassive. "I accept your resignation."

He looked as if he wanted to say more but Anne caught his eye. They had considered this option, too. She wanted no further discussion if this outcome occurred.

Leo Unwin quickly placed his papers back in his slim briefcase and, in doing so, signalled the meeting was over. But Moore didn't move. He just said, "One moment, Leo."

Unwin responded, "Andrew, we–," but was cut off.

Moore spoke over the top of him, addressing Azikiwe. "Did I give him guidance, you ask? Or comfort?"

His voice was combative; like a man in the dock just found guilty and still in denial.

"Comfort? I thought of my own girls; my oldest is fifteen. She is so trusting of our people at St. Matthew's. To think in two years or so that trust could be so vilely broken. I was utterly repulsed and then angry, really angry.

"It was so unexpected. Aster and I had enjoyed such interesting discussions in the few days together. My mind immediately went to questions like, 'how many others?' I admit I judged the man in those moments, instead of listening to him."

Anne looked at Unwin, seeing the concern on his face. She nodded at him, supporting him, in fact, that this was not needed now. It could only complicate matters. But they were both caught, she realised, in a battle between two clergymen. Moore wouldn't be stopped and Azikiwe, wanting to know the truth of how his priest performed, wouldn't stop him either.

Moore continued, "When he mentioned the name Susan, I thought of a young woman assisting at our session. They had met already, I saw. Not again, I thought; never again. I told him quite harshly that he was carrying an unbearable moral burden. He needed to find a means of atonement, a path to seek God's forgiveness. I had no answer except an offer to pray with him for guidance.

"We were at St. Anselm's at the time. We prayed together. Despite my revulsion, I tried to appear supportive but he had already seen through it; our relationship had changed in a few moments and the silence of prayer was... not healing, for either of us.

"By the time we drove back into Keswick, whatever had developed between us in the spirit of the convention had completely evaporated. It was very uncomfortable for both of us. I don't remember what we said to each other on arrival. I think each of us just wanted to get away from the other. I know that I never wanted to see him again."

James said, softly, "But that wasn't your last meeting with him, was it?"

"No. I thought about what had been revealed to me, then went to the safeguarding officer in the Keswick Ministry for clarification of UK reporting requirements. My mind was in turmoil about it. Afterwards, I just told my wife I had something to resolve and went for a walk, thinking – and ran into Duncan again on a street near the convention site.

"I said I had thought on his words, and I believed him about it not being the Susan in our session. I apologised for that but told him I had already sought advice on safeguarding reporting obligations in the UK, to be sure. I assured him that I hadn't mentioned his name, but by then he wasn't listening. He was upset by my action, as if I, not he, was somehow in the wrong!"

"Andrew; you have to stop! Right now!" Unwin was on his feet, pulling at his client's arm.

"He's right, Reverend Moore. You should stop now,"

Anne Lieberman added. She looked at Azikiwe, his head now bowed.

She engaged Unwin again. "Tell him, Leo. He has resigned. We can claim his letter hasn't been processed yet, but it is arguable in court. He said it was immediate."

Unwin spoke directly to Moore, holding his gaze, leaning across him to physically block his view of Azikiwe. "She's an officer of the court, Andrew; I am also. But I hold solicitor-client privilege with you. Mrs. Lieberman doesn't. Don't say another word."

Moore looked shocked, then realised his error in unleashing his rebuttal of Azikiwe's question.

Bishop Azikiwe suddenly looked directly to Moore.

"I pity Duncan Aster. I pray for him. He was a priest who had a serious lapse in his vows and in his ministry, one which he carried with him, in secrecy, in silence, for years. During that time, I understand, he performed his duties to his church and his bishop under that pressure and, as the court heard, a chance encounter with Susan Carlson brought it all back; the full weight of it. And she did, with grace, the one thing she could do; she forgave him and asked for forgiveness herself. If she had screamed her resentment at him in the middle of Toronto Airport it might have been easier, might it not? But she forgave him when he couldn't bear to forgive himself.

"He turned to you; not his fellow priests in the retreat; to you. And you judged him. You still do. I had hoped that we could work through this, Andrew. But we can't, yet you need help. Turn to someone; please!"

Moore stood and looked at Unwin. "Let's go. Now."

Anne couldn't read what was more dominant; Moore's anger at Aster or his irritation at his outburst, revealing it. She said quietly, "Leo, it's over; you understand?"

The lawyer nodded, signifying agreement. What she

meant was that it would not be in Moore's or the diocese's interest to discuss it further in the public arena. She knew Leo Unwin would take it the same way.

When they were alone after Unwin and Moore left, Audrey knocked and waited for a response before entering.

"Could I get you both some coffee?"

Azikiwe smiled at her, a forced response, she could see. "If you would, Audrey; thank you."

When the door closed, he sighed. "What will happen? Not in the diocese now he's gone, but with him?"

Anne replied, "That will be up to the British investigation initially. But I think you were right. He saw Aster as a criminal, a serial abuser, and lashed out at him verbally at least, in his anger. It's whatever he said, whatever he contributed to Aster's decision to commit suicide, that matters. But we have no role in that now."

James said, "What comfort did Andrew provide? Any? None? I never found that out from him, really. Which makes me think; I will revise my homily for Sunday."

The door opened as he spoke. Anne looked at him as Audrey brought in a tray. As she read his expression, the Chancellor spoke. "I said I would know when I saw it, didn't I?"

His 'banner' as a bishop, she meant.

Audrey, catching on, said, "Did I hear the word homily? Next Sunday's text was finished over a week ago. Are we going to change it?

Bishop James Azikiwe said, "Yes, we are. Right after you have processed Andrew Moore's resignation from employment in this diocese, here and with the appropriate provincial department of employment. That's the priority."

He handed over Moore's resignation letter.

"I'll get right on this," Audrey replied, with a little too much enthusiasm in her voice, Anne thought.

31 COMFORT

In the conversations before the main service at Christ's Church Cathedral on the following Sunday morning, Joanne Du Maurier scanned the areas in the narthex where people gathered; her radar checking, as usual, for who was there, who was not and who was new. The Du Maurier family was one of the mainstays of the social life of the cathedral community.

When she saw Rowena Azikiwe – or was she Atkinson now, she wasn't sure? – she headed straight over to her. They had attended the annual Youth Ministry Conference activities together for years in their teens.

"Ro! I'm not surprised that you are here today. For your dad, no doubt. It's been ages. I thought you were one of Ginny's left-footed radicals these days."

Rowena smiled and said, "Gavin and I are. But you are right. We want to hear my dad today. Joanne, this is Gavin, my husband, and these are Rabbi David Simmons and his wife Rebecca, family friends. They are here also to hear my dad. My children are around here as well, somewhere, with the others."

Joanne shook hands and said hello. She had noticed the old man in the yarmulke when he removed his outdoor hat. That explains it, she thought. She gave Rowena a knowing look then whispered, "The word is out. It should be quite a sermon, I gather. Did you see Reverend Moore and his wife? They are with the Pernell's."

Rowena smiled. She bit back the retort that Andrew Moore wouldn't be at St. Matthew's today for obvious reasons, but this was still the family's cathedral. She just said, "We are going to take our places. Audrey is saving them for us. It's good to see you."

"With your mother and aunt, in their regular spot?" Joanne asked. She wanted to buttonhole her afterwards, as they went into coffee. She had other questions.

"No, we are all on the front row today, with David and Rebecca."

"And the blonde lady with Audrey? I saw her just now; a new staff hire, perhaps?"

Rowena gave a small private laugh as she looked at her husband, who was regarding Joanne with his special stare reserved for noisy people on the morning commuter train.

"No… she's from Toronto. She works there. I'll see you later, Joanne; we need to go."

With that, they were heading towards the front of the nave. Joanne scanned the crowd close by. There must be someone who knew what was really going on today.

~~

A little later, The Right Reverend James Azikiwe had just revealed to the congregation one of his more surprising elements – his singing voice. The cathedral was packed. It was the Sunday before Christmas, so many attending were not regular members of the congregation but people feeling the need around Christmas and Easter to revisit their spiritual roots. James knew that the unknown faces would also probably be there on Christmas Eve and then evaporate into their busy lives thereafter – at least until Easter loomed.

But many who were present were there to hear him. The news of the past week; the sudden departure of Reverend Moore from St. Matthew's without any explanation by him or others, had surprised them. The bishop they thought of as sanguine had shown his mettle, and there were rumours that on Friday, at the Diocesan Finance Committee, he had spoken to them about the current strategic spending and investment plan. All committee members were tight-lipped, and some were looking grim.

People wondered what he would say today.

The order of service showed an anthem before the much-anticipated homily by the bishop. As the choir rose to sing, they paused. The bishop stood and walked across to join them. Without preamble, they launched into the work, a short but complicated six-part motet. The bishop's voice, a clear countertenor, was mostly steady but had one or two breaks, and at the end he became a little reedy. But they got through it.

In the quiet aftermath, as the choristers smiled at him and took their seats, James thanked both them and the music director as he moved to the pulpit. For some reason, those close to the front heard a woman murmuring to her partner and give a sob.

As Azikiwe took his place his eyes fell momentarily on Andrew Moore, sitting stony-faced, as he had for most of the service. Neither the Moore couple nor the Pernell's looked particularly happy. A show of St. Matthew's discontent, James concluded. It was to be expected, perhaps, given the last few months.

The bishop began his sermon with a smile. "I would like to add my warm welcome to that of the Dean for all of you here on this day, the fourth Sunday of Advent. We prepare to celebrate and rejoice this week in the birth of our Savior. It is a wonderful time.

"In our second lesson today, we heard the words of Mary. *'My soul glorifies the Lord and my spirit rejoices in God my Savior, for he has been mindful of the humble state of his servant'*. The humble state of his servant, the bible says. The perils of travel for Mary did not go smoothly; like other travellers in despair, Joseph and Mary had the tribulations associated with their inability to find anywhere for their child to be born, other than in a stable. I think of that at this time; of her very pregnant, in pain and discomfort possibly, and of the long distance they were forced to travel to meet the obligations of the Roman census.

"We must not forget the needs of those in pain and suffering, the people alone on the road, or those seeking help. If a young couple today, the man worried, the woman heavily pregnant, stopped their salt and mud-covered old car on the road right outside this cathedral looking for help, for shelter, what should I do? Not you, not us; not one of our committees, not the collective 'we'. Me."

He paused, his eyes roving around the congregation as the silence grew.

Azikiwe continued, "Well, let me first answer why I trampled my way into the choir to spoil their beautiful rendition of that motet just now."

The choir members were smiling, shaking their heads in rebuttal.

"*Haec Dicit Dominus; Circumdederunt me*, 'Thus sayeth our Lord', a lovely work by the Renaissance composer, Josquin des Prez. I won't ask you if you knew I could sing a little: the answer would come back, 'sing perhaps, but like that! No'. Ah well, once a boy soprano, always a...."

He let it trail off as the ripple of quiet laughter moved across the cathedral.

"The motet, both in its music and its words, is about comforting people who have lost children. The last time I sang this work was many years ago, in an interfaith gathering in my parish, in a small group with a man, Michael Simmons, a young man back then. Michael died suddenly not that long ago. My friend Rabbi David Simmons, his grandfather, and his wife Rebecca are here today as two of my guests."

He paused, looking directly at the couple, and smiled. Rebecca raised her joined hands fleetingly in salute.

James continued, "I wanted to bring them comfort, you see, as best as I could with that memory of Michael. When David and I met again this summer by chance, as he told me about Michael's untimely death, my phone rang. An important church matter came up and, although he understood why, I left him. I felt guilty about that, for as a Christian I must try to live as Christ would wish me to and that involves, above all, bringing comfort to people in need."

He looked away from the elderly couple to the congregation in general and paused.

"It is not just another thing we should do; it is the thing we must strive to do in the love of Christ; it is our primary purpose.

"Those words, 'primary purpose' were used by someone in another meeting held here not that long ago, one that I did not attend in person, but I heard about afterwards. Her primary purpose, that person told me later, is to help others who are suffering to find a conscious contact with a loving

God so that they may cope with their despair and affliction and lead full and happy lives, a day at a time."

He deliberately avoided looking directly at Susan Carlson. She was now sitting next to Audrey, half-way back. Susan was his other specially invited guest. But in his sweep of the church, he saw her smile. James saw some others smile also, clearly familiar with the language of Alcoholics Anonymous, the recognition showing on their faces.

"Several months ago, Reverend Genevieve Farmer, the Rector at Park Royal, called me up. Reverend Ginny wanted to help the family of Benjamin Okafor, the young man killed so tragically, you may recall. They, like my own parents, are from Nigeria, and an older family member here spoke only Hausa, a Nigerian language. So I went, playing hooky from my other duties as bishop for a brief time. At one point Benjamin's grandmother smiled at me; a smile in her unbearable pain. She was momentarily amused that a big man who spoke her language did so with the vocabulary of a little boy. It was all I learned of Hausa, you see, the language of a child.

"But I helped as best as I could to bring comfort to a person, just as the priests and many others in the parishes of this diocese do every day. It's our job, our mission, our raison-d'être."

His voice changed, lighter now. "As someone who knows me well asked, 'did I let Reverend Ginny lead or just take over; was I there as the boss or as a translator?' Yes, there are people here who will put me in my place, I assure you!"

Again, there was a ripple of laughter.

"Afterwards, I thought on that humorous question. As a bishop, translation of our complex mission as I see it, through prayer and my sacred duty, is part of my role.

Sometimes I need to do that in the simple manner of a child. I have been told on more than one occasion that I need to make more visible my thoughts on the direction for this diocese. Voices with particular interests have encouraged me to do so. I have said repeatedly, and will continue to say, I will support all who work for harmony and the well-being of this church, our diocese, and the communities near or far that we serve."

He paused.

"Let me take you back to my original question; about the couple of strangers on the street outside the cathedral needing help. Is that woman outside with her partner also called Mary, I wonder? And does that matter? What should I do, I asked?

"I think you see by now what I must do. I must help those disadvantaged people, whether on the road outside, or any road of despair. I must comfort those living in the squalor of a modern-day equivalent of that stable we focus on this week. We should celebrate our past, but keep our focus on the present, so that we may help all people in need to have a better future. Whether these people are rich or poor, whether they have spent their entire lives in our community, or it is their first minutes among us; whether they are gay or straight, black, white, or any other colour; whether they have any creed or no creed, faith or no faith, and whether Canadian or not, I must be there for them, to offer comfort, as a Christian.

At this time, as Christmas Eve approaches, we should all pray for the strength to focus on doing exactly that."

Audrey watched her boss move on to the final part of his sermon so carefully scripted some weeks ago for this occasion, making the transition from the new material seamlessly. It was not that long, it seemed, until the homily was over. As he returned in silence to his seat, she glanced at several people, watching their faces. They want a banner, well its nailed high enough now, she thought; diocesan spending priorities and action plans would be in flux.

She saw Don Pernell, the chair of the Finance Committee, and a man now out for Azikiwe's blood over the resignation of his Rector at St. Matthew's, purse his lips. Audrey concluded that Purnell was no doubt reviewing his own battle plan. The next Finance Committee meeting would not be an easy one. Reverend Moore's face was hidden; she could not see him, but his wife's head was visible. Sylvia Moore looked puzzled, if anything, as if the bishop's sermon had given her something to think about.

But Audrey found herself very happy, seeing her boss run his flag up the mast. There would be storms to come, but she could weather those with him. As her head moved, she exchanged glances with Susan Carlson. The two women smiled at each other, as if they had a secret in common that no-one else in this large gathering even knew about.

32 PASTRY

January 14, 9.29 a.m. GMT

When Harriet Calder got the call from Sammie Livermore, it was a surprise. The overnight rain had been heavy and had given way to a grey day, with ice patches and fog. Her teams were out dealing with the fender benders and related chaos. The first week or two of the New Year in Keswick was always busy, as the influx of holidaymakers and family members to the Lake District returned to their normal lives elsewhere.

"I hear you are coming over here first thing this afternoon to visit; to see DCI Trent about the Canada case."

To Penrith, to HQ.

Harriet replied, "In and out, yes. We are busy, but it is scheduled, so... are you going to be in the meeting? I thought you were off doing other things."

"I am. I was wondering; can I treat you to lunch today?"

Harriet's voice reflected her caution. "What do you want this time? I'd rather not be away from here for too long."

"Nothing on the case. I owe you one, that's all. I've talked to Jackie at The George. She'll keep that little quiet table for us; the one round the corner just after you go in. Can you be there at noon?"

It was a nice traditional pub in Penrith.

"I thought you would offer me half a pizza down the road and a selection of one of the toppings. What if I say no?"

"I would tell you to be at the Crossed Keys at 11.30. It's further out and the roads are slow in this weather, full of maniacal drivers. I want to see you before you meet up with Trent and my new boss."

Detective Sergeant Samantha Livermore is getting more assertive, it seems, thought Harriet as they closed the call.

Once they had ordered their lunches, Sammie said, "I lied. I do want something. I want you to consider being my boss."

Harriet looked at her, working it out. "In MIU? You have one, DI Cotton. Brand new and shiny, probably freshly ironed, even."

Sammie said resolutely, "He's a pain in the rear. How he made it to a post in the National Crime Agency, we can't fathom. John tried to bring in fresh blood, and it's not that; we aren't against that. Terry Cotton interviewed well, I gather, but we think someone in his last job must have sold our boss a complete bill of goods on the man. Mooney had a chat with someone he knows in NCA who knows Cotton; they are all glad to see the back of him. He isn't going to last."

"I take it you don't get on with your new boss, then?"

"There's nothing to get on with. He is like a steak and kidney pie without the filling, all flaky pastry and no substance. His only concern is whether the crust looks good. You'll see, this afternoon."

Harriet sat back, taken by surprise by it all.

"Well, you are full of it these days, I must say! Even if I wanted to be in MIU which, by the way, I don't, and John Kent knows that; having you working for me would be like grabbing a tiger by the tail. I'm not sure I am up to that. I'm happy back in Keswick, thank you very much."

As in a long tennis rally when the ball goes over the line, they just looked at each other, not sure what to say next.

"Why me?" Harriet asked suddenly. "I trample all over crime scenes, remember?"

Sammie smiled. "Don't. I'll blush. Why you? I simply think you would be great at this; you have relevant experience, are well regarded in MIU, and you are seasoned and thoughtful. You have integrity. And I suggested you some time ago to the boss and he told me you didn't want it. I think he'd have you in a flash."

"If he told you... why ask?"

Sammie looked down, composing her thoughts. "I just ask that you consider it if the job becomes vacant: not make any decision now. I talked it through with Neil."

Harriet remembered that Sammie had told her she was staying in touch with her former boss, Neil Green.

"How's he doing? I must admit I hadn't thought about Neil in the last while."

"I was his liaison after he left on long-term disability. Now there's nothing left to pick over with him, but I still see him twice a week, him, and Valerie. He won't be too long, I think, but he is hanging on, staying at home so far. I thank God it was me and not Cotton who John put as liaison."

Harriet pursed her lips then smiled. "Thank God? You, the lapsed Catholic and proud of it?"

Sammie said seriously, "Yes, I do. Lapsed or not."

"Sorry," said Harriet. "I'm glad. Honestly, I am glad you do. It's wonderful that you are helping them."

Sensing a court advantage for the next rally, Sammie said, "Neil said I should just ask. Not for him, he's past any interest in it. But he said something which really got me thinking and it may not sit well with you. But it is what made me think of asking you today."

Harriet said nothing and just nodded, seeing Sammie's apprehension.

"He said that he remembered you getting the call in the office when your husband had just got the results of his brain scan. The way your boss looked after you when you put the phone down, and he took you out and drove you to the hospital. Neil said, 'I don't think Harriet would want to return to MIU and be there every day, to be reminded.'"

She saw the prick of tears in Calder's eyes and the sudden movement of her head back and to one side. Sammie spoke more quickly to finish.

"I know I am being rude, intrusive, and I shouldn't have, but... it's been playing on my mind. I'd love you to lead our team and with you coming up this afternoon, I took the plunge. Sorry if I am being too personal, but if it is a block rather than you really wanting to be where you are now forever, I hope you will face up to it, because Cotton is not going to make it with MIU, I guarantee it. I don't need a response–."

"One oxtail soup and a side salad with cheese, and one mushroom quiche and green salad, low-fat blue cheese dressing?"

The waitress had appeared with a plate in each hand, and a third on her forearm.

"– and I've made my pitch. Thank God the food is here."

The server addressed the room. "And I have a steak and mushroom pie with chips for someone? I think Kevin took the order?"

A man alone at another table raised his hand. As she put the quiche in front of Sammie and the soup and salad in front of Harriet, she said, "I knew these two were yours."

As she walked away, Harriet smiled. "Did you check the pie?"

Sammie said, "Yes, it looked good. Looked like it had some filling in it. Good luck this afternoon."

After a moment, Harriet said, "I have my other work with my church. It fits. I have reliable shifts and Sundays off. I…"

She petered out. Sammie reached across and touched her hand. "Don't. It's OK. I just wanted you to know, that's all."

~~

DI Terence Cotton looked perfect. Clean-cut, well-dressed in a quality suit and a meticulously clear desk. When Calder had arrived at the MIU area, independently of Sammie, she went to see John's assistant, who said, "DCI Trent has Mr. Hutton in with him already. DI Cotton asked if you could pop along to his office; he could meet you and you could go in together."

Cotton was welcoming and collegial. "I read your report, Sergeant Calder; nice work!"

"Thank you."

"Then I think you know where I stand, I suspect. This should just blow away, I think. I doubt he would ever come to trial. Did you enjoy Canada, by the way?"

"Well, it was short, a little different, but yes, it was interesting."

"It's a pity I wasn't on board then. I have a cousin in Vancouver; I could have popped over for a few days after. Shall we go join DCI Trent and Mr. Hutton? Do you know the man from CPS, by the way? Do you have a read of him?"

"No, sir. I can't say I do."

"Neither do I. Pity. But you are out of Keswick, so I don't suppose CPS gets down to the local stations often."

He knocked on John Trent's door.

After they were all introduced and seated, it took a clear direction from Trent to get to the subject in hand; Cotton was prattling on to Hutton about his CPS contacts while at the National Crime Agency.

Trent said, "So, to the issue. I've asked Sergeant Calder to sit in, as she is the person with probably the best first-hand read of Andrew Moore, both here and in Canada. Although no-one said of course, from that end, I am sure Harriet's talk with the bishop had some impact. Moore resigned, after all."

Cotton spoke up, complimenting his boss. "Nice work, that, sir."

Trent looked at him, smiled, then looked at Harriet. "It was Sergeant Calder's idea; she saw the opportunity."

Harriet said, "I'm not sure whether the issue of his interaction with Aster, or the outcome of his canon court hearing was the basis for his resignation."

Trent smiled. "Good point. But let's turn to the issue of his subterfuge around the bible. His prints were on it, over-laying Aster's. And another person's; his wife, we suspect. They placed it in the church."

Tim Hutton responded indirectly, "And that's why we are here. Do we open that can of worms or not? Continue the investigation, or close it? That is your call. I can only say what we could possibly proceed with, if you are thinking about a specific charge."

DI Cotton focused on Harriet. "Sergeant Calder, how

do you rate this man Moore?"

"Rate?" she asked, surprised.

"Well, is he a priest who just slipped up, made a gaff, and then tried to cover it up? They are not very worldly, the people who go into the church, I find. Not at the gritty end, like us. Or is there something more deliberate and criminal in his intent, would you say? Although I doubt it myself, from reading the file."

Harriet blinked and looked at John Trent, who simply raised his eyebrows; as a question to her, or that he was unclear where his new DI was coming from, she wasn't sure. Terry Cotton looked as if a speck of grit wouldn't stick to him, for someone 'at the gritty end'.

For a millisecond, the image of the steak and mushroom pie crust came to mind.

After a moment she replied, "My view is that Andrew Moore has been calculating and self-preserving throughout his actions and communications. Everything during the interviews and my observations at the canon hearing suggest that. Indeed, the fact that he forced a hearing in the first place was about protecting him and his reputation."

"However, my understanding of the reason for my presence in Ontario was that we were demonstrating due diligence in the investigation on two fronts. First, was there more behind the reasons for Aster's death that should concern us? Specifically, was he possibly a serial sexual predator, either in Canada or in the UK? There is no evidence of that. In fact, from the statement by Carlson at the court hearing, I don't think there is a basis to pursue that."

Cotton jumped in. "I looked at that; it's indicative but not conclusive, I feel. I'm not sure about your conclusion there; the Safeguarding Unit may have more to do on that."

"I am," rebutted Harriet, with conviction. She looked at

Trent. Whether it was something in her voice or her eyes, he just nodded. "Keep going."

She said, "And the second reason for the trip was whether there is a real case worth pursuing against Moore. It would be a real uphill battle to make one."

Hutton nodded, as if her statement affirmed his wish to see this dropped.

"But a man died after talking to him. I have experienced Moore's anger. I know his expert knowledge of the bible and his ability to use it as a weapon. And the manner of Aster's death comes straight from the bible."

Hutton spoke up. "All it would take is for Moore to quote chapter and verse and sound like the wrath of God, telling him what his punishment was; that would be prosecutable…"

Sensing the mood in the room, DI Cotton started nodding in agreement with the prosecutor, apparently oblivious to the fact that only seconds ago he was for dropping the case against Moore.

Trent grimaced. "I hear you, Harriet. Do we have any hard evidence linking Moore to Aster's death, though, or even the manner of death, other than concealing a bible? I doubt the seriousness of the charges we could sustain at present would meet the litmus test for a prosecution of a foreign national now back in their own country. But that's Mr. Hutton's area, really. Tim?"

Cotton was nodding again. Harriet wondered if he nodded at everything.

Hutton responded, "DCI Trent is right. But to do nothing… it doesn't sit well."

In the apparent ambiguity of a path forward, Terry Cotton sat still, no longer nodding, his eyes moving between the others present. Ask Cotton what to do, thought Harriet, see where that gets us. Bits of flaky pastry all over the place.

But John Trent said, "Terry, give me the file. I will write to the Canadians. Harriet, there was one more thing I wanted to raise, though. I recall Sammie saying you were interested in the bible from the perspective of the book-marks, so I went back and looked in the evidence set. But you tell it the way you saw it."

Harriet seemed surprised by the additional point, but simply said, "Yes, sir. It is part of the reason why I feel that Aster wasn't a serial offender."

She addressed Hutton.

"There were two bookmarks: one in the Book of Matthew, but not the reference to the verse about the manner of death. I suspect it was for some other purpose. The second bookmark was the gift card from Carlson. It was not the card or the inscription, it was the placement. It's thick enough to leave an indentation, and the back of it and the page of the bible showed they have been in contact a long time, by the amount of wear. The card has been in the same place since he was given the bible, I suspect. The edge underlined a verse in First Corinthians. 'It', love that is, 'always protects, always trusts, always hopes, always perseveres'."

Terry Cotton looked at her, waiting for more, but the CPS prosecutor spoke up.

"After ten years. I wondered; you know? Carlson in her late teens, him in his mid-twenties. The poor man, not a way of life I would choose, celibacy at that age. Or any, actually. Aster was caught between a lost romance and an unbearable guilt."

Trent seemed satisfied with the situation. "So we don't proceed further with this, Tim? I'll turn what we know over to the Canadians?"

Hutton smiled and looked at the clock. "You did say less

than twenty minutes for a decision, John. I think we are there."

"So do I." Trent addressed the group. "Thank you all for your time. Terry, pass me the file, and Harriet, thanks for coming over today, it was really helpful. My wife says she will see you on Sunday."

Harriet smiled. "Yes. I'll see her then."

DI Cotton looked puzzled, then shook hands with Hutton again before, ever gallant, he opened the office door for Harriet and Tim Hutton to leave first.

As he followed Harriet out of the office, Cotton called over to Sammie, "DS Livermore, the Moore and Aster files. Please pass them to DCI Trent. He will be closing them off. NFA." No further action.

Sammie called across. "Yes, sir. Good afternoon, Harriet. Heading back to Keswick?"

"Right now, Sammie. I've things to do. And I'll keep Neil in my prayers. And Valerie. Thanks for letting me know."

She paused then added, with a twinkle in her eye. "And you also, of course."

Sammie replied, with a small smile, "Thank you. And I will keep you in mine."

As Harriet entered the corridor, DI Cotton said to Sammie, "Yes, of course; you two worked on the case together early on. I'd forgotten."

His face, however, showed he was querying their exchange of comments.

Sammie, replied woodenly, "Sergeant Calder is also a Methodist preacher, sir."

His face showed his understanding. It explained John Trent's earlier remark about his wife. He'd found out his boss was a staunch Methodist.

"Ah, I didn't know. Church of England myself; we joined St. Cuthbert's when we moved here; our Jonathon has joined the choir."

He seemed pleased, then looked at Sammie enquiringly, but didn't ask openly.

She turned away and walked back to her desk saying, "I'm a lapsed Catholic."

Cotton opened his mouth and closed it again, deciding it was improper to comment. He was fine with Catholics; but he wasn't sure about Methodists. Funny lot, despite his boss being one. Well not funny; serious, really; too serious. But he could see why Calder offered to pray for Livermore. A lapsed Catholic, indeed.

33 LETTER

February 2, 3.15 p.m. EST
The letterhead was the Cumbria Police crest, sent from an address in Penrith, UK, and was signed, Simon Nugent saw, by a Detective Chief Inspector John Trent. He read it through carefully.

Dear Bishop Tremblay,

On behalf of the Cumbria Police, I want to advise you that we have now closed the investigation into the death of Father Duncan Aster. We have pursued all known lines of enquiry, and the coroner has been informed of our findings. In due course she will report the conclusion of her own enquiry, but we have no basis to lay charges against any individual regarding Father Aster's death.

I note that the last person to speak with Father Aster was Reverend Andrew Moore. We have not been able to resolve to our complete satisfaction the conversation between the two men but have satisfied ourselves that no other person had a direct hand in the unfortunate and untimely death of Father Aster.

We also received correspondence from a Mr. Nigel Aster now resident in Lima, Peru, sent to our records unit. We now retain in our possession the Ignatius Pocket Bible uncovered in our enquiries. The Cumbria Police have no reason to retain the bible as evidence. Nor does it appear that the Aster family wishes to receive it.

When Sergeant Harriet Calder, who attended the recent hearing regarding Reverend Andrew Moore in Hamilton, Ontario, heard that Father Aster's bible may languish in a property file and later be disposed of, she suggested that I contact you in your capacity as his bishop, to seek your support for the bible being returned to the Church of St. Anselm in Bassenthwaite. As you may know, this church dates from the pre-Norman era and has served as a centre of worship of both Roman Catholic and Anglican faiths. These days it is a popular location with many people from all faiths who visit the Lakes and the region. The church maintains a set of bibles in various languages donated by others, and we feel that it is a suitable repository for Father Aster's bible.

Sergeant Calder and I have taken the liberty of removing a bookmark, a gift card, placed in First Corinthians*. I enclose that card for your disposal, as you see fit.

If I could have your written support for us to deliver the bible to St. Anselm's, I would appreciate it. If you wish, instead, for it to be sent to you or to another person, please advise me accordingly.

Yours sincerely,

John Trent (Detective Chief Inspector, Major Investigation Unit)

cc. Harriet Calder (Sergeant, Keswick Police Station).

*1 Corinthians, 13, verse 7. It [love] always protects, always trusts, always hopes, always perseveres.

Nugent's first comment to Hugh Tremblay was, "He didn't have to do this, you realise? He only had to inform the family and the OPP. He, like I, would dearly like to know what Moore said to Duncan."

"And they know about Susan, clearly," said the bishop.

Nugent sighed. "Calder is a Methodist preacher. I found that out in Hamilton, at the hearing; she's attuned. She was on the scene when the bible was discovered, and doubt-lessly saw it there. And the officer heard Susan's testimony and had the opportunity to talk further with her. I told you about that. Calder put it all together, I'm sure."

Tremblay nodded. "Still; the quote from Corinthians?"

"That's this man Trent, emphasizing the point. Can I see it; the card?"

Tremblay passed it over. Nugent looked at the front and back carefully. Then he looked at the thickness of the card.

"Do you have an Ignatius pocket version to hand?"

It took a few moments to locate one. Hugh called in his assistant in the end and the young priest found one in no time at all. When they were alone again, Simon Nugent opened it up and placed the card at the correct page in Corinthians.

He smiled and showed his bishop. "What Trent or Calder saw was this: the indentation and the wear - see the back of the card, how it has marked? Duncan had that card in the same place since Susan gave him the bible, I suspect."

Tremblay nodded, "So they know, but aren't saying anything, it seems."

Nugent let out another sigh. "With your permission, Bishop, I would like to contact Leo Unwin, Moore's lawyer. And not too gently, either."

"About Moore? To get him to tell us? I'm not sure he would do that. He has been tight-lipped throughout."

"I think I can get him to see sense."

Tremblay decided not to ask what that meant. He had seen the harder side of his lawyer on other occasions.

After a moment, Nugent said formally, "It would be best to give a simple response to the police officer, to support the bible being given to the church in Cumbria. I'll draft something for your signature?"

Tremblay nodded his agreement, lost in his own thoughts of Duncan's journey, his discussions with him over the years. Then he thought of those final phone calls without any response after he received the man's last email; the dread it instilled in him that night, the hope that he would be woken by a call back from Duncan, apologising for getting overwrought yet again.

Nugent interrupted his thoughts by reaching across and gently taking the gift card now in the bishop's hand. "And it's best, Bishop, if I keep this card, I suggest? I'll place it in Duncan's file at my office."

~~

When Simon Nugent, a senior partner in a downtown Toronto law firm, invited Leo Unwin from Hamilton for 'a drink and a little chat' at the Toronto Club, Unwin didn't say no. Not in his business.

The club's exclusive status appealed. One couldn't apply; you were invited. And to do that, you had to know people who mattered, people who were already members there. And if you accepted the invitation, you had to fork out a tidy sum up front. Unwin might run into someone there he knew and if not, having been to the Toronto Club would add to lines he could drop into conversations with prospective clients.

As it was Nugent who invited him, Leo knew what it was about. He had seen him at the Hamilton hearing but had no opportunity to talk with him. They had acknowledged each other with a brief nod.

"I want to keep life simple for both of us, Mr. Unwin."

After the opening greetings and being served their drinks, it was his first indication of the business at hand.

"Simple in what way?" asked Leo, in response to the remark from his host.

"I would like your client to tell us what transpired between him and Father Aster that wasn't discussed at the hearing. In fact, what wasn't discussed, I gather, even after the hearing; your client resigned rather than do that, I assume?"

He was suddenly smiling at someone behind Unwin. As Unwin glanced to check, he recognized the man, another lawyer. So, he acknowledged the man, too, although they hardly knew each other. On the way in, they had been stopped briefly by a city official saying hello to Nugent. Leo would enjoy a membership here.

"And why should Reverend Moore do that, Mr. Nugent?"

"Because, as you are well aware, the burden of proof in civil litigation is far less onerous than in a criminal trial. The criteria will not be 'beyond reasonable doubt' anymore. The question would be, 'is it more likely than not that Reverend Moore's interactions with Father Aster drove him to consider suicide as the only solution to his troubles'."

Unwin was taken by surprise. "You aren't serious, surely? A civil case: when there has been no evidence to suggest a criminal one?"

Nugent just waited. He didn't rebut the statement with words, just his eyes and expression.

"He was our man, Mr. Unwin. We knew Duncan Aster as a boy, as a young man, as a priest and, at the end, as only a memory in a memorial mass. The last person to talk to him was your priest. We have a moral right to know and a need to fill the void. One meeting, the truth – and no consequences."

The last phrase grabbed Unwin's interest. "No legal

follow up, no matter what?"

"Not from us and nothing instigated by us. A meeting not even under oath or recorded. In fact, it would be a meeting of gentlemen. You, me, Reverend Moore, and Bishop Tremblay."

Unwin thought about it.

"And if we don't?"

"I will assume there is something to hide that is a breach of the law, either in Canada or the UK, something that at some point could be unraveled. And I won't stop until I build the case, believe me."

Looking at Nugent's face, Unwin had no doubt that the man meant it.

He said coolly, "I'll talk to my client, but don't hold your breath."

Nugent responded, "It's Evan Goldstone who runs the civil and administrative law side of Goldstone and Unwin, I gather. If your client isn't willing to meet our reasonable expectations, I'll call him next, I take it, as this is a civil case we will be preparing.

"But Evan and I won't be meeting here, of course. That's business. And as we are done with our informal business now, would you be interested in a look around the club after our drink, perhaps? Only in the 'visitor access' areas, of course."

34 CLARITY

Andrew Moore was dressed in a business suit, without a clerical collar but wearing an expensive tie. It was a change, Simon Nugent noted, a contrast with Bishop Tremblay in his clerical attire.

In the meeting room at Geller & Thomas, Bishop Tremblay sat next to Simon, saying nothing, his eyes on Moore. It was evident that Nugent and Unwin were the main protagonists. Nugent said simply, "Let's get down to this. We are meeting today based on our agreement not to pursue litigation against your client in exchange for a full and frank explanation of the interaction between him and Father Duncan Aster."

Unwin looked at Moore, a sign he should begin.

Moore said, "You asked my lawyer two specific things. Did Duncan Aster make a confession, and what happened exactly during our last conversation? You know the rest, I gather?"

Nugent said, "We do. And if we do not it doesn't matter to us, or we will ask for clarification before this meeting is

309

finished."

Unwin interjected, "And that will be the end of it; we are agreed?"

"We are."

Moore began, "Duncan Aster made a confession to me in St. Anselm's Church. It did not begin formally, but he spoke first of his ever-present burden. Could I help him by hearing his confession? I said yes. Then he told me. I don't need to repeat that nor will I."

Tremblay simply asked, "Did you absolve him?"

Moore said, "I did. I did not use the *et ego absolvo* liturgy you use, but I read the absolution in the Book of Common Prayer. I stood to do it, as I should. To me, as an ordained priest, I absolved him."

Nugent glanced at his bishop. Tremblay asked, "Did you make the sign of the cross?"

"We both did. It was then he saw my expression. I have spoken of this to Bishop Azikiwe. I was angry and upset with what I had heard; it showed."

Tremblay gently smiled at him. "That is your sin, not Duncan Aster's. He was confessed and absolved; not by one of our own, admittedly, but... it is enough."

He looked across at Simon Nugent, who took the lead again. "And in front of the bookshop. He gave you the bible, slapped it in your hand, and–."

'Slapped it to my chest, then he placed it in my hand, to be precise. He was angry that I had spoken to the safe-guarding official at the Keswick Ministry. He retorted, 'You should really read this, you know; it doesn't help as much as you think it should. I wish it did for me, but the burden always comes back'. He turned away and I was outraged. In the heat of the moment, I replied to his back, 'The answer is always there if you look hard enough.' Then he stalked off. It was the last time I saw him. He was very disturbed."

Tremblay asked forcefully. "You told him the answer lay there; what did you mean?"

Moore lowered his head. "Nothing specific, I just objected to the dismissal of our most sacred text. The words came out before I thought of all their possible interpretations."

Tremblay read his expression. He said evenly, but with certainty, "But you knew immediately, didn't you? Given Duncan's sin and his guilt, you knew he would look for his punishment there… and what that could possibly mean?"

Andrew Moore took a breath; this was clearly difficult for him. "In the seconds afterwards, as I turned and walked away, I thought that he was angry enough to take my words the wrong way…"

He was transfixed by Tremblay's penetrating gaze, holding him, as if he couldn't turn away from it. Nugent had seen his bishop do this with others over the years, engaging them in a way that held their focus.

Moore swallowed hard. He suddenly blurted out, "The quote, Matthew 18:6, 'better to be drowned at sea' floated into my mind and I dismissed it as quickly. I was being too fanciful, I thought. He was only yards away at the time. I could have… When I heard in the police station that he had drowned, then I knew."

He stopped.

Tremblay said quietly, "I have been with Duncan on past occasions when he was in a similar state of remorse and anguish. I know how he loses perspective completely. In your anger, indeed… you failed him; and yourself. You became an emotional combatant with him. You lost your focus as a priest, did you not?"

Somehow it wasn't accusatory; it was simply a stated truth, a fact; Tremblay's understanding of what happened, knowing Duncan Aster so well. All Andrew Moore could do was nod then look down.

Nugent pressed on firmly. "And the bible being placed in St. Anselm's?"

"The police are right. I was frightened and I... lied. I told my wife that Duncan had given it to me for the church, but given the calamitous circumstances, I couldn't take it there now. She took the girls to pray there for him the following day, and she placed it on the bible shelf for me. I told her how Duncan and I had commented on that, how spiritual it felt there; a church which had served both our denominations.

"I was frightened after the interview and the police telling me that I faced another one. I thought it would be an appropriate place to leave the bible, to get rid of it."

Nugent looked at Tremblay who nodded; they were done. The lawyer said neutrally, "Thank you. From our perspective that concludes the matter."

Unwin stood. He was ready to leave. He held out his hand to Tremblay, professional to professional. "We have an understanding. Our side of it has been fulfilled, I believe. Do you agree?"

Tremblay spoke first. "We will hold to it. You have our word. To know... was very important to us."

As Moore stood also, he said suddenly, "What do I do now?"

Tremblay seemed surprised that he asked the question and answered as he interpreted it. Simon Nugent wasn't sure that was what the Anglican priest meant.

The bishop said firmly, "You are a priest. You know what you should do. Confess your own sins fully and freely. It has taken months to get these facts from you; now confess to a priest both the acts and sins behind your

actions that day, giving also the reasons for their concealment. Learn from them and please, please confess fully.
Make your penance and then let it go!"

Moore gave Tremblay a couple of quick nods, of
acquiescence, it seemed. Or of token acknowledgement,
perhaps, wondered Nugent. Andrew Moore was a very
difficult person to read.

Then within moments, Moore and Unwin were out of
the door.

~~

After the door closed, Nugent let out a sigh. "It was as
you said, more or less."

Tremblay seemed lost in his thoughts. After a moment
he said, "Two troubled priests… And this man Moore; all
the lengths he has gone to just to avoid any blame or
exposure of his error. It's more than vanity, but what, I
can't say."

"I think we need a drink," said Nugent, standing up and
moving over to open a cabinet door, showing a small
refrigerator and, above it, shelves with an array of bottles
and glasses.

A few moments later, while sipping his brandy and soda
and reflecting on the meeting, Nugent asked, "What do we
tell Bishop Azikiwe? Moore is no longer in the employ of
his diocese, but he must wonder."

Tremblay shook his head. "Nothing. It's not our place.
I'm not sure how our threat of civil litigation would be
received by the Anglicans, so no. If he calls me, I will tell
him if I see the right moment but for now, I think, we let
time pass on that one. Besides, I'm sure he had insight,
both from his own discussions with his priest and perhaps
from the British police officer who came over."

He raised his glass in a toast to Nugent. "Enough. To you, Simon. We'll have plenty of time for celebration and reminiscences."

Tremblay was now thinking of the previous evening in Montreal with his Metropolitan Bishop, and the fine dinner last night with both him and Cardinal Leigh. He would be retiring in eight months; it had been agreed. Then he would move to Quebec. But Tremblay would spend quite a bit of time further south, doing a little emeritus work in both Quebec and North Carolina.

The Cardinal had said, "It'll keep you spiritually healthy, Hugh, and give others the wisdom of your service. But as you wish, you'll get a lot of time out of harness. Unlike me."

Cardinal Leigh sounded sad about his own fate. Cardinals retired at age seventy-five. Hugh Tremblay thought that the Vatican would have to prise Jimmy Leigh out with a crowbar when that time came.

The meeting with Moore, organized to fit in with Tremblay's return to North Bay, had worked out well, thanks to Simon's usual efficiency.

Nugent raised his own glass in response. "The timing works for both of us. It'll give me a year with your successor. I have my own in mind as you know, a year for mentoring him, and then... it will be in the hands of others. We'll meet up from time to time and play golf."

Tremblay smiled. "I'll look forward to that. And somewhere further south, with a longer season than we get back north."

Nugent laughed. "A longer golf season than North Bay? That wouldn't be too hard to find."

Tremblay turned serious. "We've both done our duty to the diocese, Simon, for a long time. We are on our final stretch. It has been a privilege working closely with you through the best and the worst of it. You and your family will always be in my prayers, you know that."

Nugent said quickly, bowing his head, "Bishop, you have been the cornerstone in my service to God for so long, I am forever grateful to you."

They sat in silence for a moment, reflecting, at ease with each other.

Tremblay said, not for the first time between them, "I think back to the issue with Susan often. We did the only thing we could. Duncan was so torn, but he had taken holy orders. I'm not sure he would have survived laicization even if, in the short term, that was his wish. To marry that young woman!

"There was going to be pain either way. As it turned out, he gave years of service to God, his faith, and his congregations. It almost killed his mother at the time, just with the news about Susan Carlson. Her health never really recovered from that blow, as we both know; Duncan giving up the priesthood… she would never have survived it."

The bishop was shaking his head, but he continued the reprise of their well-worn justification firmly, "But through it all, Susan's parents stayed with the church. Aster and his family did, too!"

Nugent nodded in silent agreement. He added, "We did what we could, as you say; even if in the end the guilt of it all killed Duncan. That you couldn't reach him this time in his hour of need… it will stay with us both."

They looked at each other, knowing it to be true, and that both men carried a common burden.

Nugent sighed. "At his memorial service I had a quiet word with Nigel, of course. He is still struggling, still seeing Susan Carlson as the Jezebel; the Delilah who brought down his Samson, his brother. He knows he is bitter, and yet cannot get beyond it. I'm glad Susan wasn't at the funeral, for that reason alone."

Bishop Tremblay said firmly, "It was not her to blame. They were both young, him for a priestly life and her... But Duncan was ordained; the sin was with them both, but I see the failure as his. I understand, I forgive completely, but I won't accept the Aster family position. They know that."

He smiled, sounded more upbeat. "I spoke to the Carlson couple later at the funeral; they were at the back during the service, I saw, and they didn't stay for refreshments. But they came; I was glad. They are more healed, thank God. And so, in her way, is Susan."

Nugent said, "I told you. She spoke very well at the Anglican hearing. If there is a light in this whole sorry affair, forgive the pun, it is a dim one, but steady. We have lost her from our faith but from that wreckage she has found her own path to God and has grown in it."

Tremblay responded, "She's still young; it's far too soon to say she is lost from us. There is always hope and God's will. She may return to us; others have."

Nugent said nothing in response. Having seen Carlson in action, he wasn't convinced.

Hugh Tremblay smiled. "And we'll be playing golf – even in February, somewhere. God willing."

35 FOOTSTEPS

The Reverend Dean Donald Walters was feeling old, and more than ready for retirement. A number of things were on his mind, however. He had a funeral to prepare for that afternoon of a member of his parish, a young man who had been active in the church. After that, there were the preparations for Sunday, with two baptisms during the service. His organist had also resigned recently, leaving for a position in a larger church, and the substitute was, to say the least, well-meaning but barely competent.

On Walters' retirement his little church near Innerkip, Ontario, would end up sharing his successor with another Anglican church in the area; a big change for the congregations of both churches. With that came the issue of sharing services, new service schedules, and a different sense of church family, with the need to help people prepare for the transition.

And the first rains after the winter's snowfall had created another problem; a leak in the church roof. A roof replaced only ten years earlier, in fact. That would have to be fixed, and he wasn't sure if the warranty from the last replacement would cover it. You can't find a sense of peace and silence with a steady drip of water falling into a plastic bowl, even with someone's clever idea of placing some rags at the bottom to muffle the noise.

He heard the footsteps, and his first thought was that it wasn't anyone he recognized. As he looked up from his desk, he saw Andrew Moore standing there.

"Andrew, this is a surprise. I didn't know you were coming! I thought you had left for Calgary."

"We fly tomorrow, Don. It's a new church; a new diocese, and a new challenge for me and the family. We are out of the house now and packed. The family stayed with Sylvia's parents last night. Now we are all doing the last-minute things with a move, and I was on my way to… it doesn't matter. I came here to apologise for the way I treated you the last time we met. It wasn't at all appropriate and…"

He smiled, trailing off.

Don Walters spirits rose; he had prayed for Andrew ever since their last meeting, sensing something deeper to the issue of his refusal to speak to the bishop. Then the resignation. Don's last discussion on the subject with the bishop was brief, after the news that Moore and his family were moving west. He was appointed as rector of a church near Calgary.

Azikiwe had said, "I hope he does well there and finds some sort of peace… and forgiveness."

Don hadn't said anything in return. Now he stood, to face the man.

"Thank you, Andrew. Apology accepted, and you must think no more about that. Is there anything I can help you with? No-one else is here now, and I am not expecting anyone until closer to noon; we have a funeral at two o'clock."

Andrew Moore looked hesitant. "Could I ask you to apologize for me to Anne Lieberman as well? I won't have time to do so in person."

Don nodded, but said, "Shall I close the door, or would you like some tea or coffee? We can talk if you wish?"

His face showed that he really wanted that, for Andrew to open up more, to talk to him. He gestured at the two easy chairs in the window alcove, at an angle to each other around the small coffee table, intimate enough for a serious conversation. They were well worn, silent witness to many meetings with parishioners and Clericus members alike.

Moore hesitated. He looked away, breaking eye contact first, then glanced down at his watch.

"I've a lot to do –."

"Andrew, it won't take long, I promise you; you know that. Would you like me to hear your confession, perhaps?"

Out with it, Don Walters thought. One way or the other.

It was as if Moore had not even heard the last sentence. "I need to go. Give the bishop my good wishes. And my apology also."

It came out fast, almost staccato, and immediately after speaking he turned around. As Walters moved forward to the door of his office, he could hear the increased pace of footsteps and knew he had lost. By the hallway, he saw that Moore had reached the front door. By the door, Walters could see he was already opening his car door.

Was that it, he wondered? Was that as far as Andrew Moore's sense of self-vindication and righteousness allowed the man to repent and apologize? Walters resisted the urge to open the front door, to chase him further.

As Moore drove off, he wondered if anything positive would arise from this whole sorry affair tied to the man who died in the Lake District, for Andrew or the diocese. For anyone, in fact. While many in the diocese had bought on to the bishop's more visible call for unity and common purpose, there were still some, both clergy and laity, who were making Andrew Moore out to be a victim, a martyr.

Though he still had a lot to do himself before the forth-coming funeral, he went into the church alone and sat and prayed for acceptance and healing for all affected by Father Aster's death.

EPILOGUE. ST. ANSELM'S CHURCH

March 1, 2.56 p.m. GMT

It was that time of year; a person had to decide whether a rain jacket was needed, or a hoodie or sweater would do. Warmth was more a question of whether rain was in the air, or the sun was shining. You could still see snowdrops on walks, but the daffodils were signaling that spring was here now and in bright sunshine, they were the clarions of summer's promise.

There would be less tourists, was the good point, Harriet told Susan; but the weather, well, it wasn't predictable. But the timing of the visit was set for other reasons than sightseeing.

Harriet met the train at Penrith Station and waited, scanning the platform. Susan Carlson came out of the mix and smiled, pulling her case behind her. On seeing Harriet, Susan glanced away, taking in the surroundings rather than staring at her as she walked.

"You made the connections from Heathrow alright then, you said from the train. Welcome to Cumbria."

Harriet held out her hands, one to take Susan's, the other to rest on top of it to enhance the welcome, but the Canadian sidestepped nicely and moved in to hug her.

"Thank you. In my world, this is the way we greet friends. I'm amazed I came and... now I am here. I'm looking forward to it; even the church bit. I want to hear you speak this time."

She smiled.

Harriet thought that Susan was sounding bright, but the eyes showed she was tired. She remembered her own arrival at Toronto airport.

As they walked to Harriet's car, Susan looked across the road to the park, and the ruins of Penrith Castle up on the hill. They looked ancient.

"Well, I'm not in Kansas now, Toto. I thought that on the train. It certainly wasn't Via Rail; it was quiet as anything."

The energy and self-assurance are from her nervousness, Harriet thought. They had been through one round of 'trip on, trip off, trip on' before Susan committed to the ticket. In their conversation, the Canadian had said how her sponsor had finally bullied her into it. Recalling the AA meeting in Burlington, she thought that Miriam could probably stop her dithering.

"My home is not far; then a bath or shower, and a rest if you want. Let's start with that. See how it goes."

She put Susan's case in her car boot, and they got in the vehicle. Susan was watching the right-hand drive set-up and the surroundings, adjusting, thinking about the days ahead, but tomorrow in particular. They were going to St. Anselm's Church to help someone.

Ten days earlier, sitting in Miriam's kitchen, Susan had said, "It's a long way for one event. And I don't know her all that well."

Miriam responded, "As I read it, she was inviting you to stay for a few days' holiday as well, to see the place and let the two of you get to know each other better. And it's a bus ride at 35,000 feet, that's all. Get over it."

Miriam had been a travel agent. Out of the wreckage of her fall came her second career as a counsellor at Haydn House until her retirement. But she had contacts and experience in travel circles and had already offered Susan the airline ticket; it was only the taxes that needed to be paid.

"And she asked if you felt your participation in the service would be beneficial for you, too. You haven't said anything about that."

Susan replied, "I don't know. And I can't decide. If Duncan's death showed me one thing, it is that I got over him long before we discovered that he really hadn't got over me. We've talked about that. I had a way of doing that and people to support me through it and, despite all the trappings of the Catholic Church, Duncan didn't. It's made me grateful for what I've got."

Miriam said, "And now you are being asked if you will give some of that recovery away to another; not just to another alcoholic, but a person hurt by the same man. Isn't that so?"

Checkmate, her eyes said. But as a sponsor, she was only making a suggestion, of course.

~~

They talked at breakfast the following morning. Harriet had Friday and Saturday booked off work as holiday leave abutting Sunday, her normal day off from any police work. She was leading the service in Grange-in-Borrowdale again on Sunday morning, she told Susan, but perhaps one of the days before then they could go a bit further afield. She was thinking of driving across the Pennines to York, having a look around and visiting the cathedral, York Minster. They could do some shopping and have an early dinner before heading back home.

Harriet had finished with, "It should be lovely. The problem is it's a weekend, so the stag and hen parties will be out in force; the city is a magnet for them. Last time I was there the place was littered with people, mainly young women sitting on the cobbles, shoes off because they can't stand on their high heels any longer, drunk out of their minds. There were more Street Angels than coppers out there looking after them. It's everywhere these days in the UK; binge drinking parties at weekends and holidays. Would that bother you?"

Susan had smiled. "Street Angels? People making sure they are safe?"

"Yes. They're volunteers; they wear yellow vests, go around in pairs."

She smiled, "Some of them are even Methodists."

Susan shook her head. "No, it wouldn't bother me. Welcome to my world. I'd like to see York – and see the Street Angels, but not spend too much time in the cathedral, if you don't mind."

Her expression conveyed that she had had enough of those for a while.

"Let's see what the weather is like before we decide," Harriet had responded, and they had moved on with their preparations for the event of the morning, the one that had given rise to the invitation.

They drove a short distance from the village along the edge of Bassenthwaite Lake to the Maywood Cottage Guesthouse to meet the Kavanagh family. The children were there, taken out of school for two days so they could be with their mum and dad on this special visit to see their holiday friends. They were old enough, their mother thought; the entire family wanted to help Colin get well. Apparently, Moira Kavanagh had tried to pay the Maywood family, but the B&B owner would have none of it.

"It's not a holiday, Moira; it's for Colin."

Back in August at their lunch, Harriet had told John Trent that she had heard that Colin Kavanagh was not doing well. It was more than that. The man who had discovered Duncan Aster's body was a different person from the one Harriet had talked to eight months ago at the church, she thought. Then he had been disturbed and upset. That he was ill now was obvious to all; that he was spiritually ill was evident to her and in a somewhat different way, to Susan.

He was nervous and wouldn't make eye contact. His hands trembled a little; not from alcohol withdrawal this time, Harriet suspected, but from fear of the morning ahead. There was an atmosphere of care in the room, tinged with that slight discomfort around a person who was physically normal but mentally unwell.

As Susan and Harriet entered and were introduced to people, Colin Kavanagh started out firmly, thanking them for coming, but within a sentence was faltering, lost. His wife Moira was now used to it; she picked up the baton and kept the conversation going.

But Susan cut through that, made straight over to him, and took his hand, speaking directly to him. "I'm Susan; I'm like you. And it's going to get better. It did for me, and it will for you."

Kavanagh gave her an appraising look but continued to hold her hand. "You are an alcoholic, too. But I've got other problems also, the doctors told me; it's like PTSD.

It's not that simple."

"Nothing is around people like us. But trust me, it will get better."

Colin replied, "And you and I are going to talk later, Sergeant Calder told Moira; just us?"

She nodded. "Just us. Yes."

The conversation of others had petered out in the unusual directness of the encounter; it was not very English at all. For a fleeting moment, Harriet was taken back to the evening at the church hall in Burlington, watching Susan speak to AA newcomers there. Then a mobile rang, and the owner of the guest house answered it. "It's Reverend Chris, just checking."

She didn't need to say more. In a moment they would all be walking in the spring sunshine to St. Anselm's Church and the lakeside, the place that now haunted Colin Kavanagh.

The first news of Colin that had reached Harriet was that he had been arrested in a car park in the centre of Clitheroe, drunk in charge of a stationary vehicle. A month later, after seeing his doctor twice, he was found drunk again, collapsed inside a bus-stop shelter at two in the morning. This time they took him to the hospital, as they were worried that he wouldn't make it. From ER he was admitted to the psychiatric ward.

The dam of his contained fears about the experience in July had finally burst, and he had sought escape in the bottle. Colin hadn't been a drinker of note until then, but family secrets were peeled open to the medical staff; it emerged that both his father and his uncle had been alcoholics, and both had died at relatively young ages.

By late-October he was in a psychiatric care unit near Burnley. He was doing better, everyone thought, until he had a two-hour unsupervised walk, the first one in over five weeks. He came back not drunk but smelling of beer and crying. He could analyse and be rational about his trauma but confessed to a constant fear of being alone with access to alcohol. His transfer to an addiction recovery centre nearby had taken place in late November.

His counsellor there and his psychiatrist had come up with the suggestion to revisit Bassenthwaite for the day, hoping that the reality of the lake could dispel the memory that haunted him. Don't push it with him, they said and, if it was too much for him, don't continue. But if he went, he couldn't be alone at all on the trip. The family had discussed it from time to time over the winter, but it was in the spring, with its promise, when Colin said he would like to try. And he would like to talk again, if he could, with Sergeant Calder. Could she be there, he asked?

The Maywood family and people at St. Anselm's had organized the gathering with some of the congregation and a few others touched by the events of that sad July morning. It was Reverend Christopher Willard who invited Harriet to give a little homily. And, in agreeing to do so, Harriet thought of Susan.

Willard had said, "It won't be about Father Aster, but will focus on Colin's recovery; to give him and his family more support. From you, it may mean more, as you talked to him here at the time."

Intuitively, Harriet thought that a meeting between Susan and Colin might help also.

So, it was a private gathering, a small service of hope for recovery held in the Lake District, UK, not a grand mass celebrating the life of a priest in North Bay, Canada. But underpinning both events for some present was the fear, the dread of death by one's own hand, and its impact on others.

They began the little service with a welcome from Reverend Chris, a relaxed and empathetic priest, then a hymn and a reading from the New Testament. A late-comer, a smaller woman with dark hair, came in and waited near the door until the reading finished. She gave a small wave to Harriet and slid into the row next to her.

There was another hymn. As it ended Reverend Chris simply invited Harriet Calder to come forward.

Harriet didn't use the pulpit; she just stood at the front; her hands clasped.

"We are gathered here to ask for God's help and guidance for us all, to let us know how we may best assist Colin; that he may be restored fully to his family and to us. We are glad that he has returned to the Lake District and his friends here, the Maywood family. We pray that once again this lake outside and its surroundings may bring Colin pleasure and that he and his family can enjoy life both at home and here to the full. Part of him wants to, we know; Colin has told us so."

"Some of us face almost daily the small and large tragedies of others. We develop our coping mechanisms, whatever they may be. We need them; hospital workers, police officers, priests, and teachers, among many others, people who are there to help when such sad events occur as experienced here last summer. But such experiences take their toll and we, more than most, see often how hard these events affect those who are caught completely unawares."

She looked directly at Colin.

"Early one morning, a man came here. In his anguish and pain, we believe, he lost his life in the waters just outside. Neither his faith in his creator nor his fellow man could prevent that, it turned out; his pain was that great. Now, in God's love we believe he has found his peace. But in that lonely and final act there is a message, one that everyone here understands. In pain we need to reach out for help and, if we do, both people and our heavenly father will give it. It may not quite be the answer we want, but we need the humility to accept it, and have the honesty to recognize that we cannot carry our burden alone.

"Bassenthwaite Lake is a beautiful lake. It will continue to be so, Colin, with God's help and the vigilance of those who love it. You told me when I arrived on scene that morning you had stopped fishing to pick up a discarded lure, because it could hurt a child's foot, you worried; a piece of metal abandoned in the lake you so clearly love. The metal was, in fact, Father Aster's cross.

"In the months since that day, I have learnt more about Duncan Aster the man rather than Father Aster the priest from someone who knew him. One thing I am sure of is that he wasn't a person who wanted to inflict pain on others, in life or in death. As you set up your rod that morning you thought of this lake as your special place. It still is. And Duncan Aster would want it to continue to be so for you. He would want you restored, to enjoy it and your family. As do we all."

She moved forward from the dais, her arms now outstretched to take hands, saying, "Reverend Chris and I have asked my friend Susan Carlson to lead the closing prayer, and she asked that we do that in a circle, holding hands, if we would."

There was a shuffling of people out of the pews, the sorting of an oddly shaped circle, and the insistence of the two Kavanagh children that they be one on either side of their father. As the movements stopped, and the church became still apart from one nervous cough from a child, Susan bowed her head and said, "This is a prayer attributed to a man called Reinhold Niebuhr. You may be familiar with the first part of it."

She paused a moment, then said clearly, "God grant me the serenity to accept the things I cannot change."

Colin's voice joined in slightly behind and weak but gaining volume, as his older child, recognizing it from recent experiences, joined in, her voice strong. Susan slowed her pace a little as their voices blended.

"Courage to change the things I can...,"

Other voices, catching on now, also spoke the words.

"And the wisdom to know the difference."

Harriet thought that would be it, the Serenity Prayer she heard in the AA meeting off Guelph Line all those months ago. But Susan then went on speaking alone, continuing the prayer seamlessly beyond the well-known part.

"Living one day at a time, enjoying one moment at a time; accepting hardship as a pathway to peace; taking, as He did, this sinful world as it is, not as I would like it."

Harriet opened her eyes and looked at her new friend a quarter-way around the raggedy circle. Susan's eyes were closed as she concentrated on recalling the text from memory.

"Trusting that He will make all things right if I surrender to His will; that I may be reasonably happy in this world and supremely happy in the next."

Susan opened her eyes, seeing Harriet smiling at her as Reverend Chris said loudly, "Amen", to be echoed by others present.

He continued, "Please stay in the circle holding hands as I say the closing blessing and afterwards, if you wish, join us for refreshments and conversation."

There was tea and coffee, sandwiches, and cakes to aid the conversations of the people gathered. Susan was asked about the church she was 'a minister at back in Canada' by one person. She eased her way out of that one.

Harriet came over with the smaller woman who arrived late. "Susan, this is Samantha Livermore, a colleague. She led Duncan's investigation pretty well until it was closed."

The woman was studying Susan intently. "It's a pleasure to meet you."

Susan replied, "Thank you for all you and your team did; and Harriet of course."

Livermore nodded. "It's our job." She smiled and turned to Harriet. "John really planned to come, but at the last minute he sent me. He was called out."

Harriet didn't ask, just nodded, then rolled her eyes at a jovial older man who had now wedged himself into the conversation, his eyes on Susan, looking somewhat mischievous.

Harriet said, "What trouble are you causing now, Seymour?"

He smiled but directed his response to Carlson. "Can I ask? Are you a 'Mountie'? Seeing as our Harriet is actually a copper? Do you have some case together? She talked about Niagara Falls in one sermon not that long ago. Just putting two and two together; I'm good at that!"

He looked at Harriet and smiled truculently as she gave him a frown. Susan saw that Samantha was trying hard to keep a straight face, so she gave Seymour an innocent look.

"Well, I can't talk about that as there are secrecy provisions, you see?"

Harriet said firmly, "Seymour, she's not a copper. I'll arrest you for fraud if you spread that rumour; for claiming two and two make five."

She gave him a frosty stare and he took the hint and moved away to bother someone else, it seemed. The Canadian decided that saying nothing and holding on to the innocent look was for the best. Sammie adopted a similar face as she tried to hide the smile.

Harriet said softly to her colleague, "You are back in St. Anselm's. You. You must have caught a bug, a religious bug."

Sammie only gave her the eye, being in the presence of strangers. "Not so," she whispered.

"I saw you genuflect when you came in."

"I did not, my shoe caught, that's all!"

Susan was smiling at them.

Harriet added, "I'm going to pray for you."

Sammie laughed, "Not half as hard as I do for you. I'd better go, catch up with Detective Inspector Cotton. I'll give John some feedback, as he wanted to know how this went; just for him, nothing else."

She nodded in the direction of Colin Kavanagh, now talking with Reverend Willard.

Susan saw the two women exchange smiles.

The gathering had a quiet vivacity to it but all present were conscious of the Kavanagh family.

When Moira Kavanagh took her husband's hand and led him outside followed by their children and the Maywood family, no one else went after them. They just moved to the entrance and watched the small group walk across to the lake edge. Close to the point where Duncan Aster had lain, Colin crouched, picked up a flat stone and gave it to his daughter, talking to her. She smiled at him and threw it along the surface of the lake, the stone bouncing twice. The younger child tried unsuccessfully to do the same and within a moment the Maywood children also joined in. As the game continued and the parents watched their children, Colin Kavanagh suddenly put his arm around his wife.

As they were leaving the church a few minutes later Harriet asked Susan, "Are you sure?"

About not looking at Duncan's bible, on the shelf with

others.

"Yes, I'm better not to. It's from another life, a gift I gave away and no longer need to see. Have you decided where we will go tomorrow?"

As they walked up the path, Harriet said, "Yes, I've decided we are going to York, as the weather forecast is fine. We can give York Minster a miss even, if you really want. But it is beautiful. I thought we could do all the other things I said, but fit in another church near the castle tearooms, perhaps."

Susan's smirk gave away her thoughts. No doubt it was a Methodist Church.

Harriet didn't ask the reason for the expression on her friend's face, she just continued, "No. You are wrong on that one. It's a church that's not big and fancy; but it is old. It has an AA open meeting tomorrow at 5.00 p.m. I thought I would come with you. You can see your world in action over here. You still need to go to meetings, don't you? How about that?"

Susan pulled a face. "I'll call you Miriam!"

Harriet replied, "I'd be happy with that, from you."

Susan laughed, looking around, back at the Kavanagh family. "Anyway, I have my own little meeting later; it only takes two alcoholics together, you know!"

Her talk with Colin, she meant.

Harriet looked back at the lake, smiling at the church in the sunlight and the group of figures at the water's edge. It was a beautiful sight.

NOTES

Some of the places in this novel that are real are used entirely fictitiously. Any portrayal of a particular place or organisation as part of this work is fictional. All persons and events are the product of the author's imagination and are used fictitiously. Any resemblance to actual persons living or dead is entirely coincidental.

Keswick, Cumbria and the Lake District of England are real places, of course. There is a church of pre-Norman origin on the east side of Bassenthwaite Lake near Keswick; it is called St. Bega's, not St. Anselm's, the church portrayed in this story.

Christ's Church Cathedral in Hamilton, Ontario does exist; it is the cathedral church of the Anglican Diocese of Niagara. The Anglican Diocese of Hamilton-Brant, in which I situate the cathedral in this novel, is fictitious. Similarly, the Pro-Cathedral of the Assumption, North Bay is part of the Roman Catholic Diocese of Sault St. Marie. The Roman Catholic diocese of Greater North Bay is another fiction.

The Keswick Convention dates from 1875. I first heard of it through my grandmother. Later, a set of letters written by my godmother Lillian Bromiley, discovered many years after her death, revealed that she attended the Convention in 1937. From that specific experience, she devoted her life to missionary work in China and Malaysia. My short biography of Lillian can be found in the Biographical Dictionary of Chinese Christianity at www.bdcconline.net.

It was much later again that I discovered that an American, Frank Buchman, had also attended the Keswick Convention nearly thirty years earlier than Lillian Bromiley; in 1908. His experience there influenced him significantly. He was instrumental in establishing a Christian fellowship called the Oxford Group. Members of that relatively short-lived movement were involved in bringing together two men in Akron, Ohio; Bill Wilson (Bill. W.) and Robert Smith (Dr. Bob). It was the key formative event leading to the establishment of Alcoholics Anonymous.

The Serenity Prayer is now a hallmark of the world of addiction recovery. Its attribution to the American theologian Reinhold Niebuhr has been disputed at times but is now generally agreed. Written versions have appeared in various forms, of varying length. The version given in this book is drawn from the website of the prayerfoundation.org.

I would like to thank my friends Jack Soule and Mike Stroud for reading drafts of this book at different stages and providing valuable insight or input. Any remaining errors are entirely my own, of course.

ABOUT THE AUTHOR

Allan Jones lives in Ontario, Canada. He was born and grew up in Merseyside, England. An industrial chemist by profession, he worked for many years as a consultant on international chemical regulation.

www.ingramcontent.com/pod-product-compliance
Lightning Source LLC
Chambersburg PA
CBHW051948240626
47153CB00005B/1676